SNOW
CREEK

GREGG OLSEN

SNOW CREEK

GRAND CENTRAL
PUBLISHING

NEW YORK   BOSTON

Copyright © 2019 by Gregg Olsen
Preview of *Water's Edge* copyright © 2020 by Gregg Olsen

Cover design by Lisa Horton. Cover photos: woman and fire © Rekha Garton/Trevillion Images; frost by phive/Shutterstock.
Cover copyright © 2021 by Hachette Book Group, Inc.

Grand Central Publishing
Hachette Book Group
1290 Avenue of the Americas, New York, NY 10104
grandcentralpublishing.com
twitter.com/grandcentralpub

Originally published in the United Kingdom by Bookouture, an imprint of Storyfire Ltd., in 2019
First North American edition: August 2021

Grand Central Publishing is a division of Hachette Book Group, Inc. The Grand Central Publishing name and logo is a trademark of Hachette Book Group, Inc.

The publisher is not responsible for websites (or their content) that are not owned by the publisher.

The Hachette Speakers Bureau provides a wide range of authors for speaking events. To find out more, go to www.hachettespeakersbureau.com or call (866) 376-6591.

Library of Congress Control Number: 2021933873

ISBN: 978-1-5387-0688-6 (trade paperback)

Printed in the United States of America

LSC-C

Printing 1, 2021

For Claire Bord, who both charmed and cajoled to get the best out of me.

PROLOGUE

No deviations interrupted Regina Torrance's daily routine.

She simply couldn't allow it.

To permit any was to risk everything.

Regina had a strict mode of operation that was so rigid, so unyielding, that any, even the slightest change, could send her back to bed for a week. She lived with her wife, Amy, in a leaky cabin with an outdoor shower and an outhouse in the hills above Snow Creek. Completely self-reliant. They raised vegetables. Trapped squirrels for meat. Despite the fact that she had only one eye, Regina was an expert with a rifle.

Doves were lean, but tasty. Squirrels were oily and frequently on the chewy side. For protein, the couple relied mostly on nuts, eggs, and goat cheese from their trio of Nubians. Each had a name, though she never said them aloud.

Amy was on the sofa. She had been ill for quite some time. Her hair was long and braided, a pretty chestnut swag that ran over the pillow like a northern Pacific rattlesnake. She wore a blue nightgown trimmed with white piping. Both were convinced it was her best color, and it rotated frequently in and out of her wardrobe. She lay still while a conversation passed between them on a familiar loop.

"Brought coffee for you."

"Boy goat is rangy."

"Broke a jar of tomatoes."

"Darn it all! I'm feeling a change in the weather."

"You look like you're feeling it too."

Regina touched Amy's cheek and then bent down to kiss her. Like Regina, Amy was lean, sinewy. Her shoulders were cabinet knobs and her legs were a web of veins and scars. Amy's eyes caught the light streaming in between a narrow gap in the curtains at the window.

"Beautiful morning!"

"Indeed! Going for a walk now. Wish you were feeling up to it."

"Next time! Promise."

Regina pulled the curtains tight and went outside.

The ground around the barn was spongy from a nighttime rain, and the clouds dragged over the top of the trees, holding them up like circus tent poles. Regina fed the animals and started her walk, first along a narrow path that had once been a driveway. It had been at least a decade since cars had access to the ramshackle home the women shared. That was fine. No one lives in the hills above Snow Creek if they don't want to be alone. It's all about being isolated. It's solitary, not solidarity. People there mind their own business.

When Regina and Amy first fell in love, they just wanted to live and love. It was about being with each other. No constant avoidance of stares if they should hold hands. They didn't join in the Pride movement, because their love was about them, not about being part of a group.

Snow Creek wasn't far from Seattle, but it took a ferry ride to get there. And don't even think of finding their place without detailed directions. That's the way they liked it. Sure, in the beginning, the pair made frequent trips back to the city. In time, however, they just stopped returning to their old home.

Their abdication of city life was complete.

They said their wedding vows under a mammoth cedar that they eventually cut down for the house they built. Friends still came over at that time, though not many. Some came with skills to help with the farm, others to remind them that they were giving up the city and all that Snow Creek had to offer for a drippy forest and a meandering creek.

"We like the drippy forest," Amy told one of the doubters.

"Creek's not too bad, either," chimed Regina.

Their friends stopped coming after a couple of years, but the women didn't mind. Especially Regina. She'd been the one to first broach the subject about living off in the wilds, and Amy considered it merely an adventure. Something they'd do only for a while.

A while became forever.

As Regina continued her walk along the creek and then down through the woods, she paused for a beat. She thought she'd heard something. It was a familiar noise, but not one she'd heard in quite some time. It was the sound of traffic.

Two cars.

By Snow Creek standards it was beyond a traffic jam. Gridlock, really. Completely annoying too.

Regina looked up toward the noise, remembering that there had been a logging road in that vicinity at one time. She wondered if the loggers were scouting the area for another big green bite out of the hillside.

Please no.

She stood still. Like a deer. Her eyes scanning through a veil of evergreens. The wind picked up and the fringe of forest cover parted a little, though not enough to afford a better view. She moved a few steps closer.

Arguing.

What are they saying?

She couldn't quite hear, yet fear gripped her anyway. Something bad. Something terrible was happening.

What are they fighting about?

Next, there was the sound of a car door slamming, then another, and branches snapping and, finally, a loud whoosh as something rolled from the road down into the ravine.

A beat later, flames shot upward into the soggy sky.

Adrenaline surged through Regina's thin frame, jolting her, playing on her bones like some kind of macabre xylophone. She put her hand to her lips as though she needed to stifle a scream.

Don't want them to know I'm here!

Regina wasn't a screamer. Amy was.

Then the fireball gave way to a column of black smoke rising above the treetops. It was heavy, oily, and very scary. It took her breath away.

I need to get out of here. Wait until I tell Amy. Oh God. She probably won't even believe me.

Regina turned to leave and a voice called out from the logging road above.

"Someone's down there."

Another person called out.

"Shit no!"

"I saw something move," said the first one.

"You're crazy. You saw a deer."

"No, it was more than that."

"A bear. A cougar, then."

Regina didn't move. She wore a dark shirt and khakis that she rolled up above her dark blue Crocs. She didn't know why for certain, but she was terrified.

Stay still. Still will make it go away. Make them go away.

She wondered if the animals she'd trapped felt the same way when a snare caught their little legs.

She turned and took in a big puff of air and ran as fast as she could. She never looked back. Not even when she lost a Croc to a root over the trail. She was the rabbit that got away, though she still wasn't sure what she was running from. She carried that puff of air in her lungs, forgetting to exhale until nearly passing out. When she returned home, she noticed that her bare foot was bleeding. She'd cut it somehow. Sweat had drenched her back, leaving a racing stripe from her neck to her waist. She removed her clothes on the front porch, then let the water of the outdoor shower run over her. It was cold, spiking her body, mixing with her tears.

She hadn't cried in a long time.

There hadn't been any reason to.

Regina thought she heard Amy call out. She turned the faucet from her face, twisted off the water and retrieved a stiff, formerly white towel from a peg, wrapped it around her and went inside. She poked her head into the living room. Amy was still asleep. She didn't like to be wakened. She needed her sleep. Sleep would return her to her old self.

She'd tell her everything tomorrow.

She'd also go back and find out what had happened on what the couple had long believed was an abandoned road.

The next day, despite the excitement, as she now called it, Regina went about everything as she did every single day. No deviation whatsoever. She checked the stove and added an alder log because a good one could last all day. She went into the yard, down a slight incline, to the outhouse and relieved herself. She made a pot of coffee on the woodstove. Dressed. Returned outside and fed the animals. The female goat needed milking, so she did that too.

Back inside she told Amy everything and implored her to stay put.

"I can handle this. Don't give it a second thought. Something bad went on out there, but nothing happened to us. We're fine. We're good. Do not worry."

Amy nodded.

Regina kissed Amy and went for her long walk, her heart beating harder the closer she got to the place where everything had happened. She kept her eyes peeled for her missing Croc, though it was nowhere to be found.

That's my last pair. Maybe I can use Amy's old pair. Purple's good.

The forest was quiet, and the air had thickened. The change in weather had come. Early summer rains had finally given way to the warmth of high summer. Regina's garden had a chance now. The growing season in western Washington is somewhat short and unpredictable. Last year Regina and Amy had a bumper crop of ripe tomatoes. The year before, nothing but a bounty of the fried green variety.

She stood still and listened. *Nothing.* Then she started to climb up to the road, her eyes searching for the spot where she'd heard the couple arguing, where she heard the car and saw the channel of smoke filtered through the trees.

Tires had cut ribbons of mud, and footprints were scattered about like fallen leaves. She rested a moment, taking it all in, before making her way to the obvious location where the crash and fire had occurred. Tracks led to the edge of the rutted road.

She stood there looking down into a ravine, and once more filled her lungs out of fear.

A body, blackened and motionless, lay splayed out in the bushes.

Oh no. Oh God, no. This is horrible. Someone will come.

It took only a moment before she went into action. Regina concocted a plan to make sure that no one could find the burned-out truck or where it left the road on its way to oblivion. It would be no easy task. Concealment is hard work. She knew that from experience. She and Amy didn't want visitors. They just wanted to be left alone. Live their lives without the intrusion of the outside world.

How to do this? How to stay safe? Keep people away?

The slash pile left by the loggers beckoned her.

Erase.

She selected a skeleton-like fir tree branch from the slash. She surveyed the scene one more time, scanning for every telltale sign that someone had been there. Walking backward from the furthest edge of all indicators, she began to sweep away the muddy tire tracks. Methodically. Forcefully. It took some doing, but she worked her way to the edge of the logging road where the truck had plummeted downward. Back and forth, the fir branch swished away everything. It was sandpaper. It was a cleaning cloth. A vanishing act.

She stopped and regarded her handiwork. It wasn't perfect. Regina was fine with that. Nature isn't perfect, after all.

Brushing her forearm against her sweaty brow, she looked one last time, before disappearing down the trail, still walking backward and adjusting forest deadfall to vanquish her own tracks.

A hundred yards in, she turned around and started for home. Everything would be fine.

And indeed, it was.

That night Amy returned to their bed.

"I was so worried."

"Me too."

"Are we going to be all right, Regina?"

"Yes, love."

"No one will take me away."

"Never."

"Are you sure they won't come back?"

"No. I have a plan though. At least I think I do. I have to do something. I'll go back for the body and get rid of it once and for all."

"Too risky."

"Not now, Amy. Later. I'll wait awhile. When I'm sure that no one is coming back. When no one is looking for him."

Amy snuggled against Regina's breasts, and Regina stroked her long, shiny braid. She pulled the faded blue eiderdown to cover their shoulders. In that moment, all seemed perfect. Like nothing bad had ever happened. Or ever could. Safe and sound. Secure. Regina's hands traveled downward, pressing so lightly, so tenderly against her wife's body.

Regina breathed in Amy's sweet scent.

"I love you, Amy. Stay right here."
She kissed her tenderly.
"You are everything to me and you will always be my love."
"I love you, Regina."
"Always and forever."

CHAPTER ONE

I know it is only tomato soup left at the bottom of the cup from yesterday's rushed attempt at lunch. I know that. I *know* blood. And yet it's like a little trick to me, maybe *tic* is a better word. Something, among many, that I can't shake. I have seen so much blood. In my life. At my job, of course. As I sit at my desk at Jefferson County Sheriff's Office, with posters of the magnificent Olympic Range looming over me, I think of the things that spark a memory of blood. A child's finger painting pasted proudly in the window of her classroom. The smear of brick red lipstick on the collar of Sheriff's starched, white shirt. The explosion of juice left by falling cherries on the sidewalk in front of my home in Port Townsend, Washington.

Sometimes I wish I had been born colorblind.

Or I came from a place where the color red was meaningless. Innocuous. Just another color. Like the blue of the Pacific or the green of the firs and spruce trees that stumble down the snowy Olympic Mountains to the foothills, and finally, the meadows below.

Blood oxidizes and dries to a nice coppery brown. That's good. Dry blood doesn't cause me to catch my breath. Just fresh blood. Only cherry. Only scarlet.

The light on my desk phone flashes.

Red again.

I pick up.

"Detective Carpenter," I answer.

"My sister is missing," a woman says, pausing as if that should be enough information to catch my interest. In fact, it is. My cases of late have have been property crimes, burglary mostly, and a missing dog.

That's right. A dog.

The woman's voice is hesitant, and I can immediately tell that it took courage to call. Not because she's afraid of dialing the number, but because in doing so she's fearful of what she'll find.

What I might find.

"I'll need to know more," I say. "Ms.?"

Her words begin to tumble through the phone. "Turner. Ruth Turner. My sister Ida—Ida Wheaton—hasn't responded to anyone in the family for weeks, maybe a month. It isn't like her. Not at all."

I wonder how close Ruth could be to her sister if she's not sure when anyone has heard from her.

"I'll need more details," I tell her.

Hesitancy fills the line. "Of course," she finally answers. "I'm outside in your parking lot. Can I come in and talk to you?"

"I'll meet you at the front desk."

I hang up and catch my reflection on the surface of my now very cold coffee. My hair is dark and clipped back at the nape of my neck. I wear no makeup other than a single application of mascara and a touch of blush. My lip color is courtesy of ChapStick, owing more to the breezy weather off the water than a need for lip coloring. I know I could do more with myself, but doing more only attracts more attention from men. I don't want that right now. I doubt I ever will. I get up, bumping my desk, and the reflection disappears into a succession of ripples. My mother used to say I was beautiful. And even though that was a long time ago, and her word means very little, I know I'm many things. That might even be one of them.

I'm a little flummoxed as I make my way to reception. Outside in the parking lot? Who does that? And why didn't she just come inside?

*

Ruth Turner stands awkwardly next to the desk. She's lean, tall, gangly and hunches over to sign her name on the register. Not more than mid-fifties, her hair is gray and white and long, swirling into a bun that resembles the wasp nest that hangs over my garage. She's wearing a long dark dress over a white cotton blouse. Her shoes are black Oxfords, shiny on top yet scuffed in the places where her foot rested as she drove from wherever she came from. She wears no makeup, save for a light touch of mascara on her lashes. Despite her austere appearance, when she turns to greet me her eyes are warm and full of emotion. They radiate a combination of hope and worry.

I reach to take her hand. I feel a slight tremble in my gentle grasp.

"Detective Carpenter," she says, her eyes now puddling, "thank you for seeing me."

I don't like tears. My own or anyone's. I give her a reassuring smile and move quickly to defuse her emotion. Tears get in the way of truth sometimes. I know that from personal experience.

"Come back here with me, Ms. Turner," I say. "Let's see what we can do."

"Call me Ruth."

I nod and lead her to a room that we use mostly to interview children. The furniture is colorful, and its walls are adorned with pleasant posters of breeching orcas and lighthouses at sunset. It's a far cry from the foreboding space of the interview room next door. That one is all white and gray with a decidedly claustrophobic milieu, which is in line with its purpose.

Make the subject uncomfortable.

Help them focus.

Make them want to get the hell out of there.

In other words, get them to spill their guts.

I sit across from Ruth and I take in everything I can about her. Her body language. Her ability to look me in the eyes. Her tics; if she has any. She does. She blinks harder than necessary after each gasp of her story. I can't tell if she's trying to wring out more tears or if that's just how she is.

She tells me Ida, and her husband, Merritt Wheaton, live in the hills above Snow Creek.

It's an area with a bit of a reputation.

"Off the grid?" I ask.

"Right," she answers. "It's something that Merritt wanted to do. Ida didn't mind. We come from kind of a conservative background. Raised in Utah and Idaho. Dad hand-picked Merritt for Ida."

I bristle inside at "hand-picked," but I don't let on.

"You said on the phone that you weren't sure when the last time was that anyone had heard from your sister. Yet now you are concerned about her welfare? Did something happen?"

Ruth looks away and blinks hard. "No. Not really."

"Not really," I repeat.

"I don't know. Maybe. Last time I talked to her she was a little off."

"How so?"

She hesitates before answering. "She disrespected her husband for the way he disciplined the kids."

Up till then, Ruth hadn't mentioned any children. She sees the look on my face before I even ask her about them.

"Sarah is seventeen and Joshua is nineteen. You know teenagers can be a handful no matter how you raise them. It takes a firm hand to make sure they stay on the straight and narrow."

I asked for a definition of "firm hand."

She suddenly seems wary and pulls her arms tightly against her body. A defensive move.

"You probably wouldn't approve," she tells me, "but from where we come from, Detective, it has served us well. Our children are taught that there are consequences for misbehavior. Rules provide the structure for a holy life."

"What kind of discipline?"

"The usual," she says. "Spankings when small. That kind of thing. Withholding privileges when older. Extra chores." Ruth fidgets with her wallet. I notice that she carries no purse. She takes in more air and considers what to say. I give her the space, the time to continue. "We are Christian. Good people. We're not a part of some fundamentalist group that lives in a commune."

"I didn't mean anything by that," I say, though I did. "I was just thinking about the children. Wondering if you knew what school they attended. It might be the best place to start. We can do that with a phone call."

She looks at me right in the eye. "There is no school, except what Ida teaches. Her kids, like mine, and like my sister and me before them, are homeschooled."

Of course.

"All right," I tell her, getting up. "I'll drive out to Snow Creek for a welfare check. See what I can find."

"I'm going with you."

"Not a good idea," I tell her.

"You couldn't find it on your own. I've been there. Trust me. You need me to come along."

I don't really trust anyone.

"I'm pretty good with GPS," I say.

"That won't help you. It's my sister. I have to go."

I give in. "Fine. You'll stay in the car the whole time. All right?" She agrees.

I still don't trust her.

After letting the dispatcher know I'm headed out on a welfare check in Snow Creek, I poke my head into Sheriff Gray's office to tell him what's up, and he mutters something that sounds like approval from the online game he's playing on his phone.

"You want me to ride along?" he asks, looking up, over his glasses.

"No need. I can see you're busy."

He smiles at my jab.

In some ways, though I would never tell him, he's like family to me. He and his wife have me to dinner occasionally. We exchange not-too-personal gifts for the holidays. Candy. A windsock. A book.

I met him at the academy. He was teaching a class on the intricacies of small-town law enforcement—which it turns out isn't so intricate after all. The cases I'm assigned here are mostly domestic violence and property crimes. The domestics are easy. The property crimes almost never get solved. Meth-heads are brazen, though lucky too.

Maybe Sheriff Gray reminded me of someone. Maybe it was the way he talked to me that made me feel his interest wasn't rote, wasn't sexual, but of the kind that indicates a true connection. I told him some things about my past, how I'd erased as much of my background as I could.

"You won't tell on me?" I'd asked.

He'd shaken his head. "Hell no. We're all running from something or someone."

It was like that. He found a few things about me on the police database and deleted them. He told me that when I graduated, he'd have a job for me.

"You are right for this job," he said on my first day. "Uniquely right."

He reminds me daily—even when he says nothing—that good can come from evil.

CHAPTER TWO

My ancient tan Taurus, windows rolled up, suddenly smells of wintergreen. I lean slightly toward Ruth and sniff. Yes, it's her. It's not unpleasant, but a little curious. She's not chewing gum. Eating candy. As we drive from town, up toward the hills behind Snow Creek, she seems to notice that I'm breathing her in.

Not in a weird way, just a curious one.

"Deodorant," she announces. "I make my own for traveling. Otherwise I don't wear it. Hope it isn't too strong."

"No," I say. "It's nice."

I don't tell her that it smells a bit like a truck stop urinal cake. Naturally, I think, she makes her own deodorant. Soap too, I bet. Butchers hogs. Has a loom. Ruth is a pioneer woman living in the modern world and she's making everything herself. She was Etsy before there was such a thing.

"Look for the white-painted post of a mailbox," she says. "No box. Just the post," she tells me as I round a curve up a hill. "It's the first marker to get there."

The pavement recedes from cracked and tarred asphalt to compacted gravel. I follow the road up an incline and pass a dilapidated cabin draped in a patchwork quilt of brown and blue tarps. Then another with the same leaky roof issue. It rains a lot here in the Pacific Northwest. Some newcomers can't take the constant dousing from a soft sprinkle to a hard driving deluge.

We call them Californians.

A quarter mile or so further, we pass two mobile homes stacked on top of each other. I do a double take. Ruth does too.

"That's one way of getting a two-story," I say.

Ruth, in all her wintergreen glory, smiles. "Some people," she says.

A young doe appears at the edge of the road. I tap the brake.

"Ida made me a pair of deerskin moccasins when we were kids. Too small for me now, but I still have them. Our father said she was the best hunter of the ten of us."

"Ten," I repeat. "That's a houseful."

She nods. "Eight boys and two girls. Momma was a glutton for punishment, that's for sure. She had us girls last and always said she wished we'd been first out of the gate. Would have made things a lot easier for her."

My mom told me a hundred times that having me before my brother, Hayden, was a godsend: *Now, I have a built-in babysitter.*

The clouds start to thicken, and a light rain pelts the windshield. Ruth directs me up another incline and we pass another house; this time, smoke curls from a chimney.

"How much further?" I ask.

"I'm not sure in miles," she replies. "Maybe twenty minutes."

I look at my phone. No service. No GPS.

"You're right," I say. "I doubt I would have found your sister's place on my own."

Ruth stares out the passenger window as the green of fir, spruce, and feathery hemlock envelops us.

"That's the way she and Merritt wanted it. They didn't want the world to find them because they didn't want anything to do with its ugly and irredeemable influence."

"How is it that you could call them?" I ask her. "I don't have any reception. I expect where we are going it isn't going to be any better. There isn't a cell tower for fifty miles."

"Satellite," she says. "They're off the grid though they have internet and phone through satellite hookup. We have the same setup back home."

"You called me from the parking lot."

"I borrowed a friend's phone."

"Oh," I say, thinking that Ruth comes from a lot of rules, yet doesn't always follow them.

"Get ready to turn up this driveway," she says, abruptly.

I follow the trajectory of her stare.

I see nothing but a wall of green.

"What driveway?" I ask.

"Slow down. It's right...here."

I stop the car. I still don't see any driveway.

"Right there," she says, pointing. "See those two firs?"

I do. They have low-hanging branches that sweep against the gravel of the roadway.

"Drive between them."

Between what? I think.

"There isn't a road," I say.

"Yes, Detective. There is. Once you push through, you'll be on it."

I'm glad my car is old. I'd get out and check out the wisdom of plowing through, but the rain keeps me inside where it is warm, dry, and very wintergreen.

I turn on my headlights, though it doesn't help much, and tentatively move toward the trees. As I nudge the hood of my car closer, the branches move. It is almost like Dutch doors, opening to swallow us whole. In a second, we're through. The road beyond the firs is barely rutted, a faint wagon wheel driveway. It snakes along a creek and then opens to a clearing. Surprising, fenced. Beyond that, a farmhouse. It's lovely. Picturesque. Kind of like one of those calendar paintings of a whitewashed farmhouse with the cheerful, amber glow of a candle or kerosene lamp in the window.

I had half-expected a trio of mobile homes stacked together with a pilgrim-style stock out front ever-ready to punish the kids whenever they didn't toe the line. It was far from that. Pretty. Bucolic even. Doomsday preppers or whatever they were aside, the Wheatons had somehow managed to carve out a world of their own.

"Remember, you're to stay put," I remind Ruth.

She agrees. "You'll come and get me. You'll let me know what you find."

"No promises," I say. "Hang tight."

I get out and I hear a voice.

"Mom? Dad? Is that you?"

It's a girl's voice.

Next, I hear another.

This time a male voice.

"Sarah, be careful. It isn't them!"

CHAPTER THREE

"I'm Detective Carpenter," I say. "I'm with Jefferson County Sheriff's Office. I'm here for a welfare check on you and your parents." I motion to Ruth by rotating my shoulder in her direction. "Your aunt Ruth is worried about you... I'm here to help..."

"Sarah! Joshua! It's me!" Ruth calls out from the car.

Sarah Wheaton is lovely, as young people almost always are. Her skin is pale, freckled a little. Her hair is wet, blond and long, hanging nearly to her waist in a twisted braid. She wears jeans and a T-shirt.

Joshua is lanky and tall with long dark hair parted neatly in the middle. His features are angular and his eyes a piercing blue. His chin is shadowed by a light stubble, and he wears blue jeans, a jean jacket over a Miller High Life graphic tee. I think back to my days being homeschooled, and neither he nor his sister appear clueless about young people's fashion. They are wholesome, yes. But normal-looking. Not the wholesome that sends creepy, geeky vibes.

"Sorry," he says. "We are just scared, I guess. Don't know if something has happened to our parents. Or who you are."

"I'm your family," Ruth says, pausing to take them in before rushing to embrace them. "I was worried sick about you. You've gotten so big. I barely recognize you." Her faint smile of recognition fades. "I'm very concerned about your folks. It's not like your mother to not reach out when I send her a message."

I step back a little, allowing for the teenagers and their aunt to process their reunion before moving to the reason why we are here.

Ruth beats me to it.

"Where are they?" she asks, pulling back to get a better look at their faces.

Sarah answers. "They went on a trip three weeks ago. Going down the coast. Taking their time. Then ending up at an orphanage we support in Tijuana."

Ruth's reaction, an exhale, reveals a level of comfort in the news. "That's wonderful. Our whole family did that when we were kids. It was a grand time. Working together to help those children. It was a gift from God. How come you two didn't go?"

"Dad wanted me to take care of the livestock," Joshua replies. "Sarah has her schoolwork."

The clouds open up and the soft rain becomes a deluge.

"It's too wet out here. Can we go inside and talk?" I ask.

Joshua leads the three of us into the house. It's cozy, though on the minimalist side. Lots of wood and only a portrait of the kids, much younger, adorns a wall. There is no TV. No video games. Nothing of the outside world.

Only Joshua's graphic tee.

Ruth asks for a cup of tea. Sarah goes into the kitchen and turns on the kettle.

"My dad made all this furniture in his shop," Joshua tells me, noticing my eyes on a massive dining table. It's made of cherry with a beautiful matchbooked top. It resembles a tiger trapped inside an encasement of wood.

"Does he sell his furniture?" I ask, running my fingers over the glossy surface.

Ruth puts her hand on my shoulder.

"Merritt would never sell anything to the outside world," she says, nearly beaming.

A source of pride, I think. Tied to their beliefs and their need to unspool their lives from even the most casual encounter.

Joshua offers his aunt some taffy that Sarah made, but she declines.

"Mom's favorite," he says.

I decline too. Last time I had taffy it pulled a filling out, and it took me a month of pain and embarrassment before I could get into the dentist. The kids have nice teeth, I think, just then. I wonder how they manage that without the benefit of a dentist.

"When were your parents due back?" I ask.

"We thought they'd be back by now," Sarah says, entering the room with a tray of mugs and some sugar. "No lemon," she adds with a touch of disappointment. "We've never been able to get citrus to fruit in the greenhouse."

I nod not because I understand the self-sufficient family's setback with the lemons, but because I didn't come for a social visit. I came because a woman freaked out back in my office that something terrible had happened.

I give Joshua a card with my phone number.

"Will you please call me when your parents get back?"

"Will do," he says, looking at the card, "Detective Carpenter."

Ruth is suddenly very quiet. I assume she's still processing the trauma and worry of wondering where her sister and brother-in-law are. Considering the chilly rain outside, Mexico should be a relief, even the source of a little sisterly envy. That is, if envy wasn't a sin—which it was in any Bible I'd read in a hotel room.

I face her. "Are you going to stay with your niece and nephew?"

"No," she says, snapping herself out of her stupor. "As I said back at your office, I have to head back to Idaho for the church caucus."

"Right," I say, though I know she'd told me no such thing.

I turn to Joshua and Sarah.

Ruth tugs at me.

"Let's go now, Detective."

CHAPTER FOUR

Ruth doesn't utter a word until we are back on the gravel road. Her jaw is clenched, and I watch her grasp her hands and press them between her knees. I crack the window. Her wintergreen deodorant is working overtime.

"I'm sorry you came out all this way," I say. "The kids should have called you or something."

"Something's wrong," she says. "I know it."

I try to calm her. "The fact that their parents left them alone is wrong in my book, but Joshua is old enough to look after his sister."

I don't tell her that my own parents were far, far worse. I survived.

"Something was missing," she says. "It doesn't make sense."

I take my eyes off the road and glance at her for a split second.

"I haven't been out here for several years. Maybe six. My sister always had her wedding portrait hanging in the front room. Next to the kids' latest photographs."

"Okay," I say.

"It was gone. I think that's weird, don't you?"

"I wouldn't know," I say. "Maybe."

I don't tell her what I thought was out of place.

The T-shirt.

Maybe it was something Joshua had hidden and wore it only when his parents were away. Miller High Life didn't fit the Wheaton family at all.

"I'll check with the orphanage in Mexico," I tell her. "Name?"

"La Paloma."

"All right," I say. "If it checks out, we're good. If they aren't there—though I'm sure they are—then we'll fill out the paperwork and report them missing."

"My sister never said they were going there," she says. "She would have told me."

"Do you share everything?"

"Yes. Everything."

I look at her eyes.

"Does she know you wear mascara?"

Ruth turns away.

"No," she replies, her voice hushed. "I only do that when I travel. I like to fit in when I'm outside of my church group."

"Look," I tell her, "we don't know what happened. What we both know is that no matter how close you are with someone it's only what you think you know. Only what they choose to reveal to you."

She's upset, and I notice that she is fidgeting with the shoulder harness, pulling it up and down...almost hard enough to leave a mark against her neck. She's hurting herself. I immediately pull over and stop the car.

"Ruth, we'll figure this out. You need to trust that we will do everything we can to find your family."

Tears are flowing now. Silent tears.

"I know. I know. But..."

"Tell me."

I gently pull her hand from the shoulder belt and she quietly reaches for a tissue she has stored under her bra strap. She dabs hard at her eyes. Harder, I know, than needed.

"Don't tell my sister or my husband about the mascara."

*

By the time we get back to the office and try the number for La Paloma, the administration staff is gone for the day. I ask Ruth where she's staying for the night.

"I can't stay," she says.

"You're going back home?"

"My husband wants me back tomorrow. I'll have to drive all night as it is."

I don't understand this woman's loyalties at all. Not even a little. Her sister might be missing and she's going to leave before she finds out anything?

I don't try to persuade her.

"How can I reach you?"

"Here's my address."

She hands me a card.

"A PO Box?"

She casts her eyes downward. "Our phone service is spotty."

"I thought you have satellite and internet?"

"My husband has an account; I suppose I could give that to you. You'll only call in an emergency, correct? He's very busy and doesn't like to be disturbed."

I know that there is nothing I can do with Ruth Turner. At least not now. I'll need her later if her sister and brother-in-law are missing.

"That's fine," I tell her. "I'll be sure not to mention the mascara. Don't you worry about that. I want to find Ida and Merritt and that's all I want."

We both know what I'm doing.

She gives me a cool stare and scribbles more contact information on the card. "There," she says.

I stand and let her leave.

I don't like it when people light a fuse and then get out of the way. If you want to find out something you need to stay on it.

Never let go until you get where you need to be. Until you do what you need to do.

Tony Gray is leaning back in the world's oldest office chair with his eyes closed. The chair has been repaired so many times that it appears to be upholstered with silver vinyl. On closer inspection, it's clearly the work of a man who sees duct tape as the end-all, be-all. He's well past early retirement, is married to a nurse he met at the hospital when he had a mild heart attack. He's twenty pounds, maybe thirty, overweight and despite his constant complaining about dieting, I've never seen him eat anything that resembled doctor's orders.

He's either asleep or he's succumbed from the empty contents of the Taco Bell bag that takes up the space in front of him.

"Sheriff," I say.

His eyes flutter.

He bobs to alertness. "Detective. Just resting my eyes. Long day."

"Tell me about it. It's after six."

He looks at his watch. "So it is."

I fill him in on my adventure into the hills above Snow Creek with Wintergreen Ruth.

"I'm more of a peppermint guy myself."

"Good to know."

"Did I tell you about the time I went up there to arrest a bunch of freaks who were molesting their livestock?" he asks.

"Gross," I say.

"Yeah, I even caught one in the act."

I put my hand up. "No visuals please. But yeah, weird stuff goes on up there. Strange people. Probably more decent folks than freaks."

"Not in my book," he says. "People up there are there because they've got something to hide."

He gets up, his eyes landing on the Taco Bell bag.

"Let's not mention this to my wife."

I agree. I know about keeping secrets.

We walk outside. The air is filled with the smell of rain after a warm day. Oil leaks from cars in the parking lot are rainbow-colored. I'm quiet, thinking about those secrets of mine.

"You okay, Megan?" he asks.

"I'm fine. I'll see you tomorrow after I check out the Mexican orphanage."

"*Mañana*," he replies.

CHAPTER FIVE

I'm not fine.

Not really.

The thought of the Wheaton siblings and something sinister happening to their parents stirs something inside of me. I have a gut feeling that something terrible has happened, something beyond a late holiday or time doing good works for some Mexican orphans.

I've been there. So has my brother. One day in a blinding flash our parents were gone. We'd experienced the jagged range of emotions from fear to anger to constant dread—never really knowing what had happened.

My hands are trembling. I grip the steering wheel and turn onto the driveway.

I feel a compulsion that I've denied myself for a very long time. I'm not sure if it's the Wheatons or something else that is driving me to dig into a Pandora's box that I've carried with me from place to place for about a decade.

I rent an old Victorian in historic Port Townsend, though there's nothing quaint about it. It's cheap and needs more TLC than the landlady can afford at the moment. It's a big house, divided into two units. The old maple floors are dangerously uneven. I've tripped twice at night on my way to the tiny bathroom down the hall from my bedroom. Set a marble down and it will roll around on its own, desperate to find a level spot on which to rest. At the moment, I'm the sole tenant. The guy who lived in the other unit tired of unreliable heat in the winter and the sweltering that comes with western exposure. I don't mind. I open the windows and let whatever is outside blow over me.

I drop my purse and keys on the table by the leaded glass door, the only part of the house that has any style from a bygone era. I expect one day the place will be razed and the door will end up in some fancy home in Seattle. I lock my gun in the gun safe in my office and look at the blank screen of my laptop.

Ruth and her secrets.

Snow Creek people have theirs.

So do I.

Mine happened a lifetime ago.

I think about the box of tapes, how they have silently waited for me. I think of my psychologist, Karen Albright, and how she brought me back from the precipice that had been my world since I was born. I recollect how Dr. Albright's blue eyes scared me at first. Almost otherworldly. How her office smelled of microwave popcorn.

How much I grew to trust her.

I was twenty when I first saw her. Defensive. Closed off like a street barricade. I had never let anyone inside, but I was smart enough to know that everything inside of me—from my experiences to the bloodline of my birth—had to be exorcized somehow. I'd been traumatized, and while I couldn't see it in the mirror, others did. Night terrors are traumatic and uniquely embarrassing. You don't know what you said, if anything. You don't know if anyone heard your screams.

My roommate, Maria, did.

"Look, Megan, either you get some help, or you'll need to find someplace else to live. Your night terrors are turning into a problem for me. I'm sorry. It's the way it has to be." Maria took me to a counselor and after one session he referred me to Dr. Albright, a professor of psychology, who maintained a small practice outside of her university duties.

"She can help you better than I," the bespectacled counselor said. "Don't be afraid. You can do this."

I told myself that I've never been afraid a day in my life.

It was a lie, of course.

I open the windows and pour some iced tea that I'd made that morning before work.

The box is where I left it. How I left it. It sits in the back of the closet, taped shut.

"You'll want these someday," Dr. Albright had said.

I refused it at first. "I can't see that happening."

She smiled. "Trust me. You will. The day will come and listening to the tapes will make you even stronger."

She put her arms around me. We both cried. We held each other for a long time. I knew it wasn't goodbye forever, but it was the end of therapy that had spanned a year and a half. I was graduating from the university with a degree in criminology and had enrolled in the police academy in suburban Seattle.

I carry the small black box from the back of the closet and set it on the kitchen table. I take a kitchen knife—the irony of my action gives me pause—from the drawer and slit it open.

I draw a breath and peer inside.

More than two dozen mini cassettes, each numbered with the dates on which they were recorded. Dr. Albright had also, quite thoughtfully, enclosed a tape recorder.

I switch to wine.

My hand wobbles again as I insert a tape. Damn! My finger hovers and I push PLAY. I hear Dr. Albright's soft, kind voice. She addresses me by a name that I no longer use, a name that I hope has been forgotten by everyone who ever knew it.

Dr. A: Put me there, Rylee. Take me step by step through what happened, what you did.

Me: Okay. I got home from school, and I heard the water running in the bathroom sink. I just knew my mother would bitch at me for leaving it on. Even though I didn't. Mom had been critical of me, while praising my little brother, Hayden—despite the fact he didn't do much to deserve it. If he remembered to flush the toilet after a late-night pee, she practically did handstands the next morning. Mom had always been harder on me.

Dr. A: Why do you think that was?

Me: She always said it was because I had so much potential. Which meant that whatever I did disappointed her. Like home-schooling. Mom was big on that. She homeschooled Hayden.

Dr. A: Why didn't you want that?

Me: That's easy and pathetic. I just wanted to fit in with other people. I didn't want to be the loser at the mall who had no social skills and didn't know what's in and what isn't. How to wear my hair or whatever. You really can't learn all you need to know from TV or the internet, and contrary to what most people think—that all kids that age do is hang out online—it's not true for all of us. Not for me at least. I'm a watcher. An observer. I liked being out in the real world, mostly because my home life was always so fake.

Dr. A: You said you enrolled in school.

Me: Right. I was a sophomore at South Kitsap High School in Port Orchard. While I didn't know for sure if I was fifteen or sixteen (long pause)—it's complicated—I knew that for the first time in a long time that I actually fit in somewhere. That was no small feat. By then, we'd moved fourteen times. I think. So many times that I've lost track. But in Port Orchard, no one asked any awkward questions about where we lived before because people came and went around there all the time. Across the inlet was the naval shipyard. Moms and dads would arrive in the naval ships or go out to the Pacific on their way to the nearest war. Kids would come later and stay in crummy housing near the shipyard or the submarine base a little farther north. In a way, all the moving around that other people did made me feel as though I was actually part of something stable.

Dr. A: I understand, Rylee, I do. Let's go back to that afternoon... after you got home from school.

Me: (long pause) Right. I heard Hayden squawking as I turned off the running water in the bathroom. I looked down at the toilet bowl, the water was the color of sunshine, and I dropped the lever and the whirlpool sucked down my little brother's pee. Then...

Dr. A: Why are you stopping?

Me: It's stupid.

Dr. A: Nothing is stupid. You need to trust me and trust the process. Everything, Rylee.

Me: It is stupid, but here goes. I remember glancing at myself in the mirror above the sink. Thinking how average I was. Sometimes I had actually wished that I had a big hairy mole on my chin or something that could distinguish me from other girls. The ones who lurk in the halls at school with pleading eyes and heavy eyeliner that makes them look more glamorous than I am. At my school before Port Orchard, I adopted a kind of Goth persona and really piled on the mascara—two extra coats of the blackest I could find. My dad thought I looked kind of slutty, but I told him that's what I needed to look like in order to blend in.

Dr. A: Blend in?

Me: Right, Dr. Albright, my whole life has been about blending in, being invisible. My hair is brown now—not chestnut, not auburn, just a nondescript brown, the color of the bark of the dead tree near my dorm. My real hair color could be blond, but it has been dyed so many times I have forgotten what shade it actually is.

Dr. A: That's not stupid. It's about what you needed and how you survived. I understand completely. After you turned off the tap, what happened?

Me: My brother. He called from the kitchen. I thought he wanted me to fix him a chicken potpie or something as an afterschool snack. He was lazy that way. Home all day with a refrigerator and microwave at his disposal. He could make whatever he wanted, whenever he wanted it—the only undisputed benefit of being homeschooled. I followed the sound of Hayden's irritating and agitated voice.

Dr. A: What did you see, Rylee?

Me: Hayden was on the other side of the kitchen. He was on the floor hunched over and when he looked up, I noticed two things. First, he was crying. The second thing I saw was so puzzling that it really didn't compute. It was like my brain was stuck on a search engine to nowhere. His white T-shirt was soaked in red. I threw myself down on the floor and looked at the blank eyes of my dad, staring into space.

Dr. A: Do you need a moment? I know this is very difficult. You're doing fine. You are.

Me: No. I'm not fine, but I want to finish.

Dr. A: Drink some water. Take a deep breath. We can continue when you are ready.

Me: Okay. I'm fine. The room started to turn. Everything was spinning. I remember thinking for a second that this was what it must feel like to be really, really drunk. I pushed Hayden away and pressed my hands against Dad's face, then his neck. He was wearing a powder-blue shirt, gray trousers, and a red tie. But it wasn't a tie. It was a slash of blood that had emptied from the top of his chest, drained down his shirt, pooled onto the floor. The black handle of a knife stuck out of his chest. I didn't cry: Hayden was crying enough for the both of us. In my heart I had known that a day like that was always possible, that somehow darkness would come after my family. Our life away from others, our life blending into the background of the world, could be undone by someone. Fear and the possibility that something like that had always been there, had been what kept us together. Also, a barrier. It was what held us away from everyone that we ever pretended to know.

Dr. A: How was Hayden? What was he doing?

Me: Quiet. Real quiet. He was rocking back and forth like one of those weighted, blow-up clown figures. His light blond hair was compressed above his ears, where his hands clamped the side of his head as he tried to shut out everything. He'd done that before. We all cope in ways that we can. My heart nearly heaved from my chest, but I did what I could to reassure him. Despite the fact that our father was a bloody mess, we could survive. We had to do the right things—and do them right away. I remember leaning closer and tugging at his shoulder so that he would look up at me once more. You know, listen to me. He finally tells me he was in the bathroom when he heard something, he said, yelling, and then a crash. I asked for more and he stayed quiet. It went like that. Me asking and Hayden being mute, focused on the blade.

Dr. A: What did you do next?

Me: So, I yanked the knife from our father's chest. I wiped the blade's handle with a kitchen towel. I didn't want my fingerprints on it. Then I put it gently across my father's chest. I didn't know where else to put it. It dawned on me, right then, that our mother was gone too. Hayden and I were alone. And then, I saw it.

Dr. A: What, Rylee? Saw what?

Me: On the travertine tile that our mother went crazy over when we first moved in were three letters written in blood. Dad's blood. R-U-N.

Dr. A: Run?

Me: Right. Our family's code word. It told me everything Hayden and I needed to know. There was no calling paramedics; no 911 dispatcher to notify. There was no going through the house and pulling up family photos and squirreled-away scrapbooks. We didn't have much of that anyway. Mom used to joke that if our house was on fire, we'd have no reason to linger. I told Hayden we had to go. I reached into my father's jacket pocket and took his phone and wallet. I took his car keys from the table.

Dr. A: You must have been terrified.

Me: No. I mean yes. I want to say yes. I was in a strangely calm and frenzied state. Calm because in some peculiarly innate way I knew what I must do, and yet my heart was racing, and I was frantically trying to coordinate my uncooperative brother and get my backpack by the door where I had unceremoniously dumped it. I told Hayden we needed to go out the back door and through the woods, following the creek to the road. He asked me what would happen next and I didn't really have an answer. I was moving and thinking as fast as I could. I took a clean T-shirt from the pile on the table—our mother might have been doing laundry before our father's killer came into our house.

Dr. A: Here's a tissue.

Me: I'm not going to cry.

Dr. A: Right. Of course not. You know it's okay if you do.

Me: I'm fine, Doctor. I might be allergic to something here. I just remember my little brother looking at me with his dopey, scared eyes. I see those eyes in my mind now and then. Anyway, we bolted toward the ravine. We needed to get out of there fast.

Dr. A: I don't completely understand. Why not call 911? Why rush?

Me: (long pause) Because I knew if we stayed, we'd probably end up with knives in our chests too.

I sit in silence as the cassette hums to its conclusion. Things I'd fought so hard to set aside have returned and they play at my emotions. I want to cry, but no tears come. I look at my phone. It's late now. No time for dinner.

My eyes land once more on the box of tapes, all waiting for me. Each tape is like a knife meant to cut me open and expose whatever's inside.

One tape is enough for today. I doubt I could handle two.

I take my wine, and as I head for my bedroom, I hope with everything in my heart that none of what I revisited will come for me in my dreams.

CHAPTER SIX

The man answering the phone at La Paloma the next morning is exceedingly polite. His English is perfect too. The connection between my landline and his phone, however, is less than ideal. I ask him if he can help me get in contact with the Wheatons, who are there from the States to volunteer at the orphanage.

"What group are they with?"

"No group," I say. "I believe they came alone. Maybe two or three weeks ago."

"Do you know what skills they were providing?"

I don't, but then I think of the beautiful cherry dining table.

"Mr. Wheaton is a skilled carpenter. I don't know about Mrs. Wheaton's area of expertise or if she even had any."

"Ah," he said. "Hold on."

The phone cracks and every now and then it seems like it might have disconnected. Lucky for me it didn't.

He comes back on. "Sorry. No record. I searched our volunteer log and I see no mention of their request for credentials. Maybe it was another facility?"

"No," I tell him. "This was the one the family mentioned."

"I'm sorry I couldn't help."

I provide my contact information and tell him that if they should turn up then they need to call me.

"The family is very concerned," I say.

Not that anyone but Ruth Turner is, though the children most certainly will be.

Their parents are indeed missing.

I log the information into the missing persons report. I consider calling Ruth's husband's number, but I know she's not home yet. I'll let her know where we are tonight. I need to go back to the Wheaton place first and tell Joshua and Sarah.

I inform Sheriff Gray about what I've learned.

"Maybe they got in an accident?"

"Right. I'll check on that before I leave."

"Want me to ride out there with you?"

I almost take him up on the offer. I enjoy his company, but after listening to Dr. Albright's tape last night I have some processing to do. Alone time is completely warranted.

"No. I'm fine. Just some kids. I'll let them know what I found out and see if I can get anything more from them."

I return to my office and update the missing persons report with a query to law enforcement all along the West Coast from Bellingham, Washington, to San Diego, California. It was possible they had been in an accident somewhere between here and parts unknown.

Just where were they headed?

Why did they tell their kids that story?

I fill up the Taurus and get a cup of passable coffee from the drive-thru before heading out to the Wheaton place. Jefferson County's detective's shield or not, Snow Creek is no place anyone wants to run out of gas for a myriad of reasons. One, no cell service, and two, no Good Samaritans to be had. It's not that there aren't good people. The people who live out there have done so to be left alone. Knocking on a door at night could find you greeted by the barrel end of a rifle.

I touch my county-issue in my shoulder harness.

She's my best friend.

It's a long drive, but it feels shorter without wintergreen filling my lungs and Ruth Turner's anachronistic tale of how life should be. I know she's not completely passive. After all, she drove all the way from Idaho to check on her sister. Then again, she left without waiting for an answer.

And she doesn't have a phone of her own.

And a post office box is the preferred method of contact.

It's like she's Amish without a horse and buggy.

I find the Douglas fir covering over the driveway and I edge my Taurus onto the property. With a clear sky overhead, the scene is absolutely lovely, bucolic. No smears of rain on my windshield to cause me to lean forward to make out what's in front of me. It's truly beautiful.

Joshua and Sarah greet me at my car.

"Detective," Joshua says. "You're back so soon. Did you find out anything? Where's Aunt Ruth?"

"Back in Idaho now," I say.

They are wearing the same clothes as the day before, sans the beer T-shirt. This time Joshua is wearing a plain black tee. Sarah's hair is up in a messy bun held there by a large pink clasp.

"We didn't even get to spend any real time with her," Sarah says.

"Her husband needed her home," I say.

Joshua gives his sister a look.

"Let's go inside," he says.

We find places at the table. This time I decline the tea that's offered.

"I have some puzzling news." I choose my words carefully. I feel immediately that *puzzling* was the wrong word. There was nothing really puzzling about it. It was what it was. "I'm afraid your folks never made it to La Paloma."

"That's crazy," Joshua says.

"I'm sorry," I say.

I don't tell them that Ida and Merritt hadn't submitted the paperwork to support the orphanage. It could mean any number of things, not all nefarious.

Sarah gets up from the table and runs to a room down the hall.

"Go to her," I tell Joshua. "She's in shock."

He does as he's told. I get up and wander around the living room. I focus my attention on the wall with the photo of the siblings. In line next to it is a nail puncture and the faint rectangular shape where it appears another picture once hung. Ruth was bothered by the fact that the photo of her sister and brother-in-law was no longer hanging in the living room. I'll ask about that later. I'll also ask about the problems Joshua had with his father.

He and Sarah emerge from one of the bedrooms. Her eyes are framed in red, and he has his hand on her back.

"Where are they?" she asks.

"We've sent out a bulletin. Nothing has come in so far."

I direct my gaze first to Joshua, then to Sarah. "I'll need you—both of you—to come to the sheriff's office to make a statement that we can add to the missing persons report."

"Like when?" he says.

"Now would be best."

He nods and releases his hand from his sister's back. "Will you be okay here?"

I don't give her the space to answer. "You both need to come."

Sarah nods and disappears to retrieve a sweater. Joshua follows her out the door.

"Aren't you going to lock up?" I ask.

"Nah," he says. "Nobody but you and Aunt Ruth have been out here in years. Door doesn't even have a lock."

I bend to study the doorknob. He's right. No deadbolt either. It passes through my mind just then that country living is not for me. I like locks. I like people around me. Even when I don't speak to them. There's safety in numbers.

They follow my Taurus in a white Chevy Cavalier that had been parked in the barn. I can be a bit of a lead-foot, so I keep my eye on the rearview mirror. I don't want to lose them. I shouldn't have worried. Joshua drives like I do, and we get to the office in record time.

I get a couple of Cokes from the vending machine, and we sit in the same interview room as Ruth and I had. I can still smell her. I add to what they already told me, this time digging deeper.

"Did Mom or Dad have any tattoos or distinguishing birthmarks or scars?"

Joshua answers. "Tattoos are not allowed. Dad had a scar through his right eyebrow. It only shows up in the summer when he gets a tan outside working. I've never seen my mom naked, so I wouldn't know."

Sarah follows up. "Mom didn't have any scars or anything. She was perfect."

After gathering more details that would help identify the missing couple, I move on to the biggest question mark in my investigative mind.

"Let's say they weren't going to La Paloma," I say. "Let's say they were going somewhere else. Can you think of where it might be?"

Joshua answers first, his eyes fixed on mine. "That's what they told us. Why would they lie?"

"Yeah," Sarah added. "They would never lie. Our parents are all about the truth. It is the foundation of our faith. We don't just *believe* in God's existence and plan for us, Detective. We *know* it. Knowing is truth."

I tell them what I know.

"La Paloma said they hadn't registered to come. It's a requirement."

Joshua pipes up. "They are wrong. They'd planned it for weeks. Mom wouldn't mess up on something like that."

I catch the fear in his eyes.

"We double- and triple-checked, Joshua."

He looks away from me, down at the table. "I don't understand."

"None of this makes sense," Sarah says, this time holding her brother's hand. "It has to be a mistake."

"We'll figure it out," I tell them. The room feels warm, and I know that the two across from me are upset and confused. "I need to ask you about a few more things. Is that okay?"

Joshua nods. So does his sister.

"These might seem trivial to you, but they could also be important."

"Okay," Joshua says.

"Were your folks getting along?"

Sarah answers. "Yes. I mean, they disagreed about things, but they never really fought. Did they, Josh?"

"Maybe some little things now and then bugged them, but not much," Joshua says.

"What kind of little things?"

"I don't know. Mom wanted to spend more time with Dad."

I wonder how that would be possible since they never went anywhere.

"What did he say?"

"That they would go on a trip to Mexico. The orphanage. It was going to be like a second honeymoon," he says.

"They never really had a first one," Sarah adds. "There wasn't a lot of what most people would consider fun in either of their families. That's why they moved to Washington. Trying to make a better life. A happier one."

I press her. "Was it happy?"

This time Joshua answers. "I think so. I mean mostly. Maybe not as much after I graduated from high school."

"What happened then?"

"I wanted to be like other kids. I didn't want to wait until I was twenty-one to get married and start a life."

"What did your father and mother think of that?"

He pauses for a very long time. "Mom was okay with it. Dad, not so much. They argued. Gave me extra chores. Dad said more work would keep my mind from thinking about anything else."

"Did he punish you, outside of extra chores?"

Sarah squeezes her brother's hand. "Yes. He was punished. But he deserved it; right, Joshua?"

"Right," he says, finally looking up from the table. "He whipped my ass pretty good. Sarah's right, though, I deserved it. I don't have any issues with my dad or mom. She didn't like it, but it wasn't her role to stop it. So, yeah, he beat me. It just made me a better man. I don't even think about it anymore."

These two don't even know they've been abused. Just like I didn't know the way my folks lived their lives was narcissistic and utterly out of line. Kids accept so much. They want to please. They want approval.

Joshua, Sarah, and I are alike in that way.

I switch subjects. "It troubled your aunt that the portrait of your parents was missing from its place in the front room. She couldn't understand why that was."

They exchange looks.

"That's my fault, Detective Carpenter," Sarah says. "It fell when I was dusting the frame. The glass shattered, and I haven't found another piece big enough to replace it." She turns to Joshua. "Now that we're here in town, maybe we could buy some glass."

"Good idea," he says.

Then I give them potentially more bad news.

"Joshua," I say, "you're a legal adult so this doesn't apply to you." I direct my gaze to Sarah. "You're only seventeen," I start. "That means you're a minor and, though you are seventeen, the state might require a temporary guardian until your folks get home."

She pushes back from the table.

"I'm staying with Joshua. I'm not a kid."

"I agree you're mature for your age. The court will take that into account."

Sarah reaches to her brother's arm and pulls him up. Her face is red. "You can't do this. We didn't do anything wrong."

I can't back down. I try to calm her. "It's not about that, Sarah. It's the law."

"Our parents are gone. We are alone. And you want to do this?"

"As I said, it's the law."

"It's a cruel law. I thought you were going to help us. Not hurt us even more!"

It's like I'd invited a firing squad. I wish I'd never brought it up. I wish that I'd let Juvenile handle it.

Joshua speaks up. "We're going through enough shit right now."

"I know, I'm sorry."

Sarah glares at me. I don't deflect.

"When will all of this happen?"

"It may not happen," I remind them. "As I said, the judge will decide what's best."

"Right," Joshua says looking at his now inconsolable sister. "Someone else will decide what's best. That's just perfect."

On my way to my car, I feel the size of a gnat. I'd spoken the truth, of course. At the same time, I've frightened them. I did that once before with my brother when I ran and left him in foster care. I'd miscalculated the impact of what I thought was best.

And every day since, I've paid the price.

CHAPTER SEVEN

It had been two days since the pickup truck crashed downward from the logging road into the woods. While Regina Torrance had done all she could to obscure it from discovery, she knew that in time someone would come. She also did her best to keep Amy from worrying.

"I'm going to get the body and get rid of it."

"Just leave it."

"No. If they find it then we'll be ground zero for a murder investigation. Can you imagine how that would play out? The police would harp on us; the media would come calling for a quote. The world would find us."

Amy finally agreed. Begrudgingly, but consented, nevertheless.

Regina completed her morning routine, and left Amy with eggs and bacon served on her mother's dishes, Franciscan Ivy pattern. She remembered how one of their moving helpers had dropped the box with the dishes, breaking a big platter and sending Amy to bed in tears. Regina fixed the platter, making the spiderweb cracks barely noticeable.

She could fix the problem of the dead body too. Indeed, it might even be an easier endeavor than the platter. It still showed some cracks through the green of the ivy pattern.

The woods were not nearly as muggy that morning. The forest floor had dried like a kitchen sponge left on a counter for a couple of days. It smelled of living things. Regina was grateful about that. Mud would be an unnecessary complication, literally mucking up what she'd set out to do. As she snaked her way down the trail, Regina shifted her armload of supplies: a hacksaw, a bolt cutter, plastic garbage bags, an old tarp and painter's respirator.

Approaching the vicinity of the truck, she reminded herself to breathe through her mouth when she went about her business.

Her effort at concealment had been effective. She squinted her eye to make sure she was headed right to it. A deer had passed through the area, leaving tiny chiseled hoofprints in the now-drying mud.

Nothing else.

No one else.

She stripped off her clothes, put them inside the plastic bag. She spread out the tarp and stood naked over her tools. She halted her breathing and listened with all the concentration she could gather.

No one was there.

Just birds.

Only squirrels.

And the dead man.

Pulling off the cover of branches and ferns over the body, she gave it a careful look. She hadn't made time for that when she'd made the discovery and considered the implications of what might happen if someone found it. It was badly burned, but she could tell it was a man. His shoulders were broad, and hips narrow. Not a woman. Her eyes traveled downward for further confirmation. She found it. A nob of charcoaled flesh indicated what was left of his penis. He wasn't very tall, as men go. Maybe five foot eight. His clothes had melted onto his skin or had been completely incinerated. In a few places he wasn't burned as badly. He was white. It appeared that he wore glasses because lines seared around his eyes bore the distinct traces of frames. Regina made a note to look for them when she was finished.

She put the respirator on and bent over the body, hacksaw in hand.

I'm doing this for me and Amy. I didn't kill him. I'm only doing what I know I must do to protect us. This is ugly, but it isn't wrong when so much is at stake.

Regina started with the head because all of her years butchering animals on the farm had taught her that was the most difficult area to work—physically and emotionally. It took some doing, but she managed to sever the head just where the neck met the shoulders. She knew that blood cooked in the fire oozed rather than splattered.

Thank you, God.

She put the head on the tarp, facedown. No need to look at the face. Even though she didn't know him, it felt invasive. Too personal.

Regina took air in through her mouth. The hands were easily snipped off at the wrists with the bolt cutters. She deposited them on the tarp with the head. She took in another gulp of air and listened. Nothing.

I can do this!

She tried the cutters on the arm bones, but the dead man was too large for the blades. She reverted to the hacksaw. Up and down. Up and down. The blade wasn't as sharp as it needed to be for efficient cutting, yet it worked. In time, Regina butchered the increasingly fetid body into manageable pieces. By the end of it, her hands and arms were covered in blood and body fluids. Some spatter even freckled her face. That was fine, she thought. She could wash away everything in the outdoor shower. Her clothing would never betray what she did and how.

Amy didn't need to know how far Regina would go for love.

Neither did the Jefferson County sheriff.

It took her two trips to bring the body parts to the firepit, a location that had been the center of activity when she and Amy still had visitors. S'mores. Puffs of marijuana. Long, drunken stories about people they loved and hated.

Regina used some fat rendered from a goat she'd slaughtered to help ignite the pieces of what remained of the nameless dead man. She piled on the wood and set the fire. She knew it would take a long time, probably all night. When they first moved there one of their friends hit a doe and someone came up with the bright idea of cremating the animal's remains. The worst idea ever. It sent up a stream of acrid smoke and the fire hissed as the animal's fat was consumed. A person's pre-burned body couldn't be that bad. Or could it? When the night was over the deer was gone. Even some of the bones had burned. *Gone.* That's just what she needed. She knew that no one would pay any attention to the pyre. Once she'd burned a mattress, sending a tornado of black smoke into the sky. No one said a word. No one complained of the smell either. In Snow Creek, she mused, burning a body was a private, do-not-disturb affair. Like a lot of things out there. She watched the blaze take off and then hurried inside to tell Amy that she was finally getting to some of that trash that had piled up in the barn.

"How'd it go? Did you bury the body?"

"Yes. I did."

"In the woods?"

"Yes, baby, in the woods."

Regina felt Amy's lips against hers. So warm and lovely. So perfect.

"You get some rest. I'm going to watch the fire."

"I love you."

"I love you forever and a day."

Their love, they both knew, was everlasting.

CHAPTER EIGHT

Not a single cloud marred the blue of the sky the morning Dante York and his off-and-on girlfriend, Maddie Cohen, took off from Port Hadlock to scope out the wilds above Snow Creek. Dante had become obsessed with cryptozoology. He was sure that he could be the first person to get an irrefutable photograph of a Sasquatch. Maddie was pretty interested in the idea too, although she felt that the new fascination was taking up too much time out of their romantic life.

Everything they did lately centered around Sasquatch.

A logger had reported seeing tracks there in the late eighties. Sam Otis had even been photographed and featured in the Port Townsend *Leader*.

PT Man Says He Found Bigfoot Tracks

Last Friday was like any other day for Sam Otis, 36, of Port Townsend, with one big exception.

Make that one Bigfoot exception.

Otis had just got off his shift as a sawyer for Puget Logging Co. at the timber giant's Snow Creek property. While returning to his truck, he says he stumbled upon a trail of large humanoid tracks.

"I knew what I was seeing right away," he told the Leader. *"I've always had a feeling that Bigfoot was out there, you know, watching the crew. Now there's proof."*

Otis's proof is in the form of two photographs of the tracks.
In one, he put a dollar bill in the frame to show scale…

"We're going to find something," Dante insisted as he downed a bottle of Mexican Coke.

Maddie smiled encouragingly from her cell phone.

"Yeah," she said as she clicked a deluge of Likes on her friend's Instagram posts. "Something."

The ride was rough going up the old logging road. Puget Logging had intended to harvest more timber there, but an endangered species, the spotted owl, put an abrupt stop to those plans. The irony was the little bird was discovered by a group of crypto-hunters in search of Sasquatch.

Sam Otis's story cost him and everyone on his crew their jobs.

Maddie looked down at her phone.

"No service," she announced.

Dante looked over at her. "You don't always need to be on your phone. Let's enjoy the moment."

It was a familiar refrain. She was on her phone a lot. More so with Dante's new obsession taking center stage.

Maybe they weren't right for each other after all?

She glanced away from her nonfunctioning Samsung and thought it over. Dante was handsome. Kind. Had a good job. *What more could she want?*

The terrain grew rougher, steeper, and the roadway narrowed.

"I feel like I'm in a NutriBullet," she finally said.

"Yeah. Shocks are shitty on this car."

That's true, she thought. *His car is shitty. That's a solid strike against him.*

"Let's pull over," she said.

"Nah. Can't here, but up ahead I see a wider spot."

A minute later, they stopped next to a slash pile of stumps and other refuse from the forest. It had been there such a long time that a Douglas fir seedling managed to get a foothold and rose like a Christmas tree topper from the wood rubble.

"I got to take a leak," Dante said, on his way to the other side of the road.

I need to figure out where this relationship is going, Maddie thought as she perched on a sun-bleached log.

Dante stood in the familiar stance, legs planted apart, rinsing the road dust from a natural hedge of Himalayan blackberry bushes. The razor-wire-like brambles were laden with ripening fruit. The aroma of sun-warmed blackberries is many Pacific Northwesterner's idea of summertime heaven.

"Hey, we should pick some berries."

"Not over there," Maddie shot back, making a disgusted face. "You're gross, Dante."

Dante rolled his eyes. "I didn't mean right here." When he dropped his knees a little to zip up and looked down past the blackberries, a glint of silver struck his eyes. He craned his neck to see better.

"Maddie," he said, turning to face her, "there's a pickup truck down there. Let's go check it out."

It wasn't Bigfoot, but it was something more interesting than just standing around waiting for something to happen, so Maddie agreed.

"Maybe someone junked it here when the logging stopped?" she offered.

"Sounds reasonable," he said, as they slid down the ravine.

As they got closer, Dante could make out the tailgate.

"It's a GMC," he said. "This truck's only a few years old."

He started pulling off branches.

"Someone ditched it here," she said.

"Wonder why? Better than my POS of a car."

"No argument there, Dante."

They walked around the vehicle. It was blackened by fire and the windows were broken out. Driver's door hung open. In the truck bed, a mishmash of carpet and paint cans.

"Remodeler's truck?" Maddie suggested, flicking away a yellow jacket.

Dante assessed the contents and gave her a quick nod.

"Stolen," she said.

"Yeah, someone took it for some fun up here and ran it off the road."

Maddie poked at the contents in the truck bed with a stick.

"Nothing to salvage here," she said.

All of a sudden, her eyes locked on something in the truck bed. She stood frozen for a beat. Her eyes locked. She started to scream. It was a horror movie scream, the kind that slides up and down in volume and doesn't seem to stop.

Dante, who was looking for a registration to see who the truck belonged to, hurried to where she was standing.

"You okay? Did you get stung?" He wrapped his arms around Maddie and tried to calm her.

Maddie stepped away from the truck; though her mouth was moving, she remained mute. All she could do was point the stick at something in the back of the truck.

He drew closer.

"What is it?"

"There," she said, taking the stick and tapping against what she wanted him to see.

A desiccated human hand protruded from the carpet scraps. It was small, a child's or a woman's. The fingers were curved and crab-like.

"Holy shit," Dante said looking at his girlfriend as she leaned into a sword fern and vomited.

CHAPTER NINE

A young state patrolman catches my eye and motions in my direction as I climb out of my car. He's not alone. There are three more cars, two of which belong to Jefferson County sheriff's deputies. A third, I can tell, belongs to the young couple who made the call. It's a ten-year-old Buick Skylark, brick red in color. It must have been a hand-me-down car from a grandparent or something. The couple standing next to it are young.

The female is petite with light brown hair and white skin. The male has black hair and dark skin. She looks toward the ravine. He keeps his eyes on me as I approach.

"I'm Detective Carpenter," I say. "I know today has been traumatic for both of you"—my eyes take them in—"but I need you both to tell me how you found the victim."

The two of them tell me their story. It's a Wimbledon tennis match, with Maddie and Dante taking turns filling me in.

"Sasquatch."

"Proof."

"Road sucked."

"Wanted to go home."

"Had to pee."

"He called over to me."

"Truck."

"Like it was hidden."

Maddie stops for a second before starting up again. She looks down at the powdery dirt road. I know she's remembering. Dante wraps his arm around her shoulder.

"Hand like a claw."

"Heard scream."

And that was that.

We're finishing up as the coroner's plain white van pulls in, and I take down Maddie and Dante's contact information and tell them to go home.

"This is a murder case, right?" Dante asks before turning to leave.

"We don't know that yet," I say.

Really, I do *know*. I can't think of a scenario in which the whole thing was the result of a freak accident. Like maybe someone got caught in a carpet roll at Home Depot and a worker found the body and was fearful they'd be blamed. And maybe fired. That's stupid. Honestly, why else would anyone wrap up a body in carpet and set the thing on fire, and push it off the road? Murder, most likely.

Jerry Larsen approaches. He's in his sixties. He's been our coroner for more than half his life. Since the position is very part time, he and his wife run a drugstore downtown. He makes me think of Santa Claus every time I see him. His hair is white, and he has a silky, six-inch white beard. Jerry's not the least bit fat, but with his twinkly eyes, white hair, and pink cheeks, in my mind, I think of him as Merry Larsen. I never say that aloud.

"Detective," he says, "what have we got here?"

I lead him to where the state patrol has been working the scene. This is our case, our jurisdiction. Even so, the truth is we're in a kind of no-man's land here. Our small budget means we rely on the state patrol and the crime lab in Olympia and assists from Kitsap and Clallam counties. Jerry Larsen is a coroner, not a pathologist. He'll transfer custody of the body to one of the counties or the state and retrieve it when cause of death is determined.

The climb down to the scene is steep and I worry that Jerry might slip, yet I don't dare offer him a hand. He's sweet, but old-school. Old-school sometimes offends. Sweet is fine. Jerry, I think, is sugarplum sweet.

I recognize the patrol officers and they back off to let me do my work.

"We've searched fifty yards around the truck," one says.

"Let's do a hundred," I say.

"VIN removed," another says. "Plates too."

I pull latex gloves from my pocket and find my way to the back of the truck. *Good*, I think. Only the hand is revealed from the carpet. Just as Maddie found it. No one here tried to do my job. I climb into the back of the truck, careful not to move anything any more than necessary.

Jerry assists me with photos.

"Is there something in her hand?" he asks.

I lean in closer. The putrid scent of the body is overwhelming. I don't let on. It's the worst odor in the world and it stays in your nose for a week, particles of the dead clinging to your cilia like parasites that exist to remind you.

Of her.

Or him.

Or them.

The dead who want you to capture their killers.

"Doesn't appear to be," I tell Jerry.

I lean in and peel back the carpet very carefully. Some of the victim's flesh adheres to the backing and it takes a little effort.

Unrolled from her carpet pupa, the woman is nude and partially burned. Her eyes are fused closed and her mouth gives out a silent scream. Jerry turns away for a split second before he resumes recording what's in front of us with his camera.

She's thin with pendulant breasts. Her abdomen is a pattern of stretchmarks. She's someone's mother. Her hands are claws, but they are calloused at the fingertips from hard work. She wears no jewelry. Her hair is long and blond. I stand still and for a second the woods around me goes silent.

I look over at Jerry. His pink cheeks are suddenly ashen.

In my gut I already know who this woman is.

What did he do to you? And where is he now?

I look over at the men standing around me.

"Everything here is evidence. I know you know that."

I say that because sometimes they don't know.

"We need everything preserved for the lab. That means every bit of carpet. Scrap of paper. Gum if there's any in the cab. Coffee cups. The condition is unimportant right now. If you think anything is trash, then you should get another job. We need to ensure that nothing slips through the cracks here. That means the truck too."

I'm pretty sure someone mutters the word *bitch*. That's fine. That means I made an impression. I'm not here for a date anyway. I'm here for justice for the dead woman.

"Did anyone find anything on the perimeter?"

The trooper who met me when I first arrived pipes up.

"I did," he says. "I found a plastic shoe."

He holds up a clear plastic bag.

"Trooper, that's a Croc."

"Sorry," he says. "I thought it could be helpful."

Everyone laughs. His face goes scarlet.

"It might be," I say with a reassuring nod. "That's the brand of the shoe."

CHAPTER TEN

The forest is full of eyes. Tiny eyes. Bigger ones. When an intruder or a pack of them find their way into the dark world of green with its sweet, musky smells, watchers track every movement. Every interloper is a threat. To the single eye that tracked the police, nothing was more dangerous than what was transpiring over by the truck she'd carefully hidden. She watched, unblinking, as the coroner and another deputy carried something away on a stretcher.

Another body?

Regina couldn't believe what she saw. How did she miss that? How was it that there were two? Her attempt at concealment was a devastating failure, one that could ruin her life with Amy.

Damn!

Fuck!

What can I do? What will I say if they come calling?

That night, she carried Amy to the barn. She was asleep, and the weight of her body was heavy in Regina's arms. She made some soft wheezing sounds and to Regina the noise was as lovely as an aria.

Amy opened her eyes.

"I love you, baby."

"I love you more."

Regina could feel Amy's gentle, almost timid, embrace. She longed for the day when she'd be better, and they could live with carefree abandon. They could live as they did before that terrible day two years before.

"I'm going to put a note on the door that we're away for the rest of the summer."

"Good idea, Regina."

"I try. Besides, we used to love sleeping up here anyway."

Amy smiled as Regina lifted her onto a mound of straw she'd fashioned into a bed in the loft of the small barn they'd built so many years ago. It was like a homecoming of sorts. Memories of those early days were magical. The best years of their lives.

She put Amy to bed and went down to the kitchen in the house and wrote out a note.

> *Reminder: Amy and I are out of town traveling with our friends in their RV. Jared is taking care of the animals so no worries. We'll be back in September or thereabouts.*
> *Love, Reggie and Amy*

The way Regina saw it as she stuck the message on the front door, the ruse would buy the sheriff enough time to find the answers to what happened with the truck without trampling on their privacy. They had made their own world, and the outside was not invited in.

Especially law enforcement.

Regina peeled back her thoughts two years, to the last time she left the farm in the woods for town. She remembered how she felt. Alone. Strange. Different. She walked the streets of Port Townsend in a daze. It was as though she'd never been there. An alien. Everything and everywhere was so loud. So irritating. She wondered why she needed to be party to a stranger's phone call as a young man passed by yakking about some woman he'd "boned" the night before, bragging that he'd already ghosted the "skank." It made Regina grimace. A mother whisper-yelled into her phone about her child's latest tantrum and how she was at her wits' end and wished she'd adopted a Korean baby instead of a Russian one. A man in his seventies stopped in front of a girl, not more than twenty, selling seascape paintings and proceeded to tell her in no uncertain terms that the colors she had selected clashed.

"I don't know if you're going for realism or kitsch, but either way, you're way off," he said.

It was missing the mark. Unnecessary. Everyone seemed to trample over each other's privacy as if they'd been invited to do so. Amy would hate the way it was out there. She really would. Regina knew that was truer than anything she could measure as she gathered supplies. She hoped that it would be another two years before she needed to make the trip to PT.

She ordered a mocha with whipped cream, and an avocado and cream cheese sandwich from a downtown deli. With each sip of the mocha, each bite of the sandwich, she vowed it was the last she'd have from another's hand. She and Amy were self-sufficient. More so every day. They had a robust vegetable garden. A flock of chickens for eggs and meat. Goats provided milk, cheese, and meat. They even grew their own wheat in a field behind the barn. Before she closed the trunk, she surveyed the results of her shopping trip, things that she and her wife couldn't raise or grow but needed.

The list was quite small, yet in its own way, crucial—olive oil, cornmeal, tissue paper, some plastic piping, and a box of activated charcoal.

Satisfied, she snapped the trunk shut.

Regina started the car and turned on the radio. Seattle news filled her ears, and its droning newscaster made her resolve to leave the world behind even stronger. She pressed the pedal with the ball of her foot and watched Port Townsend's pretty Victorian homes—painted ladies of every conceivable hue—and the façades of its quaint brick and stone downtown buildings fade from the rearview mirror.

Regina caught her own image just then. She cocked her head. She looked good. Tan, fit. Her eyebrows could use some shaping, though Amy didn't complain about them, so why should she worry? Even her missing eye didn't eat away at her sliding vanity. Her one eye was full of life. Full of hope. Wonderment, even.

You only need one eye to see the world clearly. To see what matters most.

Regina Torrance never felt better in her entire life.

She rolled down the window and allowed the soft sea-scented breeze to flow over her face.

Life was so good.

No more drama.

Regina crawled under the covers. Amy was asleep. It passed through her mind that something was physically wrong with Amy, but she didn't let the thought take root. It was too much for her. She'd done everything she could to help her recover from whatever it was that had been ailing her. For a time, she thought things were getting better. She prayed on it. She whispered in Amy's ear that there was nothing that could keep them apart, not sickness. Not anything worse.

We belong together.

Amy murmured and stirred.

Regina whispered some more.

"I want to make love with you. My tongue misses you. Wants to taste you. Make you writhe like it's the first time we've ever loved each other."

There was no response for the longest time. Finally, Amy shook her head.

"I'm sorry. I love you. I don't feel like that right now. Kiss me. Hold me. Touch me. I'm not ready for anything more."

Regina leaned over and kissed Amy's cheek. Every night had been like that for a very long time. Regina told herself that it didn't matter, that loving Amy any way she preferred was good and if there was a barrier at the moment, in time they'd cross it. Real love prevails. The world survived only because of that singular truth.

The morning after staying in the barn, Regina went about her regimented routine. The only deviation were the thoughts in her head. She wondered if she'd done the right thing. If she'd have to pay for her deeds or if Amy would be made to pay. She patted her favorite goat.

"We're safe, right?"

The goat looked at her with her devil-like eyes.

"That's enough out of you," she said.

She finished in the barn, collected the eggs from the coop, and walked over to the firepit to examine the ashes for the umpteenth time.

It was clean.

We're safe. We're all safe.

CHAPTER ELEVEN

It was no real surprise when Jerry called me from the coroner's office. He'd received the preliminary reports from the pathologist.

"We've got a homicide."

What else could it be?

"Cause?"

"Blunt force trauma to the back of the head. Dr. Andrade suspects the claw end of a hammer. Skull had tool marks from the blow. Besides the fracture, of course."

"That's brutal," I say. "Anything on tox?"

"Too early."

"How about prints?"

"They pulled palms, but the fingertips were burned pretty bad. Nothing there."

"Just the fingers?"

"Yeah," he says. "Some burns on the face too. Andrade thinks a blowtorch was used."

"Torture?"

"Likely post mortem."

That's a relief, I think. Getting beaten with a hammer is beyond belief, using an acetylene flame on a woman is the stuff of slasher films.

"Still processing the truck," he says. "More on that in a day or two. Pretty backed up down there. We're lucky they processed her as fast as they did. We have two rape kits that have been on ice there for almost six months. Prosecutor pushes, but they've got so much backlog and not enough staff."

"That's an excuse," I say. "They spend their money where they want to. Guess rapes don't mean as much as new highway projects."

"And murders," he adds. "Those still move the needle down there."

I can feel where this is going and it's all my fault. I opened the door. Jerry is on the edge of a rant about government waste. I shift the conversation back to the murder victim.

"Send me all you've got."

"I already did. One step ahead of you, Detective."

I go on to the county server, enter my credentials and password. In my folder I find a PDF of the reports from Olympia. I get the printer humming and head down the hall to the coffee room. Sheriff is pressing the button on the candy machine when I arrive.

"Damn thing never works," he says.

"Maybe that's a good thing."

He ignores my remark.

"How's Snow Creek doing?" he asks.

"Printing out the coroner's report now. Give me a bit to absorb it. I'll swing by later."

He nods, and I take my coffee and leave. I can hear him back at the machine as I return to my desk.

I read through the report page by page. Dr. Andrade's words tell a complete story, yet it's his photos that really hold my attention. The victim's burns had to be post mortem. They were so clear, so precise. I flip through them one by one. The face. The arms. The back of the head. When I get to her feet, I do a double take. I pull the photocopy a little closer. I can't be sure, but it appears that the victim is missing a toe.

I see no mention of that in the report.

Gulping some coffee, I dial Dr. Andrade's office.

He's on the line right away.

"Doctor, there's a discrepancy in your report. There's no notation—that I could find—that indicated the woman had a missing toe."

I hear him tapping away on his keyboard. A pause. Maybe even a sigh. Hard to tell over the phone.

"Missing baby toe on the right foot, yes, yes," he says.

"It's not in the report, Doctor."

"My bad," he says with obvious regret, before throwing an employee under the bus. "I have a new transcriptionist and he has missed a few things. Not terrible, but not great either."

I wonder why people don't just admit their mistakes.

People like me.

"Post mortem?" I ask.

"No," he says. "Not at all. There was scar tissue where the toe should be. Jane Doe lost her toe probably as a child."

"What else did he miss?"

"The back of her heels collected some soil. It's on the photographs, but not in the report."

"She was dragged?"

"Likely."

"She was only 122 pounds. Not that heavy."

"Dead weight though. It's not easy."

I'm exasperated yet also intrigued.

"Will you amend your report?" I ask.

Long pause. Everyone in three counties knows he hates amending anything. He's right. Always. Never, ever wrong.

"All right, Detective. I'll do it. Just for you." His tone carries a hint of sarcasm.

Do it for the victim, I want to say. But I don't. Instead, I thank him and hang up.

Later as I head for home, I stop in to brief the sheriff.

He's up to his neck with paperwork. He looks up with those kind eyes and gives me a nod.

"How's the carpet case moving along?"

"Not much to report. Ms. Wheaton never had a driver's license. Nothing from the DMV to help figure if the victim is her. Maybe one thing: She was missing a toe on her right foot. Kids didn't mention that. I'll round them up tomorrow."

"Sounds good," he says, lowering his wire frames. "How are you doing, Megan? You stressed?"

Tony Gray does know me. What I *allow* him to know. He's seen something on my face that I didn't hide from him. Or maybe couldn't. It's true I'm stressed. I guess, with the Wheaton case, things that I'd forgotten, suppressed, have come at me with a vengeance.

"I'm fine," I tell him. "Just need to confirm our vic and find her husband."

CHAPTER TWELVE

Back in my kitchen I rifle through my completely subpar pantry for something to eat, though I'm not really that hungry. The photos of Jane Doe have worked as an appetite suppressant, which would be some kind of benefit if I were overweight. But I'm not. The indignity of murder doesn't stop at the point where life ceases to exist. It's a continuum. The victim from Snow Creek was treated like trash. Disposed of. Like she was nothing. Killers like hers invite others to enjoy the impact of the crime. The kids who found her. The team that investigates the crime and goes home to their wives or sisters with the picture of what happened to Jane forever in their consciousness.

And then the line becomes a circle when the loved ones learn what happened.

I know all of that.

I've experienced all of that.

Now I wonder if that little tape recorder and the box of tapes had been a good idea. It's brought me back to a time and place that I've wanted to forget yet can't. I look around for something stronger than wine, but in reality, I'm not much of a drinker. I should be. I have reason to. I should be a raging alcoholic by now. No one would blame me if I were. Sure, they'd feel sorry for me.

If they knew.

Only three people know the sum of everything I've done. Hayden, Dr. Albright, and me.

A few like the sheriff know the end of my story, but not the beginning. As I swallow my wine and stare at the box, I hope more than ever that no one knows the middle. That's the part that makes me question who I really am.

And why I did what I did.

My hand swipes lightly over the tapes. They are numbered by date. I take a deep breath as I pull out the one from my second session with Dr. Albright. I remember thinking at the time that she had the kind of affect that suggested she was a genuine do-gooder, not some poseur there to enjoy the troubles of others, as though what unfolded during each session was only about entertainment.

I take a breath and press the button.

I hear her calming voice reminding me.

Dr. A: Rylee, you know I'm recording you, right?

Me: Yes. I know that. What are you going to do with the tapes? I was thinking about that after our first, ah, session.

Dr. A: They are only for me. They won't be played for anyone else. Someday, when the time is right or when I die, they'll go back to you.

Me: Okay. I guess.

Dr. A: Last session we talked about how you found your father—stepfather—and how you and Hayden made it to the waterfront of Port Orchard. Put me there, Rylee. Tell me what you remember.

Me: (short pause) Okay. It's silly but I still remember this seagull fighting with another, smaller, shorebird over a french fry on the bench beside me and Hayden. The fight was occupying Hayden's attention, which was good. I remember hugging him. Telling him we would be all right. I put my arm around his shoulder, feeling his bones underneath his dark blue hoodie and the clean T-shirt we exchanged for the bloody one I buried in the woods.

Dr. A: Your brother means a lot to you.

Me: (crying) Everything. He's small. He's been my baby since the day my mom brought him home. He trusted me. I would have done anything I could for him. I didn't nuzzle him or hold him. I wanted to. We're not the touchy-feely kind of brother and sister.

Dr. A: Put me there. What did you see? How did you feel?

Me: We watched a green and white Washington State ferry chug through the choppy waters to the dock in Bremerton. We sat in silence as the cars unloaded. Feel? Scared and empty inside, but I didn't show it.

Dr. A: You wanted to protect your brother.

Me: Yes and no. It's just the way I am. I once saw a girl get hit by a car and I didn't even yelp. I was ten and back then my name was Jessica. I know it's dumb, but I loved that name. I remember watching a green Honda Civic smack into that girl in jeans and a pretty pink top. I didn't even flinch. I didn't go to her. A lady standing next to me by the side of the street where it happened must have thought that my nonresponse was a result of shock, but it wasn't anything like that.

Dr. A: What was it?

Me: When you have to pretend that you're someone or something that you're not you get pretty good at concealing emotions. Reactions, my dad used to say, are for amateurs.

Dr. A: Are you hiding your feelings now?

Me: Do I look like it, Doctor?

Dr. A: Sorry. Please go on, Rylee.

Me: Maybe we shouldn't do this. Maybe it won't help me.

Dr. A: I can't promise anything. I believe it will. I believe that it will help you move forward. Your past has a hold on you in ways you might not even understand. Please, go on.

Me: Hayden kept saying that maybe our dad wasn't dead. He was hoping. And I went along with his hope, just for him. But not for long. I knew we had to get out of there. We had Dad's credit cards, some money, and even my mom's driver's license.

Dr. A: Her license?

Me: Right—a duplicate. Hers. It puzzled me for a minute then I figured it out. I knew the credit cards were useless. They could and would be traced. I knew the eighty dollars we had would run out. And I knew that we didn't have anyone we could trust, Doctor. (pause) Trusting anyone was against our family's rules.

Dr. A: I understand. Trust can only be earned.

I remember thinking about that exchange. I was unsure of Karen Albright back then. I still am.

I continue listening. I told her about the trip to the drugstore to buy hair dye and scissors. Gum for Hayden. How, all the while, I remember thinking we needed a place to stay.

Dr. A: Tell me more about your family, the rules you mentioned earlier.

Me: It sounds silly. We weren't in some cult. I mean, don't you have to have other members besides just us? We were isolated. If I hadn't attended a public school, I wouldn't have had any idea of what the world was like.

Dr. A: That must have been very hard for you.

Me: When you don't know anything different, whatever weirdness your parents put into your life seems normal. Your normal. You know what I mean?

Dr. A: I do. Did, for example, it seem normal to your parents? The rules?

Me: When I think about it, it's hard to say. Even now. I can almost see the look on Dad's face when it was time to leave whenever we were on the run. His anxiety. The way his eyes narrowed and sweat collected at his temples and he'd withdraw a little. He was worried that we'd be found.

Dr. A: How did you decide where to go?

Me: It seems so stupid now. But also, in its own way, smart. We called the nights before we moved to another place "the switch." We had a glass bowl with a bunch of names of towns that were written by Mom on small, fortune-cookie-sized pieces of paper. I once asked my mom why it was that we did all of that. She told me, and I'll never forget it, that there was security in randomness.

I press STOP on the recorder. It's getting late. I'm tired. My mind needs a break. And yet I can't stop thinking of my mother. How she made me believe in so many things.

If we are thinking of a place, making plans for a place, then it can be found out, she said. *If we are random, no one can know where we're going, honey. You know, because even we don't know until we make the switch.*

I remember thinking how it all made sense, in the way that parents sometimes can make the most ridiculous things seem normal. Like the Easter Bunny. Like the fact that only old people die. Or that all dogs go to heaven.

Speaking with convincing authority was my mother's forte.

I'm dizzy from the wine or the memories that have bombarded me. It's hard to know which. Wine, I hope. I want to think of myself as a strong person. That's what makes me good at my job. I look down. My hands are shaking. I know why. The tape has sparked so many memories of Hayden. I miss my brother so much as I think of him as that little boy back in Port Orchard. Everything that happened after he found our father was my doing. He was a little kid. I dragged him along on my odyssey and dropped him off the first chance I had.

He didn't deserve that.

I pad down the hall to a second bedroom that I use for an office. The scene there is chaotic. I've turned an entire room into the proverbial junk drawer. Little things, big things. Nothing put where it belongs. Most of the stuff is junk, yet because I have so little of my early years, I keep it all—a necklace I wore the day we left the house, vintage Foster Grant sunglasses, my ASB card from South Kitsap.

And a news clipping I tore from an old bound edition of the *Oregonian* from Portland State University archives.

My laptop beckons from the desk.

I slide into the chair and open my email account. Nothing but the usual offers from stores that I was stupid enough to give my email address. I'd rather not have ten percent off anything if it means you'll spam me every single day of my life.

Even though risk always looms with any technology, especially the use of email, I start typing, keeping things vague and free of details that could hurt either one of us. It is my only hope to reach him.

Hayden,

You don't have to answer. Please read all the way to the end. Please don't let this email bounce back because you've blocked me or relegated me to your SPAM folder. I'm missing you so much right now. I just wanted to let you know that I'm doing okay. You'd like Port Townsend so much. It's got some cool old architecture like Wallace. Lots of restaurants and bars too. I have a spare room. When your deployment ends maybe you can come here and stay awhile. Like I said, you don't have to answer.

I love you,
Rylee

I reread the email. I note where I tell him—no less than twice—that no response is required. That's really not for him, but for me. I doubt he will reply. I write those words so I don't check my email obsessively. Even though I will.

I put my fingertip on SEND and go back to bed knowing that I'll check my email first thing in the morning.

CHAPTER THIRTEEN

Jane Doe's face is so badly beaten and burned that there's nothing for a forensic artist to work with. No photos of Ms. Wheaton exist online. I wonder how anyone could escape social media these days—even if you want to be anonymous, someone somewhere is going to take a picture and post it. Except the Wheatons. None of them have any kind of digital presence.

I listen to the news as I return to their place in Snow Creek. It's Seattle news, of course. It's like the news bureaus have erected a wall around the city and declared that nothing outside it is worth reporting. The reporter for the Port Townsend *Leader* will do a story on the body found off the logging road when he finally sobers up and checks the log at the department. I'm thinking he'll get around to that tomorrow. Always on top of it.

Sarah is in the yard pushing an old-fashioned rotary mower. She's wearing jeans and the Miller High Life tee that her brother had worn the other day. Her long hair is pulled back and beads of sweat sparkle on her brow.

She runs over to my car as I pull in.

"Have you found them?"

Joshua appears in the doorway and joins Sarah.

"Detective, do you have some news?" he asks.

"You can tell us," Sarah says. "We're not little kids. Were they in an accident? Are they in the hospital? Where are they?"

"Let's sit here," I say as we start for the front porch. I motion to a bench by the door.

"When we talked at the sheriff's department," I go on, "you said your mother had no distinguishing features."

"Right," Joshua says. "No tattoos. Nothing like that."

"That's right," I say. "Was there anything else about her that would be different than most people? Maybe something about her body."

Sarah looks at her brother, then back at me.

"Mom was super self-conscious about her foot," Joshua says. "She wouldn't want to bring it up. She was very embarrassed."

My stomach drops. I look at their faces. They are about to receive the worst possible news. I've made visits to the families of people who had died in traffic accidents. Mothers and fathers who have to be told their child had been found in a school bathroom or a county park, dead of an overdose.

Never have I told two children that their mother was murdered.

"What was it about her foot?" I ask, knowing the answer, knowing that Ida Wheaton had been found.

"Her baby toe. She had an accident with a mower when she was five." Joshua looks over at the mower Sarah had been using. "That's why she wears those."

Sarah indicates the heavy, lace-up boots on her feet.

He's reading me now.

"You found her," Joshua says. "Didn't you?"

"We think so. We can't be one hundred percent sure."

"Where is she?" Sarah asks, bunching her hands together. "Is she in the hospital? Is she going to be okay? Where's Dad?"

"We don't know where your father is," I say. "But no, she's not in the hospital. I'm very sorry to tell you this, we think that a body recovered from Puget Logging's old property not far from here could be your mom."

Sarah lets out a cry, and Joshua reaches out to comfort her. Her shoulders melt into her body as she shrinks downward on the bench.

I give them a moment to process.

"I'm very sorry," I say.

Joshua nods. "I think we're in shock. Is our dad in the hospital?"

"No, he's not," I say.

"He killed Mom, didn't he?" Sarah says.

"We don't know that," I say, switching the subject, admittedly awkwardly so. "What kind of car did he drive?"

"A GMC pickup," Joshua says. "Are you looking for it?"

I shake my head. "No, we found it. Dumped off the logging road."

Joshua stares at me. His eyes are glistening, yet he's not yet crying. He's being brave for his sister.

Like I'd been for my brother.

"You found Mom, but not Dad?" he asks.

"Yes, and as I said, it might not be your mom. We have to confirm."

"You want us to come to town and look at her? I don't know if I can do that," Sarah says, through her tears.

"No," I say, softening my voice. "I would not recommend that. The body is not in any condition that you should view."

"I don't understand," she says.

"There was a fire at the scene where the truck was found."

Sarah wails and Joshua puts his arm around her, tighter. He whispers in her ear that everything will be all right.

"Maybe it's not her," he says.

I give them some time, before speaking again.

"I need something with your mother's DNA. A hairbrush would be good. Or a toothbrush."

Joshua gets up and disappears into the house. A minute later, he comes out with a tortoiseshell hairbrush. Strands of blond hair catch the light of the sun.

I put it into a plastic bag and seal it.

"I need one more thing," I tell them. "I need some DNA from one of you. It will be compared against your mother's, so we can determine a match, all right?"

I pull the swab and vial from my pocket.

Sarah is closest to me, but she's suddenly inconsolable.

"I can't believe this is happening."

She gets up and runs into the house.

"I'll do it," Joshua says.

I hold out the swab, and he opens his mouth like a baby bird. A severely injured bird. I feel my hand shake a little as flashes of my own life come back to me. I know what's coming next for them. It won't be easy. It will leave a scar for the rest of their lives.

"It won't hurt," I say. "I'll just rub the tip against your cheek."

I finish and put the swab into the kit and seal it.

"Our dad had his issues, but he wouldn't hurt our mom. Not like that. His kind of hurt was not talking to her for days. Never even yelled at her."

I won't tell him what I'm thinking. The strong silent type is often silent because to give words to what's in his mind would shock his audience. Ted Bundy never said a cross word to his girlfriend, but inside he was reliving the things he did to the girl he'd just left, skull shattered, head severed, in the woods. Gary Ridgway had his son in the truck when he picked up women to murder and dump along the Green River. *Wait here*, he'd say. *Me and my friend are taking a walk.* After raping and strangling her, he'd take his boy for an ice cream, playing the murder like a silent movie in his head while the boy ate his cone.

"I'll call your aunt Ruth," I say, "but it would take her a day at best to get here."

Joshua nods. "Yeah. Thank you."

"Do you have anyone in the neighborhood you can be with?"

He shakes his head.

"I mean there are people around here, but we only know them in passing. I don't even know their names."

"Are you going to be all right? Should I send someone out here tonight? Otherwise, I'll be back when I have more news. You call me if you need anything, Joshua?"

"We'll be fine," he says, tucking his shoulder-length hair behind an ear. He's acting strong for my benefit, showing me that he can deal with the tragedy. I also see the hope in his eyes. "Our dad has to be out there," he says. "Someone must have abducted them. Maybe he escaped or something?"

I doubt it, though I don't say so.

"We'll do our best to find him."

CHAPTER FOURTEEN

I try Ruth Turner three times but no one picks up. Maybe she's at the church caucus, whatever that is. Or her husband won't allow her to take my call. There's no answer on her so-called borrowed cell phone, either. Though I wonder how close the sisters actually were—after all, she hadn't been to Snow Creek in a half dozen years, I know that my words will crush her.

I order a pizza from an Italian place across from the courthouse on my way home. I want thick crust with a mountain of cheese and pepperoni. I'll probably burn the roof of my mouth with the oil that pools on each little round slice of pepperoni. I don't care. The pizza is so good and maybe I deserve a little pain to shift me from what I know I'll do when I get home.

I pull a triangle of cheesy goodness from the box and eat it as I drive. Oh perfect, I think...I feel a burn.

The house is surprisingly cool when I go inside and I set down the pizza box next to the tapes. Analog tapes. I suddenly feel old. The world today is a vapor. Nothing, not even photographs, exists in tangible form. Just ether floating around your phone or computer. I crack a cold beer and open the windows to suck in the maritime breeze.

My fingertips roll over the little rectangles, each like a pair of coiled snakes in a clear, plastic case.

I insert the next one into the little recorder.

Dr. Albright tells me to take off my shoes. The command puzzles me for a moment. What kind of therapy was I getting anyway? What else did I forget? I breathe a sigh of relief when it dawns on me that there'd been a cloudburst on my way to my appointment that afternoon. My hair, my feet and the front of my shirt where my jacket was unzipped were sopping.

"Feel better?" she asks.

"Thanks," I say. *"It was a dumb day for sandals."*

She murmurs something that I can't make out.

"Let's start where we left off last time. Close your eyes and tell me everything; tell me the story that you've held inside all these years, Rylee. I want to see what you saw, hear how you felt. Put me right there in real time."

"Okay," my younger self says.

I drink my beer, the first of several I'll have. The pizza, which I told myself when I ordered it would be great for lunch the next day, will be nearly gone.

I tell her about how Hayden and I slept in the bathroom of the *Walla Walla*, the ferry from Bremerton to Seattle. I mention the sepia-toned photograph of Princess Angeline and how she watched me.

Dr. A: Tell me more about that.

Me: Princess Angeline, Chief Seattle's daughter, was born in 1820, died in 1896. I remember looking at her picture. She had skin weathered like silver driftwood and her eyes were wide and light in color—like amber beach glass, I think. I felt like she was watching me as I plotted my way to the end of the night.

Dr. A: You didn't really think that, did you?

Me: I'm messed up, Doctor. I've done crazy things, but no, I'm not crazy.

Dr. Albright offers an apology, and I carry on with my story. I tell her how I monitored the cleaning crew's routine with the bathrooms, going in and out, with a mop and bucket every fifteen minutes.

I knew that inside the door was a sheet of paper that indicated when the restroom was last cleaned. It was a farce, of course. They were only in there long enough to sign their name to the card affixed on to the back of the door that indicated they'd done what the captain had asked.

Me: So, I told Hayden to plug up a toilet with a bunch of toilet paper, flush, then hide in a storage cabinet. He got mad because I made him hide in the women's room. I told him it's the only way we can be safe. A man will come in there and shut down the toilet's water flow. And since it's the last run of the night, he'd leave the mess for the morning crew to clean up.

My voice goes soft and then stops.

Dr. A: Do you need to take a break, Rylee?
Me: Just thinking about my brother. His trust in me. Hayden was so scared. I remember how I acted so tough because I knew that I was near breaking too. I just did my best to hold my emotions inside because that's the only way anyone can get through the really hard stuff. Our mother told me that. Mom told me that she learned to actually control her feelings. She said that she knew that emotions only made the punishment greater. Dr. Albright, can we stop? I feel sick.

I hear Dr. Albright shift in her chair. She says that remembering buried things can do that, but promises it will get better. She pulls a tissue from the box and says I could call her if I need to talk before our time together the following week.

Me: I carry your number with me, Doctor. I haven't used it yet.
Dr. A: But you can. You need to know that, Rylee.

*

I check my email. Once more, nothing from my brother, Hayden.

My nearly empty glass follows me to my bedroom, and I lie there, half asleep, half woozy from too much alcohol. I run my hand through my hair. I'm back on the *Walla Walla*. The images are fuzzy, like an old VHS tape.

Hayden is asleep, and I gently lift him away, deeper into a nest of paper towels. I turn in the dim light of the ferry bathroom and hold up my hair with one hand. I reach for the scissors and start cutting. Locks fall like autumn leaves over the dingy countertop and into the bottom of the pitted white sink. I cut, and I cut. Tears roll down my cheeks, but I don't make a sound.

I open a box of dye and apply it with the thin plastic gloves that come in the box. I smell the chemicals as my hair eclipses from brown to blond. I rinse in the sink, the acrid odor wafting through the still air of the bathroom. I tear a ream of paper towels to wring out the water and then, in what I think is a brilliant move, I turn on the hand dryer and rotate my head against the hot spray of air. I am in Maui. I am in Tahiti. I'm on the beach and I have a tan. A handsome boy looks at me and I smile.

The dryer stops, and I look in the mirror and I see her. *Mom.* I look just like my mother. It was unintended genius.

Hayden, now awake, seems to agree.

"I miss Mom. Do you think they found Dad?"

I indicate the second box of hair dye. "Your turn, Hayden."

He climbs up on the counter and lays his head in the sink as I wet his hair with lukewarm water. It reminds me of when he was a baby and Mom washed him in the sink instead of the tub. He scrunches his eyes shut as I rub in the dye. When I'm done, he will be transformed. He'll no longer be the little boy with the shock of blond hair, the one that makes him look like he's stepped out of the page of a cute kids' clothing website.

I look down at the name on the dye box.

Dark and Dangerous.

The tape in my head spins to the end and all I can think about is Hayden. We had a blowout of a fight the last time we saw each other. It was my fault. All of it. I was like some insidious weed that took over every inch of his life. We'd met in a crowded bar near SeaTac airport. He was all grown up, going on a vacation to Cabo before deploying for the Middle East. Things were going well for us, I thought. We'd moved on and made something of ourselves.

I don't know why it happened, but it did.

All it took was four words from my little brother.

"Mom really misses you," he said.

"I can't go there, Hayden."

"Why?" he asked, leaning closer to me, scanning my face. "She's our mom, Rylee. She hasn't had it easy. She misses you. Don't you even love her a little?"

I didn't. Not even a drop of love for her. I couldn't tell Hayden why.

"You're one selfish bitch of a sister," he said. "After all we've been through, you don't care about anyone. Do you?"

I put down my gin and tonic. "I care about you."

Hayden shook his head. "Really? That's funny. You've only seen me three times since foster care."

The thought of him in foster care stabs at me, even now. It was my fault. I own it. Nevertheless, he didn't need to bring it up.

"You know, Rylee," he told me. "I looked up to you. Now when I see you, I realize I don't know who you are. I don't know if you're even capable of being a sister or daughter or anything."

My eyes were damp, but I didn't let a single tear fall down my cheeks. I want to cry ugly—it's how I felt inside.

My brother got up and turned to me.

"See you around, sister."

Nothing came out of my mouth. It was not my style to say sorry. Or to beg for forgiveness. Why should it be? I remember thinking. I did what I had to do. I can't take it back.

And then Hayden disappeared through the labyrinth of tables and the cacophony of people who laugh as though whatever their drinking partner has said is the funniest thing they've ever heard.

I finished my drink and got up to pay.

Nothing's funny about my life. Never has been.

That's the last time I saw him.

CHAPTER FIFTEEN

Snow Creek was punched into the hills and mountains by logging companies more than fifty years ago. After the spotted owl put a halt to things, Olympic, Weyerhaeuser, and Puget Logging sold off parcels at bargain rates—because there were no public utilities like water or power or sewer. That was fine for the folks that decided they'd rather live in a lonely world of their own making than the cookie-cutter places they came from. Some were hippie types—at least by the looks of them. Beads, flannel shirts, and jeans so dirty they could walk across town on their own. Others came to do things verboten in the outside world. Pot growers, mostly. Some were believers in the occult—or at least pretended to be. A writhing mass of naked people under the moon was something no one would ever see in suburbia, where the nosy neighbors lived with 911 on speed dial.

Everyone who came sought seclusion.

As I drive from the Wheatons' place I make a left, looking for the closest neighbors on that side of their farm. The woods break to a field punctuated with massive stumps, then back again to a black wall of old-growth timber. I can see where the loggers gave up and moved on. One tree looks big enough to tunnel through like the famous Redwoods in California. I slow to take it in. The first driveway is a quarter mile or so farther. I follow it up to a small log cabin dripping in ferns and emerald moss. Smoke curls from the river rock chimney. *It's a pancake syrup commercial,* I think.

As I open the car door, I'm immediately yanked from the quaintness of the scene.

Cats.

A lot of cats.

I can smell them. Anyone within fifty yards could.

An elderly woman peers from the window. I motion to her and she comes to the door.

She's in her eighties if she's a day. She's wearing a pretty pink robe and boots. Her hair is black and white, almost skunk-like.

I'd rather smell a skunk right now, I think.

She squints at me.

"Do I know you?" she asks.

"No," I tell her. "I'm Detective Megan Carpenter, from Jefferson County Sheriff's Office, ma'am. I'm here on police business. Can we talk?"

Her lips tighten to a straight line. "I'm not getting rid of my cats. You can't make me."

"Oh, no. Of course not. I'm not here about your animals."

"My babies," she corrects me.

I ask her for her name.

"Maxine Jacobson," she says.

"Ms. Jacobson, I'm here about your neighbors."

"What neighbors?"

"The Wheatons."

"Oh them. Religious weirdos. Don't have much else to say about 'em. The girl and the boy are all right. Came over here a few times with food for my cats. Want to come inside and see them?"

I know I will throw up if I get any closer to that door; the acrid smell of feline urine is literally punching at my nostrils. I'd give anything for Ruth Turner's wintergreen deodorant right now. I'd shove the whole stick up my nose.

"No," I say. "Thank you. I'm highly allergic."

It's a lie. I actually like cats. Not a hundred at a time, though.

"That's too bad. After my husband died, a pregnant cat showed up and, you know how it goes. Ten become twenty. Then more. I'm probably the luckiest woman on the planet. Never, ever lonely."

I turn the conversation back to the Wheatons.

"Did you meet Ida and Merritt? What was your take on them?"

"Why are you asking about them? Folks out here don't have block parties. We mind our own business."

"I imagine that's very true," I say as a cat circles my legs, leaving a trail of gray fur on my pants.

"Cotton likes you," she says.

The acknowledgment softens Maxine.

"She's beautiful," I say. "I so wish I wasn't allergic."

Maxine nods. "The Wheatons were weird. He did all the talking. His wife just stood around and looked lost. I couldn't figure out the relationship. I even asked the kids one time if things were okay at home."

"What did they say?" I ask.

She picks up Cotton and a cloud of fur scatters in the breeze. "Nothing really. It was a while ago. It was the last time I saw 'em too. They were real regular visitors. After that, nothing. Why all the questions, Detective—"

"Carpenter," I tell her, giving her a card. "The parents are missing. Been gone for a few weeks now. Supposed to be in Mexico at an orphanage. Never got there."

"Orphanage? What for? To get another worker?"

I look at her eyes. They're slits now, but she's studying me.

"No, to do some work for charity."

Maxine lets Cotton slide from her arms to the ground.

"That's a crock," she says. "That man had a mouth like a sailor. Always yelling at those kids, especially his wife and the boy. Charity? What a joke that is. I bet they were headed down there to get another boy. Joshua wanted to bolt."

Cotton is back to rubbing against my legs.

Help me, I think.

"He told you that?" I ask.

"Yes, he did," Maxine went on. "He told me that he didn't want to live out here. It's not for everyone. Kids don't have a choice. Parents get to decide everything. My husband moved us out here and I hated it for the first twenty years; now I wouldn't trade places with the queen of England."

I imagine the queen would feel the same way.

I ask her if there are any other neighbors up the road, off the grid.

"Not anymore. Since marijuana became legal in Washington, our local growers packed their tent—and I do mean a tent—and moved on. Nice couple. No one else up this far. Few folks back the way you came. Saw 'em a time or two, but don't know them by name. Not even by sight. Sorry."

I thank her, nudge Cotton away, and head to the car.

"Come by again, Detective. Haven't had a visitor out here for a year or so."

I tell her I will, but I hope I don't ever have to. I'm sure I smell of cat pee.

I wind my way down the bumpy road, stopping at a couple of places. No one seems to be home. One mobile home looks abandoned. Yet it hasn't been. I peer through the window after I knock and see a sweet potato vine growing suspended by three toothpicks over some water. The water's full. I leave my card with a note to tell them to call, though I doubt whoever lives there has a phone.

When I get to my office, I fill out the paperwork for the lab work on the samples. The courier hasn't left, so Joshua's cheek swab and his mother's hair will be in Olympia tonight.

I write an email to the crime lab:

RUSH NEEDED.

The DNA samples I'm sending your way need your urgent attention. Looking for evidence of a familial match. Please do it first thing. We have a dead woman and a missing man out here and we need confirmation from you.

That night I eat the one slice of pizza I somehow managed to resist the night before. I sit at the table in my underwear, windows wide open and a fan blowing over my body. I hear the sound of the washer down the hall, separating Cotton's fur from my black pants. I catch my reflection on the open windowpane. I look tired. The roots of my hair are showing. I'll need to get to the salon. Maybe I should get some Dark and Dangerous.

CHAPTER SIXTEEN

Sheriff and I arrive at the office at the same time the next morning, an unusual occurrence. Port Townsend's only all-season panhandler is setting up by a fountain that no longer spouts anything but a green swill of algae.

"Morning, Chad," Sheriff says.

"Going to rain today," Chad says, looking skyward, as he unfolds the cardboard sign that hits all the right notes for his job.

ARMY VET. PLEASE HELP. FAMILY NEEDS FOOD.

I give him a side eye. He drives a better car than I do. Better apartment too.

Nan looks up from her keyboard, while the modern jazz she prefers leaks out of her headphones.

"Lab tried to reach you, Sheriff. You too, Detective," she says, adjusting an owl pendant that hangs from her neck. "I told 'em that you were on assignment in a remote part of the county."

Sheriff gives her an affirming nod. "What did they say?"

"Shooting at one of the malls in Tacoma. Case came in and crime lab gave them priority. Lots to process." She looks down at her notes. "Late tomorrow. Next day. Can call in the morning for a better idea."

The DNA results will only confirm what I know to be true. The missing persons report and BOLO for the Wheatons will become a murder case with a chief suspect.

CHAPTER SEVENTEEN

Regina looked at her wife and smiled reassuringly. They were still in the bed, curtains pulled, doors locked.

Regina got up and poured water onto a towel from a pitcher on Amy's nightstand. Amy sat up and let Regina wash her.

"Feels so good. I wish we could go swim in the creek like we used to."

"When you're stronger," Regina said, dabbing the moistened towel over Amy's brow, then down her cheeks to her neck. Next, she put a very small amount of olive oil on her palms and worked it gently into her skin.

"Stop that, Reggie. You're making me feel sexy."

"It's what I do," she said.

Amy snuggled tighter against Regina.

"I'm so sorry for everything. Your eye. The things I said."

A tear fell from Regina's eye. She put her fingertips against Amy's lips.

"Shhh...I don't want to cover this ground ever again. We can be sorry and wallow in our own self-pity or we can move on and love each other forever. It's what we chose to do, babe. Remember? We chose love."

Amy didn't say anything more.

Regina stayed quiet too. She had said everything that truly mattered. Their love was stronger than any disagreement ever could be.

CHAPTER EIGHTEEN

This is how my brain works. Little things spark big things. It would be far easier for me if I could just forget. Forget who I am. Where I come from. That my brother hates me. That I haven't had a boyfriend for three years—and that's being generous. A one-night stand from a Tinder pickup doesn't really count, right?

Make that five years.

I think of Maxine Jacobson and all those cats. I think of Joshua and Sarah. The case is spooling through my head. The sweet potato vine. I grew one just like that when I was a girl.

I text Sheriff a reminder that we'll need a search warrant.

We need to find the hammer.

DNA results will be all we need. Have a good night. Enjoying a bowl of rabbit food for dinner, wishing for a taco.

Your wife wants you to stick around. We all do. Good night, Bugs.

I reach for the next tape and slide it into the recorder. Dr. Albright is telling me to lie back and tell me what happened after we got off the ferry.

Me: Okay. I remember seeing the front page of the Seattle Times. *It was right there, you know. Staring at us. It was our house. Our photographs. I remember the headline: "Port Orchard Murder Mystery Stuns Neighborhood. Father Dead, Mother and Children Missing." (pause: noise of static on the tape) Sorry. Just thinking of how real it all became. I knew it was real, of course. It was that by seeing our photos and Dad's name and Mom's and reading what the neighbors thought of us. Just made it real.*

Dr. A: I'll need to turn the tape over now.

Me: Okay.

As I do the same, my mind wanders back to that time. How I looped through the ferry collecting all the newspapers and tossing them in the recycle box. I knew that I looked different than the photograph. Hayden too. But I wasn't about to take a chance.

The tape starts playing again.

Dr. A: You were on the ferry. You were making a plan, isn't that right?

Me: I was. Or I was trying to. I knew that the key I had since I was eleven was to the safe deposit box. I knew I had to get there. Hayden is only thinking about Mom and Dad. I was thinking about them too.

Dr. A: What were you thinking, Rylee, when it came to your mother at that time?

Me: At that time? Right. I was just thinking about how we needed to find her.

Dr. A: Why?

Me: Like I said before, I knew he took her. I knew that she was alive because he wouldn't kill her. He wanted her. Killing her would take away his motivation. His reason for being.

Dr. A: Which was?

Me: Owning her.

*

I remember the reason for the long pause that fills the tape just then. Dr. Albright looked at me with a mix of horror and disbelief. I wasn't sure if it was because I'd said "owning her" with a bizarre casualness or if it was because the very idea of it shocked her.

That's enough; I remove the tape and put it back inside its little clear plastic holder.

The breeze moves the kitchen curtain and the sound of laughter from the kids next door wafts into the room.

I was about seven when I first started to understand that we were a little different from other families. It might have been earlier, but when you're not of school age, you don't mark time the same way. Seasons blend together, and time seems to go on forever. No rituals divide the months. No back-to-school shopping. No carnivals. No winter breaks. I'm not even sure where we were living then, except I remember the smells of the country. Cow smells. A dairy farm was nearby. The land was flat, long and green all the way to the edge of the horizon. Later, I learned we had been living in eastern Nebraska, not far from the Iowa border.

Mom was on the sofa talking to somebody on the phone. It wasn't a cell phone, but a landline that ran from the wall in the kitchen all the way to the living room. Her voice carried a sharp edge that brought me from my bedroom upstairs. She was crying. Seeing Mom cry made me cry too. I watched from the hallway. Something told me to stay put. Just listen.

"...what am I supposed to do now?" she was asking.

I moved a little closer, though still out of view. It was nighttime, and I was wearing a pale yellow flannel nightgown. On my feet were slippers made to look like pink bunny rabbits. I loved those slippers more than anything. I never saw them again after that night.

"...tell me just how that's supposed to work?"

After a long silence, Mom hung up the phone. She stayed very still on the sofa and wrapped an old crocheted blanket around her shoulders.

I remember something else just then. *It was Christmastime.* Our tree was up next to the fireplace. Why hadn't I remembered this before?

I take my mind back to that place. I stood there frozen, watching Mom. I had the impulse to run over and hug her, but I was too scared. Later, when I thought about the reasons for my reluctance to interfere, I figured that it had to do with the fact that my mother was a private person. To see her crying almost seemed like a violation of her privacy.

Then she saw me. I felt a jolt go through my body. I was caught. She recovered a little and motioned for me to come closer. I followed the trajectory of her finger to a spot next to her on the sofa.

"Honey," she told me, "I'm all right, but I do have something to tell you. It's about tomorrow. We're going to take a little trip tomorrow. It'll be fun."

Her eyes were red and nothing that came from her lips seemed like it could possibly be fun.

"Where?" I asked.

"That's the fun part," she said, trying to sound upbeat. "I don't know. *We* don't know." Her eyes left mine and wandered around the room. I followed them until her gaze stood still.

On our coffee table was a travel magazine with the image of a log cabin in the woods.

"We're going out west," she said.

Her random choice scared me. It felt desperate. "Why?" Yet my mother had pulled herself together now. She was in full-on survival mode, an affectation that I later knew to be a complete façade. "Because we have to get away from someone. Someone bad. Someone who wants to hurt me."

I didn't understand what she meant. The funny thing about it was that I didn't even ask. I just accepted it. The next morning, I found her in front of the fireplace burning papers and photographs.

I watched my own image get licked and then devoured by orange and blue flames.

Ten minutes later, we were gone, and my name was no longer Shelly. We took nothing with us. Not even those pink bunny slippers. I always missed those slippers so much.

"Anna," she said, trying out my new name as we drove toward the highway, "starting over will save us. Starting over is the only way we can survive."

My pizza is long gone. Two beers too.

I think of Joshua and Sarah and how they'll have to start over their lives. Just like Hayden and I did. Depending on how the family court judge rules, it is possible that Sarah will go into foster care until more permanent arrangements can be made. Among the list of things that Hayden hated me for was how he had to, as he said, "serve time" in foster care. I was out there somewhere, and he was alone with strangers. It was my doing. I left him. He didn't know why.

Not then.

CHAPTER NINETEEN

The night had been a rough one. I doubt I slept more than two or three hours. I tossed and turned and struggled to find the cool side of my pillow. I dreamed of cats and Hayden. I pick up my phone and open my email. Nothing but a bunch of spam offering me things I don't need and don't want. Nothing from my brother. I remind myself, as I put my feet on the floor and head to the bathroom, that someday he'll write me back. He *has* to. He's my blood. He's all I have.

I put a pod in the coffeemaker and wait while it pushes hot water through the ground coffee. My phone pings and my heart skips a beat.

Hayden?

I look down. It's not my brother. It's an update from the crime lab.

We will run the samples this morning. Expect a call after lunch.

I finish my coffee, take a quick shower, and dress for work. My first stop is at the community planning office, where I'll ask for a printout of the property owners closest to the Wheatons, before heading out to Snow Creek.

The printout is scant in information. There are only four property owners—Maxine and Earl Jacobson, Ida and Merritt Wheaton, Regina and Amy Torrance, and Daniel Anderson. The house with the sweet potato vine is a ghost on the page. A squatter, I think. A notation indicates that the previous owners had left the area before we went digital. They owed back taxes to the tune of $2,024 and apparently felt the tax bill didn't justify the reality of what they had.

I completely agree.

As I get up to leave for Snow Creek, Sheriff appears in my doorway.

"Want some company?" he asks.

I smile.

"Sure. I'll even let you drive."

As we drive, I tell him about Maxine and her cats.

"Seriously? More than a hundred?"

"I didn't exactly count them, but that's my guess."

"Wife and I are more dog people."

Second-growth firs are a ribbon of green from my passenger window. The view from where I sit as Sheriff drives is stunning. Really. The forest is a massive green wall on either side of the road, every now and then giving way to the shimmering waters of Snow Creek. We had a small creek in Port Orchard. Hayden loved looking for salamanders there.

Sheriff slams on the brakes as a doe jumps into the roadway.

"Jesus! We almost hit her."

"We didn't," I say.

He looks ashen and reaches over. "Are you okay?"

I exhale. "Fine. We're all fine."

"I don't like close calls," he says.

I know he's thinking of the car accident that left him with a metal plate riveted to his skull. He jokes about setting off the metal detector at the courthouse. It's not really funny. He'd veered off the highway and hit the barrier. *Hard.* A few in the office gossiped that he'd been drinking at the Indian casino and the state patrol covered it up.

It helps having friends in law enforcement.

Drunks, criminals, and people looking for a second chance know that.

Like me.

It was Tony Gray who somehow managed to excise details of my life from law enforcement files. I didn't ask how. I assume someone helped him. He's not what anyone would call a digital native. He's what I call, however, the man who gave me a chance to live a life in which I could be the best part of me. He saw it in me, before I really did.

He eases his foot onto the gas pedal, while I look down at the plat map.

"Slow down," I say as we start moving. "The Anderson property is right here, on the left."

We proceed up a slight incline. As driveways go around here, this is the nicest one by far. It's not paved, of course, but its compacted gravel makes for a smoother ride than the rutted-out ingress of his neighbors.

He studies me. "You sure there's a house up here?"

"Folks out here have a thing for long, winding roads," I say.

My eyes widen as the house comes into view.

"I didn't expect that," I say.

"Impressive," he says.

What held our attention wasn't the Anderson house, though it was nice. It was a small two-story, painted white, with black shutters. More Nantucket than, say, backwoods Washington.

The yard was filled with wood carvings done with a chainsaw. There were bears, eagles, totems, and more. Some were painted with bright colors of marine paint. While chainsaw art isn't my thing, the collection here was carved by a master—if there's such a thing. A Smee-like character from *Peter Pan* looked like he could speak. I did a double take at a sea otter because I actually thought it was real.

"Some serious talent here," Sheriff says.

"No shit," I say.

Daniel Anderson emerges from the house and walks toward us. He seems normal. No gun. He has a neatly trimmed beard on a square jaw. It looks authentic. Not like the hipsters that flock to Port Townsend on the weekends to pose as lumberjacks or mariners. He's lean and has close-cropped dark brown hair. He's wearing Carhartt jeans and a purple University of Washington shirt emblazoned with the university's mascot: a husky. When he smiles, I notice straight away that he has all his teeth.

"You folks from the fair committee?" he asks as he approaches.

His eyes are blue. The kind of blue that's not really found in nature. Dark, with violet undertones. I break my gaze and Sheriff speaks up.

"No," he tells him, holding out his badge. I do the same. "I'm Sheriff Tony Gray and this is Detective Megan Carpenter. Your work's awesome, really. Daniel Anderson, right?"

"Call me Dan. I have a business license," he says. "Take me a minute to get it."

"No," I tell him as he turns to go inside. "We're not here about that, Dan."

He stops and looks at me warily. "Then why are you here?"

We tell him about the Wheatons, though not everything. If he gets the *Leader* or reads news online, he'll know about the body found off the logging road. Since we don't know for sure that it's Ida, I won't volunteer anything. Rumors thrive in the dark, unknown places like Snow Creek.

"Did you know them?" I ask, omitting the word "well" because no one seems to know anyone out here other than to wave to now and again.

But Dan does.

"Yeah, Merritt used to come down here. We both dug working with wood. He's a furniture maker and he'd bring pieces over to me to sell for him. Didn't like dealing with outsiders. Funny that way. I told him he was a commune leader without a real commune one time. That pissed him off."

Sheriff interjects. "You were close?"

"No," Dan says. "I wouldn't say that. He came down here to unload his tables and stuff. We had a beer a time or two. His favorite was Miller. Tastes like piss to me, but hey, I stocked up some and we shot the breeze."

"Did you know Ida? The kids?" I ask as he leads us over to a bench carved in the shape of an orca. I run my fingers over the grain of the wood. Smooth as satin.

He sits on a stump ready for carving and faces us.

"No. Not really. I was thinking of inviting them over one time for a barbecue. You know, to be neighborly. He wouldn't have anything to do with that. Said his wife was shy and his kids were too unruly to take anywhere. I never saw anything like that in them. Always seemed like a nice family."

"Ever say he was unhappy with his marriage?" I ask.

Dan doesn't answer right away.

I give him a little push. He's holding back. "What's on your mind, Dan?"

"Oh, I don't know. One time he told me, now he was a little drunk, he said that Ida didn't always do what he wanted her to do."

"What did he mean, if you know?" Sheriff asks.

Dan looks at me. He's embarrassed about something.

"It's fine. Go ahead."

He nods. "Okay. It creeped me out. He told me that he'd trained her to do what he wanted and lately she'd been holding back."

Ruth Turner's "hand-picked" comes to mind just then.

"You mean sexually?" I ask.

He nods again, his face now pink. "Yeah, that's the way I took it."

We talk a bit more, mostly about his artwork. Sheriff asks if he knows any of the other neighbors and if they were close to the Wheatons.

"Old Maxine used to have the kids over," Dan says. "Said they were nice kids. That relationship fizzled out; not sure why."

"I chatted with her already," I say.

He gives me a smile that's almost a wink. It's disarming. "You see her cats? Merritt called her Crazy Cat Lady."

I smile. "I thought one of them was going to go home with me. Or at the very least attach itself to my calf."

"No shit," he says. "I have one showing up here every now and then. I imagine cats don't like living in those conditions. Her heart is in the right place, but anything over two cats is too many."

"Do you know the people holed up in the mobile home?" I ask.

"Nope," he says. "Place has been abandoned for years. No power. Surprised it's still intact. Guess some people just need a roof over their heads and don't care what it's like. Meth-heads stayed there for a few months. They're gone now. I think whoever has it now uses it on weekends only."

"Some vacation getaway," Sheriff says.

"I guess you could call it that," Dan says.

"What about the Torrances?"

"Those gals keep to themselves. Just like everybody out here, I guess. I haven't seen either in months. Last time I was over there was to return one of their Nubians. She got loose, ended up way over here. Regina was glad to get her back. Amy was inside and didn't come out to say hello. Regina went in and got me a nice brick of their cheese. Give a big hello from me, when you speak to them. Always liked those girls and how they ditched the city to make a life out here. Kind of like *Little House in the Big Woods*."

Sheriff and I thank him for his time. I hand him my card.

"Please call if you have anything to add," I say.

He smiles at me.

Sheriff looks at me and I turn to leave.

"When they turn up," Dan calls out, looking up from my card, "tell Merritt that I've got some dough for the live edge dining table."

As the sheriff backs up the car to turn around, he glances at me with a sheepish grin.

"Don't say anything," I say.

He does anyway.

"You like him," he says.

I ignore his remark.

"Let's get going."

CHAPTER TWENTY

I'm on edge. Teetering. When it comes to gut feelings as I work a case, I'm not infallible. I've been wrong a few times. Two, in fact. This one, however, I know what I know inside. I just need confirmation because the law requires it. I'm learning how to follow the rules, something I avoided completely when I was younger. I look at the dead, black mirror of my phone. I want to see the DNA results to confirm who Jane Doe is.

Even though I know who it is.

"How do people live out here without phones that work?" I ask as we pull away from Dan Anderson's place on our way to the Torrance property.

Sheriff pops another cherry candy into his mouth.

"Waiting on those reports?"

He reads me. He is the only one who can. Though only as much as I allow.

"Of course. We'll need the warrant right away."

"Theory?" he asks.

"It's all about the claw hammer. I think that Merritt Wheaton killed Ida and wrapped her up in the carpet."

"Where? In his workshop in the Quonset hut, or in the barn?"

I nod. "She was hit in the back of the head. Had to be at home. No one carries a hammer around."

"Carpenters do."

I make an annoyed face. "I guess so. But not this control freak. He's going to kill her where no one can hear or see anything."

"Motive?"

He's lobbing the easy ones at me. I answer anyway.

"Like I said, control freak. You heard Dan. He said Ida was pushing back on her duties, I guess. They come from a fundamentalist sect that, as far as I can tell, is their own invention. No church that I can find. After spending time with Ida's sister Ruth, I definitely got a *Children of the Corn* vibe."

He smiles at the reference.

"There," I point, "that's the Torrance place. Pull in there."

"You sure?"

I look at the plat map. "Yes. And by the looks of it, this driveway is about a mile long."

"More like a road than driveway," he says.

"Apparently that's the way they like it out here."

The road, or whatever it is, is deeply rutted. No effort has been made to stabilize its surface. Sheriff expertly navigates the deep dips. He slows to cross a pool of mud and water.

"Shouldn't have had my car washed yesterday," he says.

I see a potato chip bag stuffed next to the console.

Shouldn't be eating chips, I think.

"Well looky here," he says as the barn and house come into view. "A real house."

I'm surprised too. The sight of the Torrance farm is unexpected and makes me think of a bias that I have about Snow Creek. Yes, they are off the grid. Yes, they want to be by themselves. Dan, Maxine, the Wheatons, and now Regina and Amy Torrance... they carved out their own lives in the woods. They weren't living in squalor—with the exception of Maxine's herd of cats—like a bunch of tweakers or head- and neck-tatted white supremacists.

We get out and go to the door where we find a note referencing an RV trip and someone named Jared, who was watching the animals.

"No one on the county property rolls around here with that name," I say.

"He must be from town," Sheriff says, peering through the window on the door. "A caretaker, I guess. Someone has to be taking care of the animals around here."

A hint of smoke from the barely burning embers of a firepit across the yard between the house and the goat barn fills my lungs.

"Must have just missed 'em," I say. "I'll leave a note for Jared to call me."

I tuck my card with a message into the door jamb next to the note.

"No one's in trouble," I write. "Just trying to find out if anyone knows anything about the Wheatons. Please call me."

Just as we hit the highway off Snow Creek Road, my phone pings. I feel an adrenaline surge even before I play the voice message from the crime lab on speaker.

It's the call that I've been waiting for.

"Hey, Detective Carpenter," the lab tech supervisor, Marley Yang, says, *"we got a match. It's mother and son. This is no guess. Real thing. No doubts. Your victim is Ida Wheaton. Good luck with the case. Find the son of a bitch who killed her. There, I said it. Bye now."*

"Let's go get a warrant," Sheriff says.

My phone pings again. It's from a number I don't know. This time I put the phone to my ear and listen.

It's Dan Anderson.

"A . . . Detective, I saw you admiring some of my work. Would like to give you a carving. No charge. OK? Unless that's against some county government policy. If it is, it's a dumb one. Let me know. Okay? Bye. It's Dan. Dan Anderson."

"Everything okay?" Sheriff says. "You're suddenly very quiet. That's a trait I'd never ascribe to you, Megan."

I look at him, then out the window. "Nothing. Landlord's going to fix the broken window in the basement."

It's a lie. I suspect he knows it. He doesn't pry. I like Dan Anderson. Though I don't like relationships; I know most people would chide me for even thinking that's his intention. Egotistical. Narcissistic. Whatever. If anything, I know people and the way they think. My mother taught me that. She might not have known it at the time, but she did.

This time Sheriff has his ear pressed to the phone. I watch him as he drives. I know he cares about me. He's the closest thing I have to family. Or a friend. A relationship. A lifeline. Hayden is off in the desert and I wonder if he ever thinks about me.

"Warrant tomorrow," he says looking over at me.

"We need to notify Joshua and Sarah and Ruth that Ida was murdered. I've tried Ruth's husband's phone multiple times and no one picks up. I want to be the one to notify."

"Not my favorite thing to do," he says. "But it does come with the job every now and then."

I'm thankful that murder in Jefferson County is a rare occurrence. There has only been one since Sheriff Gray gave me the job I was meant to do. It was the wife of a tourist from Indiana. Her body had been found at low tide off the ferry dock. She'd been strangled. He'd been found in his hotel room, dead of a self-inflicted gunshot wound.

We pull into the parking lot and I tell him that tomorrow will be the first step in getting justice for Ida Wheaton.

"It won't be easy telling those kids their mom is dead," he says.

Understatement, I think.

"It'll be even harder to tell them that we think the killer is their father," I say.

CHAPTER TWENTY-ONE

After trying every Jared in Jefferson County and reaching six of the seven, I call it a day and head for home without knowing who he is. The seventh is on a cruise, so I think he's likely another no. Who would leave a note for someone who was gone for four weeks? It has to be a Jared from outside the county.

Persistence sometimes feels like disappointment.

Tonight, Chinese takeout from Happy Dragon. I normally order moo shu pork, but I don't this time. The girl running the drive-thru tells me the pork is "not so good today." *Good to know,* I think. If I weren't in the drive-thru queue, I'd probably bolt, yet I don't. Instead, I ask for the walnut shrimp.

The girl on the speaker tells me walnut chicken is a better choice. Not really that word, she actually said *fresher*. I reluctantly order and vow that, no matter how lazy I am about cooking, I'll never go back.

Happy Dragon, not so happy, I think.

I take the food home and study it carefully before I eat. I'm not super handy with chopsticks, yet somehow I think I can avoid food poisoning if I use chopsticks instead of a fork. Like a fork would tell the walnut chicken that I deserved to get sick.

That might not make sense to anyone, yet it does to me.

The tapes beckon as I pour the chardonnay that I hadn't bothered to chill in the refrigerator. It's bad, but I drink it anyway. As I sip, I lie to myself as I eat that I don't need the drama of my own, younger life. Since I started listening to the tapes, images of my brother, mom, father have been coming back to me.

Especially my dad. My *real* dad. He's the reason that I'm somewhat screwed up when it comes to love and the trust that's needed to make it flourish. I don't save Dan Anderson's number in my phone. I delete his voice message after listening to it one more time.

I push PLAY on the next tape, and I'm instantly back with my little brother, trying to keep us safe.

Dr. Albright's soothing voice recounts the date and the time. She asks me to continue, but I don't answer. The tape hisses for what seems like a very long time.

Dr. A: Go on Rylee, you can do this.

Her voice soothes.
Leads.
I knew she wanted to help me.

Me: What if I don't want to?
Dr. A: There isn't a choice. We can't free you from the past without acknowledging it. Go on. Tell me about what happened after you got off the boat.
Me: I needed to look like Mom in order to get into the safe deposit. I had her ID and my hair was pretty much Mom-ready. I needed clothes though. I dragged Hayden to the Lost and Found office in the ferry terminal at Seattle's Colman Dock, where I told the attendant that our mom had lost her jacket. I grabbed a bag. I still have it. It's black leather with a fake Chanel clasp. Oh...I managed to find a white silk scarf and a pair of vintage Foster Grant sunglasses.

*

The clerk, a young man with an X-Acto-blade-sharp nose and unibrow, looks over my ID and compares it with the signature card that he pulls from a file cabinet behind him. It seems like a very, very long time, but it was probably only a second. His hair is blond—golden, really. I wonder if my hair looks as bad as his.

"This doesn't look like you," he says curtly.

"I get that a lot," I answer in a throatier version of my voice, one that I assume sounds like my mother—or at least someone older than fifteen. I offer no excuse. Sometimes the less you say, the better the odds are of getting what you want.

"Hair looks better the way it is now," he says.

I wonder if he's hitting on me and if he is, he is breaking the law. I am underage, no matter what that ID card states.

He leads me to a doorway and turns to face me. "Passcode?"

"What?" I ask.

"You need to enter your passcode," he says, his eyes riveted to mine.

I feel sweat collect on the back of my neck. Passcode? I don't have any passcode. His nicotine-stained index finger points at a keypad.

I think hard and fast. Now my face is hot. It must be red. Great. Nothing's coming to me and I think Unibrow knows it.

He shifts his weight. "If you don't have the passcode, you can't go inside."

Think. Think.

"You only have three chances and if you don't get it right, we'll need to arrange for the bank manager to create you a new one. He's a real stickler for security around here."

I know I'll like the bank manager even less than Unibrow, who, by the way, is now in my personal top five of all annoying people.

I punch in my brother's birthday.

"Let's go see the manager," he says. A slight smile on his face indicates that he's happy that I can't remember the code. He must want to go on a smoke break, because he smells like an ashtray to me.

Then it comes to me. My mind flashes to the day that my mom and dad set up the router for our internet connection. The password they used was the same one they used on everything—whenever anything required some kind of security code.

"Wait!" I say. "I have it."

My finger goes to the keypad:

LY4E1234

Love you forever, and a digit for each member of our family.
A green light flickers on the keypad display.

I pause the tape and go to my office, where I dig deep into the bottom drawer of the Goodwill desk that I bought when I first came to Port Townsend. What I'm looking for is buried in a grave of other papers and clippings. I feel my muscles tighten even after all these years. There it is. It is a letter that I've folded, cried over, even once thrown away—only to retrieve it moments later. I no longer have the envelope that it came in, but I remember what it said in my mother's handwriting: "For my daughter's eyes only. Do not read this in front of the bank employees. There is a camera in the corner of the room. Turn your back to the camera before you read any more."

There was a second one too: "For my son's eyes only."

I burned that one.

I carefully unfold the letter, knowing that Hayden might have been the one to go to the safe deposit box one day. I know with certainty that my mom and my stepdad had considered I might be a casualty of their choices, their lives.

Honey,

If you are reading the letter, then I am gone. As I write this, I don't know what exactly that might really mean. It is one of two possibilities. He has captured me, or he has killed me. I know you will want to find out where I am; if I'm alive. I know that I cannot stop you from doing so. I am sorry that there is very little here to tell you where I might be. I have put some information into some other envelopes. I want you to take those along with this when you leave. Do not show any of it to anyone. If you do, not only will I die, you probably will too. Please sit down. There is a chair on the other side of this room.

I stop reading to take a moment to remember my fifteen-year-old self. How lost I was at that time. I feel that shiver looking at that letter. It's like I'm in a car, driving past the worst, bloodiest car accident ever.

Honey, I have lied to you. I didn't mean for my lies to spin out of control and frame so much of our lives. You have to believe me when I say that being a liar isn't what I set out to be. I lied because it was the only course of action to save you, save me, save Hayden. I used to think that by ignoring the truth just maybe a little of my nightmare would go away. Pay attention to my words and remember the need for forgiveness. It is real. It is the only way to salvation.

The man who we have been running from our entire lives was not a jilted boyfriend. Not a stalker. At least not the kind of stalker that you—or I—could ever imagine. I felt as though you only needed to know a part of the story. You were so young when I started telling you the story, that I knew you would believe it. Two words here. Forgiveness and strength. For you to survive you must embrace both.

I set it down. I haven't been breathing. I suck in more air as my mind races back to a conversation my mother and I had when I was around eleven. Maybe twelve. We were sitting outside on the back patio watching fireflies as they zipped through the lowest hanging branches of a big oak that spread over our entire backyard like it was protecting us. I loved that tree so much. When we moved that time, I vowed I'd live in a place again someday with a tree that had branches that functioned like caring arms. That afternoon a TV talk show did a segment about the impact of being a child star in Hollywood. It stayed on my mind well past dinner.

"Sometimes I feel like those kids on TV," I told her.

Mom looked at me, the light from the flame of a small citronella candle playing off her beautiful, even features.

"What do you mean?"

"Those kids," I said a little tentatively. Not because I felt tentative about what I was saying, but because I felt like I was lighting a fuse. "They are born into something. Their parents wanted to be a part of something. They didn't have a choice."

She looked at me with those penetrating eyes of hers, and then returned her attention to the fireflies and our beloved oak tree.

"Honey, you really feel that way?"

There was remorse in her voice, but not too much. Just a hint of regret. In some ways that was all I ever wanted from her. I wanted her to tell me that she was sorry our lives had been so screwed up. That she shouldered some of the blame. Even if she didn't, really. "Sometimes," I lied. I felt that way all the time. My mother's choices had dragged me into a life that left me without any history of my own. I tried not to resent her, because I loved her so much. Yet, there were times when I just hated her for what she'd done to me, and to Hayden. As I grew older, I sometimes allowed myself to see her side of things. The reasons why she did what she did. My mother's story was flimsy, but since she told it with such evasive conviction, I never really questioned it.

Those memories attack my brain with the ferocity of a thousand ice picks. I shake my head as if to free myself from a firestorm of nerves and questions, but I know I need to remember what happened in that bank vault: the day everything changed.

I sit in the corner of the vault with the letter in my hand. I need to face it. My heart rate is going faster. I look down on the paper and a tear drops on it. It leaves a shiny pool. I'm almost afraid to read on. I'm worried that her words will break my heart, that the betrayal she's hinting at will be too great.

> *We've been running our whole lives from your father. It makes me ill to put those words to paper, but that's the truth.*

My father? My father is dead. He was an army enlistee who died in Iraq. I have carried his picture in my wallet for as long as I've had one. I have another reminder. I press my fingertips against the dog tags that hang around my neck on a silver braided chain that I'd saved up to buy from the Macy's jewelry counter in Minneapolis.

The first tag has his name, enlistment number, and blood type.

WALTERS, WILLIAM J.
FG123456Z
A NEG

On the second one was the next of kin:

GINGER WALTERS 1337 MAPLE LANE TACOMA, WA

For a moment anger and confusion well up as my emotions battle for some kind of strange supremacy. I have no idea where this is going, so I read on. I take in the last words in big, oxygen-free gulps.

What I have to tell you does not define who you are. Not at all. You are my beautiful daughter. I have done everything I can to spare you the reality of your conception. But you are here reading this, and you deserve to know the truth. You also can decide if you want to help me. If you don't, I will die loving you anyway. If you don't, please take care of your brother. Take him to my sister Ginger Rhodes' place in Wallace, Idaho, and leave him there until after you are sure I am safe or dead. Your birth father will never harm him.

I'm reeling. We had no family. We never did. Mom said that her parents and siblings died in a car crash when she was a little girl. Seven, I think. Though now I am beginning to question everything I thought I knew. And as I do, my eyes take in a sentence that no one should have to read.

Your father is Alex Richard Rader. He is a serial killer. I was the victim who got away.

I want to scream, but I don't. Tears stream down my face and I half-glance at the bank's camera trained right at me. I feel scared, paranoid, and very, very angry. The words feel toxic. Serial killer? Victim? Got away? Each syllable comes at me like a bullet to my temple. I almost wish they were bullets. Abruptly, my skin feels dirty and itchy. My hands are shaking. She could have told me. She *should* have trusted me. She made our vagabond lives utter hell. Why didn't she just go to the police? She had always said that her stalker was an ex-boyfriend, a man who had come into her life after my father. She'd been kind to him and he just wouldn't let up. We were living in military housing in Fort Lewis, south of Tacoma, then. I was barely out of diapers. She said that the police on the base refused to do anything to help her, that her stalker hadn't broken any laws. And yet she felt so threatened that she thought that being on the run was the only solution for our safety. I want to laugh out loud now about the absurdity of her story, but she'd been so unbelievably convincing. Every time a freak would stalk and kill someone when a restraining order had been put in place, she would point to it as an example of the world we lived in—and the danger of living life out in the open.

"No one can help a victim until it is too late. It's a chance we're never going to take," she'd said on those occasions.

I bought into it. I guess the drumming of the same thing over and over ensured my complete acceptance. Like those kids we had seen on TV years ago. They had no other frame of reference for the world. They believed everything they were told. Even when the stories were stretched to breaking point, they still believed.

I know what I know, honey. So please give me that. I know that Alex has killed three girls and those cases were never truthfully solved. I also know why. I know his friends on the police force tampered with evidence. I know all of this because he told me when he held me captive when I was sixteen. I could draw you a picture about what happened during those dark days, but I don't think I need to. You were conceived in the worst horror imaginable. But I would never want to live without you. I don't see him when I look into your eyes. I see the face of the daughter that I will always love.

If you decide to try to find me alive—I know I can't stop you—you will need to follow his trail. I don't know where he is. I don't know where I am. But I do know two things: I have seven days. He killed each girl after holding them for seven days. A week. Look into the victims' pasts to find me.

I go back to my office, to the bottom desk drawer and pull out more paper, clippings from various newspapers. Though the images have yellowed with age, any one of them could have been a ringer for my mother. Shannon Blume, sixteen; Megan Moriarty, sixteen; Leanne Delmont, sixteen. All were from the Seattle-Tacoma area. All of these murder cases were attributed to different men. All cases were closed. According to the newspaper clippings, none of the men who killed any of the girls was named Alex Rader.

I scoop it all up and return to the kitchen table and restart the tape. I hear my voice talking about my confusion, how stunned I was that one of the other items in the safe deposit box was a gun.

Me: I didn't get it. I didn't really get any of this. I was confused, shocked.

Dr. A: Of course, you were, Rylee. You'd been traumatized in multiple ways within a very short time. You were piecing together bits and pieces that had been your life up to that point. You were a strong girl. Incredibly so.

Me: I didn't feel so strong. I felt sick. I kept thinking over and over that who your parents are doesn't need to define you and the rest of your life.

Dr. A: Yes. And look at you now. You're in college. You're moving forward in ways that you might have not ever imagined.

Me: (crying softly)

Dr. A: You will be fine, Rylee.

Me: I hope so.

Dr. A: I know so.

Me: Thank you.

I'd continued telling the story of how we made our way to Idaho to see our unheard-of aunt Ginger. How I felt disoriented. So much had been crammed into my head, a mass of loose ends that felt like they'd coagulated inside my throat, that I could barely speak. I remember sitting in the back of the second car.

I let Hayden have the window. He was tired, and I was hoping the monotonous beat of a rolling train would lull him to sleep. It worked. I pulled out the envelopes and papers from the safe deposit box and consumed the information on each page as if I were a human scanner. I am, sort of. I've always had the ability to remember things. I know that I possess a photographic memory. I never say so aloud. It sounds too conceited, but I do. While I took everything inside, while I felt the gun in its paper wrapper, I was thinking over and over about what was happening to Mom. I was so angry at her for the lies she'd told me. I felt foolish too. I imagined the father I never knew, the soldier, and how he'd fought for our country. He was a hero. When I was small, I used to pretend that I was talking to him on the phone all the way across the world. He was dodging bullets, bombs. He was facing death inside some burned-out village in the Middle East, but he stopped everything to talk to me. I saw my father as a kind of superhero worthy of respect, love, and a movie. All of that had been a figment of my imagination.

My stepfather was a good guy. Decent. Yet still a mystery.

Why would he take us on? There had to be something wrong with a man who would carry such a burden as to live on the run with my mother, me, and later, Hayden. I loved him in the way that one loves a trusted pet—one who might bite you, so you never get too close. He was solid. Caring. Yet he wasn't my dad. He was Hayden's dad. My stomach roils as I think of him nearly pinned to the floor of the kitchen with a knife, like some moth specimen in biology class at South Kitsap. I want to cry for him right now. He deserves that much, but I don't.

I can't think of anything but my biological dad and who he was. He was not dog-tag material. He was not the hero. Far, far from that. He was the villain, the worst, most despicable kind ever. The feeling that overtakes me right then as Hayden sleeps in the seat next to me is a mix of sadness, anger, and confusion: If

I'm not the daughter of a hero, but the daughter of a killer, then what kind of person am I?

I sit motionless for a very long time. I almost don't know the girl on the recording, what she's thinking, where she's going. How she plans to use that gun. It's scary. Even though she's a stranger to me, I know she is still deep inside me. I don't blame her for what she's about to do. I wish that I had one of Maxine's cats right now. I'd hold it in my arms and tell it how much it means to have someone you can depend on. I'd pet it softly and take in the purrs, the motor-like sounds that would reassure me that there was more good to the world than the evil that seems to surround me.

I pour another tepid glass of wine and head for bed, hoping that slumber will give me relief from what I know is about to come.

Not from the Wheaton case.

I can handle that.

It's what the tapes are about to disclose.

Who I am.

CHAPTER TWENTY-TWO

Warrant in hand, I don't drive alone to the Wheaton place. I bring Bernadine Chesterfield, a social worker and victim's advocate, a fixture at the county before I arrived. She's in her late forties with bright red hair and eye shadow that I seriously think would scare off a victim. It's an iridescent blue. Or is it purple? Pink? I honestly don't know what hue it is or why she wears it with such abandon. She talks about her son in the Coast Guard. Her daughter lives in Portland and crafts beeswax candles.

"I always knew that my beautiful little dreamers would do great things someday."

"You are so lucky," I tell her.

Okay, serving our country in the Coast Guard carries real honor, but beeswax candles? I think.

She goes on a bit more and then stops as we pull off the highway and head up Snow Creek Road.

"Confession, Megan."

"Go on," I tell her.

"There's some weird stuff going on out here. Gives me the willies. Like *Deliverance*. Do you know that old movie?"

I shake my head.

"You should stream it. Seriously, you never know what you'll find far away from town. Out here."

"In the middle of nowhere?"

"Exactly."

We pass Dan Anderson's place. *Yeah*, I think, *you never know what you'll find.*

I review what we're doing. I do this because Bernie, as she likes to be called, is something of a loose cannon. She likes to play cop as much as she seems to enjoy her court-appointed duties. She also has a strange effect when comforting a victim; it's almost like she's enjoying her role too much. Like she's getting off on the misery of someone facing the worst conceivable outcome after a tortuous wait, bouncing from hope to the inevitable reality of what's really happening.

"Sarah is underage and we'll need to consider that," I say. "She's scared about what might have happened to her mother and father. This will crush her. Joshua too. He's mature, but still, he's only nineteen. The implications of their mother's murder will not be lost on either one. While we are looking for their dad, we are not naming him a suspect. He's a missing person."

"A person of interest?" she asks.

I shake my head. "Let's avoid the terminology, all right?"

She gives me a cool look, her eye shadow only adding to the effect. "Fine, though if they bring it up, our victim's advocacy code says to always tell the truth. Never lie or trick the victim. That's your job."

I ignore her little snipe.

"Deputies Davis and Copsey will meet us there. They'll work with me on the search. You'll be there for the kids, all right?"

"Fine, but I have had some police training, you know. I could do more."

Bernie brings up her extensive training all the time. Really. All the time. She had one class at the academy in Burien. *It was one class!*

"What you're doing for the victims is far greater than anything I could do," I say.

Stay in your lane, I think.

"I think you're right," she says, as we pass the cruiser with the deputies. "There really is nothing more important than lifting up the hurt and demoralized. It's really who I am."

Inside, I roll my eyes upward.

"I told them to wait on the road," I say. "We're going in first."

Sarah is picking blueberries, and Joshua is burning trash in a burn barrel: a practice the county has prohibited for a decade or more. The folks of Snow Creek do what they need to do to get by. Going to the dump or, God forbid, having trash pickup doesn't cross their minds.

Joshua looks over and joins his sister as they approach the car.

"You know something, Detective?" he says.

Sarah sends silent tears down her cheeks.

"I'm afraid we do," I say.

I turn to Bernie and introduce her.

"She's here to help you. We both are."

"What do you know?" Joshua repeats.

"Let's go inside," I say, nudging them toward the front door.

My words unleash Sarah's tears.

"Mom's dead," she says. "Dad killed her. Didn't he?"

"We don't know what happened," I tell her, looking over at the world's worst victims' advocate. She isn't saying anything. Just standing there letting me deliver the bad news. *Seriously*, I think. *This is how you answer your calling? Really? Like a statue?*

We take seats at the table Merritt made.

"I'm really sorry, but the DNA samples we collected confirm that it was your mother who was out on Puget Sound logging road north of here."

Joshua stays stoic. Sarah not so much.

"How did she die?" he asks.

"We've only started our investigation, Joshua. In fact, we have a warrant to search the property," I reply.

I hand the paper over to Joshua and he skims it.

"You think our mom was killed here at home?" He touches his sister's shoulder. "We'd have heard something, right?"

Sarah, still sobbing, doesn't respond.

"The search warrant is for your father's workshop," I say.

Joshua gets up from the table. "I'll show it to you."

Sarah, who has been silent, save for her tears, speaks up.

"Our father was an asshole, Detective," she says. "If Mom was murdered it was he who did it."

Her out-of-nowhere candor startles me.

I prod for more. "What do you mean?"

Sarah dries her eyes on her shirt sleeve and pushes her long braid over her shoulder. "Our dad wasn't the man he pretended to be. He was an abuser. He was the kind of man who thought love meant hurting someone. Our mother lived with it. We all did. She never fought back. Not really."

Joshua shoots darts at his sister.

She doesn't seem to care. "They are going to find out, Joshua. They are going to find out that our father was a piece of shit. We know it. Mom knew it. I was surprised that Aunt Ruth showed up here. He'd told her that she was going to rot in hell for the way she treated her husband. Running around. Slutty like a common whore. He called her a Mary Magdalene reject. His favorite was calling Mom Ida-Ho or Ida-Whore. When Mom pushed back, he just laughed and said he'd cut off another toe."

I'm glad I'm sitting. Bernie, on the other hand, looks like she's at her own birthday party.

"I thought it was a mowing accident."

Joshua's eyes are riveted to his sister. "Don't do this, Sarah."

"Josh," she says. "We have to. Dad killed Mom. You know it. Detective Carpenter knows it."

"Please," he says. "Don't."

She looks at him with the saddest eyes I've ever seen.

"Too late, brother. I already did."

CHAPTER TWENTY-THREE

The judge was very specific, as he or she must be. I'm a stickler for following the rules of law. I don't want to be the person who screws things up on a technicality. We asked for a broader search of the property, the Chevy, of course, but the mention of the hammer keeps our focus on where tools might be found.

I lead the deputies, armed with cameras, into the barn. It's a peculiar space because it doesn't appear that it is in much use for an off-the-grid family. There's a single stall with a milk cow and a few Sussex chickens. One is a broody hen and she stays put on her clutch of eggs as we pass by.

"This isn't a one bite of the apple, guys," I say. "I want to wallpaper our office with all the photos you take. We might see something later that we miss right now. It happens."

"We got it, Detective Carpenter," Deputy Copsey says.

It enters my mind just then how much I like the sound of that. There's no sarcasm, no phoniness in his voice. I am a detective. I am going to solve this case.

My eyes are lasers. I absolutely will not miss anything.

"Davis," I say, looking up at the hayloft, "check out every square inch. Run your fingertips through the straw up there. Be careful. Tell yourself that you will be the man who solves this case."

Davis is younger than me. He has black hair and a mustache that screams seventies porn star or cop. Cop, I think. His gut hangs over his belt. He's earnest and a total pleaser.

"Yes, ma'am. On it right now."

I give Copsey a smile. He gets it. At least, I think so. I'm too young to be a ma'am.

"While your partner is poking around up there," I say, "let's check out the shop."

"Sounds good," he says as we leave the barn. Copsey is older, hard to say how much. Maybe five years. No more than ten. He's a strawberry blond with biceps that are barely contained by his uniform. He speaks with a slight lisp that I find charming.

Merritt's woodworking shop is in an aluminum Quonset hut. Its form reminds me of the arching ribs of a chicken carcass. My mother wasn't much of a cook, but whenever she made her favorite—and no one else's—she started by simmering a whole chicken in a pot with onions and carrots. And, yes, her chicken and dumplings smelled so good. Her dumplings never came out of the pot tender. Always hard, like little doughy rocks.

Like her heart.

Merritt's shop is filled with the odor of cedar and fir. Balsam, I think. It's like one huge potpourri bag that I wish I was able to give to Maxine. I can't, of course. The thought that passes through my mind is only good, not snarky. I liked Maxine. I didn't like how her place assaulted my olfactory senses.

I tell Copsey to search the north side. I note a flattened area on the floor, an imprint of something that had been there a long time.

Carpet?

"I'll start here, on this end. We'll meet in the middle. Seriously, Deputy, if the hammer we're looking for is anywhere on the property, it will be here."

"Got it, ma'am."

"Please," I say. "No more ma'ams."

"Yes, sir," he says.

I keep my mouth shut and wonder if I should grow my hair longer. Or maybe slather on the peacock shadow.

There are a bevy of galvanized storage bins on Copsey's side.

We search by grid, first sweeping every inch in a methodical manner. We take photos too. Not of everything. Copsey also uses a metal detector. I didn't think to bring one. I make my way around a couple of chairs and a table, works in progress, toward the wide workbench that runs the length of that side of the hut. Merritt Wheaton might have been a monster, but it was clear that he was a very neat one. An array of tools hangs neatly on hooks against a pegboard. He'd outlined with a Sharpie each tool.

In the row of hammers, I note several with the distinctive claw that the coroner indicated was the cause of death.

One in particular draws me close. As I lean over the bench, an errant nail cuts through my clothing.

"Shit!"

Startled, Copsey looks up from the hovering head of the metal detector.

"You okay, Detective?"

I grimace as I touch the tear in my shirt. Thankfully, it didn't puncture the skin. My father's DNA would really confuse this crime scene.

"Okay."

"Gotcha," he says.

I fumble with my phone to turn on the flashlight app. Its tiny beam is all that I need to be sure.

Blood.

A few strands of hair too.

"I think we've found our murder weapon, Deputy."

Copsey ambles over as I put on my latex gloves and take the hammer from the pegboard. Davis joins us too.

I turn the hammer in the light. It is unmistakable. The long blond hairs wrapped around the picks of the hammer are the same color as Ida Wheaton's. There are a million ways to kill someone. At that moment I cannot think of a worse one. I almost say a prayer, but I don't pray. If I did, it would be simple:

Dear God, let the first blow from that motherfucker be the one that killed his wife.

Copsey holds out a large brown paper bag and I carefully place the hammer inside.

"Holy crap!"

It's Joshua. He stands in the entrance. He looks like he's about to crumble.

"He really did it. He beat Mom. Didn't he?" His eyes are red, and he's obviously been crying. "He killed our mom here. Right here."

Bernadine appears and puts her hand on the teen's shoulder.

"Let's go back inside, Joshua. Let me help you and your sister."

I lock eyes with her and nod. Her iridescent lids shutter. I can tell she's within a beat of crying too.

I tell the deputies to secure the scene. We'll get a tech over here to see what story Luminol will tell us.

Inside the house, Bernie and the kids are in the living room. Joshua, who's calmed considerably, moves from a recliner to the sofa. Sarah has pulled herself together too. She's sitting on the floor, her back leaning against the sofa. Bernie sits across from them, like a sympathy Buddha, if there were such a thing.

My eyes glide over all of them. "I'm really sorry."

Bernie unfolds her arms. "It's a terrible tragedy," she says. She's about to say more, but Joshua cuts her off.

"You're going to find him, right?" he asks, his tone more hopeful than angry. "He really needs to pay for what he did."

"We've got a BOLO all along the West Coast. His picture. Everything we have on him. This will likely hit the news tonight and I expect social media will follow suit. Everyone will know he's out there and we have reason to believe he's dangerous."

"What about Mom?" Sarah asks. "We want to bring her home."

"The funeral home will take care of things."

"No," Joshua says, "no funeral home. Home. Here. She wanted a green burial. We all do."

I'd never heard of anyone doing green burial and I ask him for details. Joshua tells me that the body—not embalmed—is wrapped in a mushroom-spore-infused shroud and is deposited just below the surface of the ground. It's watered daily during dry months—which is where we are now—and as the body decomposes, it nourishes the soil. I can see the appeal, but I don't think it would be for me. I don't like the idea of being food for mushrooms.

Actually, I don't like mushrooms at all.

It's a texture thing.

"Would you like me to notify your aunt Ruth?" I ask. "Or do you want to call? I know she would want to be here for her sister's memorial service."

"She can come, of course," Joshua says, "but there's no big service."

The space above the sofa catches my eye.

"You got the photo reframed."

"Just new glass," Sarah says, shifting her gaze to the portrait behind her. Her eyes land there only a second before looking away like she's seen something terrible. "And a lot of good that we fixed it. I'm going to burn it in the trash barrel after you leave. Can't stand looking at our dad."

I tell them what will happen next, how a crime technician team will be out and go over the scene with a chemical that illuminates blood.

The two exchange looks.

"I know it's hard," I say. "I know all of this is a shock and there will be more to come. It will get easier. That might take a long, long time."

"We know," Joshua says. "It's just the idea—"

Sarah jumps in as her brother buries his face in his hands. "It's the idea that our father killed our mother. Right here. All the time we were waiting for them to come home, we collected eggs, milked Noelle... all the time we were in the place where it all happened."

"I'm so sorry. The forensic exam will give us more answers. Some of those will be painful. But we need to know what happened," I go on. "I need you both to stay clear, all right?"

Joshua, now looking up, nods.

"Ms. Chesterfield is going to stay with you while all this is going on, then she'll make a recommendation to the judge regarding you, Sarah."

Bernie gives the girl a warm, reassuring smile.

I already know what her recommendation will be.

CHAPTER TWENTY-FOUR

I hear the crushing noise of gravel under car tires, rumbling, nearly like thunder somewhere in the foothills above Snow Creek. Sheriff Gray and Mindy Newsom have arrived. She's following his vehicle in her white van—the same one she uses for flower arrangement deliveries. I've known Mindy for years. We used to go out drinking when I first moved to Port Townsend. She was Mindy Scott back then. She'd just graduated from the University of Washington with a degree in forensic science. Our connection was immediate. I was new and so was she. At the time she had the office next door to me, and Sheriff Gray converted one of the old conference rooms to a lab. He had big dreams then. So did she. Mindy was certified by the state and put everything she had into being a skillful criminalist. She didn't know it would be a part-time job.

Yet that's how it turned out.

Seems that Jefferson County crimes with the need of her tools of the trade are few and far between. Mindy got married, had a baby, went on family leave, and opened up a flower shop downtown.

She brightens when she sees me.

"It's been eons, Megan."

I give her a hug. I've missed our friendship. I'm not really close to any other women. Not many men either.

"Far too long," I say.

We talk about her daughter, and she asks if I've met anyone. My mind flashes to Dan Anderson, but that thought is fleeting and completely idiotic. I give her the bag with the hammer, and she puts it in a red and white camping cooler in the back of her van.

"You got me on a good day," she says. "No weddings this coming weekend."

I tell the two of them what I know so far. I watch as Mindy eyes the house and shakes her head at the tragedy that has befallen the occupants of the pretty house in the middle of nowhere. It was worse than a tornado. A fire. A devastating earthquake. It was a decisive kind of evil from within the walls of the house itself.

"Not that it will do much good," she says, indicating the barn, the workshop and the two deputies. "I brought a couple of clean suits."

She looks at the sheriff.

"Sorry," she says, "I don't have one that'll fit you."

He pats his belly. "Now my size is interfering with my work. My wife's going to kill me."

"I hope she doesn't," Mindy says. "You'd have to get a new criminalist because there's no way that I would ever want to process your scene. Especially if she shoots you in the shower."

He scratches his head and makes a face. "Yeah, she's a neat freak. She'd probably do something like that."

The deputies have already taped the windows with black plastic in anticipation of the Luminol test. I thank them and tell them to search the property while Mindy and I get dressed for the hut.

Once inside, she opens her kit and double-checks its contents. "Luminol is not a failsafe detector of the presence of blood, Megan. If a killer attempts to conceal his or her crime by using bleach to clean up blood, it can give an erroneous read. In some cases, Luminol can destroy DNA."

She's told me all of this before. I think of it as her way to move the gerbera daisies and fern fronds from her consciousness. Mindy hasn't worked a case in quite some time. "Hammer was recovered here," I say pointing, then turning. "And over here, see that rectangular space on the floor?"

She nods.

"Mrs. Wheaton was found rolled up in carpet. Looks like that space had something covering it."

"All right," Mindy says. "I'll spray here around the workbench. We'll see what we get and then move over to the section where you think the carpet was. I'll spray. You'll shut the door. I'll photograph whatever turns up. Remember, we'll only have twenty or thirty seconds."

Mindy motions for me to stand back and she starts spraying the area where the hammer was found. She's not a tall woman with long arms, but somehow, she manages to sweep in very large, even movements, depositing the misty chemical that reacts to iron in blood.

"This being a working space," she says, "we might get a lot of false positives."

"Metals?" I ask.

"Who knows what they did in here."

She looks at me, picks up her camera and I shut the door.

Blue glows in the shape of an arc, revealing a couple of smears and some spatter freckles: errant castoff from what I'm sure is the hammer, on the lower half of the workbench.

The camera's digital and set on a slow speed. Even so, Mindy's emits the clicking sound of an SLR.

"I'd say you found your crime scene," she says.

I drop markers in the areas that reacted with the Luminol and we move to the space on the floor.

I turn on my flashlight app and direct its soft beam to the floor. Mindy starts spraying, so evenly, so precisely that I wonder if she should have become an airbrush artist instead of a florist. There is no overlap. No place where her spray isn't anything but perfect. I turn off my phone's flashlight.

Right away a pale blue line appears on the edge of the rectangle closest to the front of the hut.

"Good eye, Megan," she says as she photographs the space.

I set a marker.

"I'll collect samples," she goes on.

"I'll tell Sheriff."

I find him standing outside with Bernie.

We don't need to speak. He can read my face.

"Oh shit," he says.

"I'll go inside and check on Joshua and Sarah," Bernie says, disappearing through the front door, the screen door screeching like a bird of prey.

"It's like we thought," I say as we walk toward the barn, where Mindy is now collecting samples for the lab. "The Luminol lit up that workshop like the Fourth of July. Seriously. Spatter and castoff are clear as could be. Merritt hit his wife with the hammer. He dragged her over to the carpet and rolled her up."

"Things like that don't happen around here," Sheriff says. "Not on my watch, anyway."

I know he wants to believe that, of course. Truth is, places like the woods around Jefferson County are full of nefarious doings. We just don't hear about them. Nobody calls in their neighbor to find out if something bad happened.

I think I heard a shot.

Someone screamed in the middle of the night next door. Bloody murder scream.

Haven't seen anyone at their place for months.

Mindy is finishing up.

"What happened here was brutal," she says. "The velocity and trajectory of the spatter shows some major rage."

"Kids say their father was very demanding, even cruel to his wife," Sheriff says.

"Let's be direct," I say. "He cut off one of her toes as punishment for some made-up infraction."

"Infraction? Was he running a prison camp here?" Mindy asks as she continues to record samples for chain of custody. Her writing is precise, somewhere between cursive and printed. Everything about Mindy is precise. Even the way she arranges flowers. No loosey-goosey English garden bouquets with a sprig of this and bunch of that. Hers are always perfectly proportioned, symmetric, and, very often, single-hued.

"You could call it that," I say. "Family is a mix of doomsday preppers, cult-like religion, and prison camp. Very little contact with the outside world."

"Sheriff, this is going to hit the news. I need to call Ida's sister, Ruth."

He gives me a knowing look. He hates making family notifications. No one likes to. It's the worst part of the job. But one of the most important parts.

I get back to the office. It's stone-cold quiet, except for the hum of our relic of a refrigerator—harvest gold—which is like an outboard motor on the other side of a lake. You don't hear it unless you mistakenly hear it, and then, it's all you hear. I settle in at my desk and once more dial Ruth Turner, on a number that she doesn't want me to use.

Unless I really have to.

Her sister being murdered by her husband qualifies in anyone's book.

There is no local police station or sheriff department in 150 miles. I can't send an officer in time to tell her in person, as customary in cases like this, as it will be picked up by the media pretty soon.

I dial the 208 number she gave me.

A man answers. "Who gave you this number?"

I'd have preferred hello. The man's voice is gruff and dismissive. I'm thinking that Ruth might have the same issue with her hand-picked husband as Ida. I decide not to tell him that Ruth had come out to Port Townsend to see me. Maybe he didn't know.

Like the way she hid wearing mascara.

"Mr. Turner, I'm Detective Megan Carpenter from Jefferson County Sheriff's Office in Washington. I have some news I need to tell Mrs. Ruth Turner. There's some urgency here."

"Tell me," he says.

"She reported her sister missing, so it's my duty to speak with her."

"You can tell me. I'll tell her."

"It's the law, sir."

It wasn't but Mr. Turner was acting like the biggest ass in the Gem State. Maybe the whole Pacific Northwest.

"It's not the way we do things in Idaho, miss."

"Detective, please."

There's a slight pause. He says something under his breath, but the refrigerator hum cancels his epithet.

"Ruth, get over here. Some detective in Washington is on my phone. Be quick about it. Someone might be calling for me."

"Hello?"

"Mrs. Turner," I say, "there is no easy way to give news like this to anyone."

"Yes."

"Is there someone there to be with you?" I purposely act like Mr. Turner isn't even an option, because honestly, in my heart I doubt that he is.

"My husband and my oldest daughter are here."

Her voice is cracking. She knows part of what's coming. The other part, I doubt she could even conceive of it.

"Ruth..." I say.

She starts crying before I can say any more, and I hear a young woman hurrying to her, asking what's wrong. I also hear Mr. Turner telling her to lower her volume. It's interfering with whatever he's watching on TV.

Her questions come in bursts between guttural sobs.

"What happened? Is Merritt in the hospital?"

I wish with all my heart that I was there with her.

"I'm sorry, Ruth. The evidence is that she was murdered. Merritt is still missing."

Silence.

"Are you still there?"

"Yes," she says, trying to pull herself together. "I am. I am. This is such a shock."

The phone drops to the floor.

"I'm here, Mother."

It's the girl's voice.

"Oh, Eve," Ruth answers as she gets back on the phone. "Do you think Merritt has something to do with her…her… death?"

"We're searching for him now. Yes, we do."

I let that soak in a moment and she doesn't react to it. The walls around the Wheatons and Turners are high and seemingly impenetrable.

"Joshua and Sarah?"

"A social worker is with them now. They are in a world of hurt, but they are being looked after until things get sorted out with the judge."

She doesn't ask about any of that.

Again silence.

I fill the pause with a change in topic.

"They're arranging a green burial for your sister."

"I don't know what that is," she says.

I tell her, seeming like an expert, when I knew nothing much about it until a few hours ago.

"Oh," she says. "My sister," she says, before letting out a cry, "would have liked that. She loved nature and all of God's wonderments."

It is an odd response; however, these are odd people.

"All right then," I say.

"Eve and I will be there. Nothing—and no one—could stop me. She was everything to me."

I say goodbye and hang up.

No one. She meant her husband, of course. *Everything to her?* And she hadn't seen her in years?

I haven't seen my brother in years. It's not for lack of trying. Maybe Ruth's husband forbade it, and only now did she have the courage to break away.

Good for her.

The county plat map of the Snow Creek area stares up at me from my desk. I take a yellow marker and circle where the body was found on the logging road. I put an X through the locations of the various neighbors' landholdings. I find a pink marker and I draw the only way that Merritt Wheaton could have taken his truck to dump his wife's body. The properties are not that far apart as the crow flies. In reality, they bunch up at the logging road. I ponder that. I'd been thinking that he had brought a bike or something to ride away from the scene. Or had another vehicle stashed up there.

The kids said there was no car missing other than the pickup.

He easily could have walked out of that remote area and worked his way down through the forest and even into town. The plat map shows that, if he did, he passed through property owned by Dan Anderson or Amy and Regina Torrance.

I weigh that for a moment. Dan never mentioned anything. So I scratch him off the list. But the women. No one has seen either Amy or Regina for a while.

I take a deep breath. Having done what he did to his wife, literally from head to toe, I doubt there's nothing Merritt Wheaton wouldn't do.

Steal a car.

Break in a house to hide out.

Or maybe something worse.

As I'm pondering all this, a news alert from the *Leader* appears on my phone. I click the link.

MURDER MYSTERY IN THE WOODS OF SNOW CREEK

A woman's body was found by two Bigfoot hunters in the vicinity of the abandoned Puget Logging tract north of Snow Creek.

She has been identified as Ida Wheaton, 40, of Snow Creek Rd. Ms. Wheaton was reported missing by a relative earlier this week, according to sources.

Her husband, Merritt Wheaton, 53, is missing.

The couple left Snow Creek more than a month ago to volunteer at an orphanage in Mexico. They told their two children that they would be gone several weeks, taking time to drive down the West Coast.

A search was made of the Wheaton family farm and property earlier today. Several items were seized as possible evidence.

Bernadine Chesterfield, Jefferson County victim's advocate, spoke on behalf of the family tonight.

"These kids have been traumatized," Chesterfield said. "They are dealing with an unimaginable amount of pain. Please respect their privacy as they conduct a memorial service tomorrow afternoon."

I roll my eyes upward. Of course, Bernadine is the source. She's always on the edge of violating county privacy rules. I don't even have to call her to find out what tactic she employed to get in the news, so she could send the link to her Coast Guard son and candlemaker daughter.

"The kids wanted me to let the community know of their loss and memorial service. You know how misleading social media can be."

She's always thinking of others.

CHAPTER TWENTY-FIVE

I take the tape recorder with the next tape to bed. I'm too tired to sit at the kitchen table. Its proximity to my room-temp wine hasn't been helping matters. I undress and put on my Portland State University T-shirt. I haven't donned it for quite some time, and I wonder if my subconscious is working on everything I do.

Portland State University is where I was treated by Dr. Albright, of course. The shirt is pulling me back there in its own way.

I don't make friends because I was trained not to trust people.

I don't cook because my mother used me like a slave.

I don't even own a TV because, when I did, certain things triggered me a little. All right, a lot. Hair dye, for one. A Kit Kat candy bar commercial. It's the little things that add up. Those things treat my body like a voodoo doll, poking me until I cry out.

Silently, of course.

I know the work that I do is a kind of lifelong atonement for the sum of what I did. Who I really am.

The poison that circulates in my blood.

I lay my head on the pillow and look around; my eyes scrape past the recorder. The room is pale blue, kind of a soothing robin's egg hue. The ceiling is high and every time I look up, I make a mental note to get a broom and stepladder, so I can swipe away the cobwebs. On my dresser there are two pictures of my brother, one taken at our aunt's place in Idaho. Another when he graduated from high school. On the back is a note that was meant to wound me.

Rylee, I'm graduating today. You are not here (as always). My foster parents are nice people, but they don't replace my family. Thanks for taking all of that away from me.
   Hayden

I don't even have to pop the photograph from the frame to read it anymore. I've memorized every single word of it.

He hates me.

I don't doubt that I deserve it.

And still I check my email twice a day to see if he's written back.

On the wall next to the door with its vintage crystal knob is a painting of a sailboat. It came with the place. Sometimes I imagine myself on that boat, sailing away, never to return.

I press PLAY and I turn off the light next to my bed. I lie there, like a child listening to a scary story. *My story.*

Dr. Albright starts things off with a reminder that she is on this journey with me. That I'm strong and that I'm on a pathway to healing. I remember wanting to believe her so much, but also thinking it was complete bullshit. That I'd never be fully healed. She tells me to close my eyes and bring her with me. Hearing her voice so full of concern makes me think of the Wheaton kids and how alone they must be feeling. How huge their tragedy is and how it will forever be etched on their minds. How I hope they will find someone like Karen Albright to help them move through life.

   Dr. A: Tell me about finding Aunt Ginger.
   Me: It was flat-out weird. I'd never even heard of her and Hayden and I were about to knock on her door. I didn't know how we'd feel. How she would feel. Or even if she knew about me and Hayden. So much of our lives had been compartmentalized. I remember standing outside, looking at her gray two-story. It was tucked into the base of a ridge down from the mountains.

It was old. But in decent repair. I'd seen an episode of Dr. Phil in which some kids went looking for their birth parents only to find out they were living in a rusted-out trailer on some riverbank somewhere. The kids on the show had decided that their adoptive parents weren't so bad after all.

Dr. A: It's good to be grateful for what you have.

Me: I am alive. And I'm grateful for that. (pause) I remember when she opened the door, how much she looked like me and my mom. She was about my height. Her hair was long, not Mormon-sister-wife long, but close. I remember how she reacted when I told her who we were.

Dr. A: Go on, Rylee. What did she do?

Me: She looked nervous. Scared. Anxious. Her light blue eyes narrowed, and I watched her eyelids flutter. She looked around the street, her yard, the driveway, and told us to hurry inside. The first thing she asked was where her sister was. I told her, "He's got her." And then she did something weird.

Dr. A: Weird? How so?

Me: It was something no one other than my parents had ever done. She hugged me. I didn't know her. But I just started crying. I mean, tears just streaming down my face. Hayden too. In fact, all three of us just sobbed. I melt into her arms and I cry harder than I ever have since the ordeal began. I can cry loudly because I feel that someone cares and that even though I'm in a stranger's place, I'm with family. It wasn't a reunion of joy, but something completely different. We are a sobbing mass of pain, loss, and fear.

I tell Dr. Albright how strange it was to hear this newfound aunt call our mother Courtney. *Her real name.* Not the one engraved on the dog tags that I wore around my neck. My mother's name wasn't Ginger. Ginger was my aunt. What's more, I was stunned by her reaction to us appearing on her doorstep. *She wasn't shocked.*

*

Me: But I was. Hayden and I had been kept away from her for our entire lives and she went along with it. I wanted to be kind. I wanted to think that all of that had been for our own good, but I wasn't sure. The betrayal was so deep, and apparently, shared. And then she dropped the bomb. She said, "The last time I saw your mother—last Labor Day—she told me that she thought you'd have to move again soon. She thought he was closing in on her. I told her that she was paranoid, you know, more paranoid than cautious. I told her to stay put. I told her that his threats would never evolve into reality. I..." Aunt Ginger was shaking as she spoke. I didn't want to confront her right then, but I thought, really? Really? Did she see our mother last Labor Day? Did this aunt who we never knew existed up until twenty-four hours ago stay in touch with our mother, and she never bothered to tell us?

I asked her if she knew where my mom was, where he could have taken her. But she shook her head. Didn't know where he lived. And when I asked if she'd help us to find her, she said, "Let's figure it out later."

"There is no later," I say in the most direct way that I can.

She bites down on her lower lip before speaking. "I mean, after you eat and rest."

I don't understand her peculiar reluctance. Her sister has been abducted by a serial killer. Why is she being so weird?

Hayden's eyes landed on a cheese sandwich and a stack of Pringles potato chips that our aunt has set on two cornflower-blue plates that she's placed on an enormous table in the kitchen. On the wall adjacent to the table are some photographs. Lots of them. My heart skips a beat and I feel a surge of bewilderment. My school photo is among a bunch of images of complete strangers. There's an old picture of Hayden, too. We were part of a family. We just didn't know it.

Aunt Ginger turns to me and mouths some words. She says, "After he's in bed, we'll talk then."

I sit down across from my brother while our aunt pours milk from a glass bottle. I don't even like milk, but I say nothing. I sit there thinking of how the forces have collided to make my life worse than it has ever been.

And how my mother has less than six days to stay alive if I don't do something about it.

The air from the open window passes over me. I check my phone before I turn out the light.

Again, nothing.

Is that all I am to him?

I go to Hayden's Instagram feed. He doesn't know I'm a follower. My handle was meant to be an inside joke.

Twisted Sister.

CHAPTER TWENTY-SIX

Just when you need it, the marine layer from the straits sends a blanket of air that drops temperatures by at least ten degrees. Sometimes twenty. I dress in a blue suit. Sheriff Gray and I are attending the memorial. I expect Bernadine to be there too. I'll be sure to thank her for being such a great advocate—and news source for the *Leader*.

And though it is a long shot, I wonder if the killer will come. Maybe watching from afar? Enjoying the results of his handiwork. It has happened, many times, though mostly in cases with a larger pool of possible suspects.

Merritt stands alone.

I go over the case in my mind as I drink a cup of coffee, spread blackberry jam on toast.

Evidence from the Wheaton farm is being processed and I expect some preliminary results some time this afternoon. Too bad I won't be able to get an update in the cell phone iron curtain of Snow Creek. I have time to make a run at the Torrance place before the memorial.

I open my email. Again, nothing other than a bunch of offers for discontinued furniture from Pottery Barn. Half off a red and white checked sofa is half off nothing anyone would ever want.

That's why it's discontinued.

I check my teeth in the bathroom mirror before leaving. Good thing. Blackberry seeds have found a home on my front tooth. Not a good look for a memorial service.

*

The offices of the Jefferson County sheriff sound so much better than the night before. The refrigerator hum is definitely in the background where it belongs as deputies, clerks, and ringing phones take the forefront. Everyone is talking about the Wheaton case, of course. It's the biggest thing we've had around here in I don't know how long. Maybe forever. Nan at the front desk looks especially excited.

"A producer from Seattle's KING-TV called. Wants to come out and do some interviews on how the murder of Mrs. Wheaton is affecting the town," she says.

"We shouldn't be doing interviews," I say.

She shrinks like a popped balloon.

"Bernadine did one already."

"That's Bernie. Not us. We drive the media story when we need to. Not to serve their ratings, Nan."

She still looks deflated, but she nods.

I poke my head into Sheriff's office. He's finishing a call.

"I told Nan no interviews," I say.

Now he looks deflated.

"Yeah, you're right. I like that gal they were going to send out."

I don't respond.

"Anything from the lab?"

"Not yet," I say.

He looks me over, like he's seeing me for the first time.

"I remember that suit. That's what you wore to the interview."

I shrug. "Not much need for one around here. Besides, nothing goes out of style. I saw a guy in a leisure suit the other day when I was getting coffee."

"No shit," he says. "I used to have a few of those back in the day."

I suspect he still does.

I tell him that I'm going back to Snow Creek before the memorial and I'll meet up with him around one or so.

He gives me a sly smile. "Leaving no stone unturned, Megan?"

"That's me," I say.

In fact, I nearly live for turning stones to see what ugly thing crawls out from under. I did it with abandon when I was fifteen. Or sixteen.

The ride back to Snow Creek is now autopilot easy. I play Adele on the CD player. Her voice soothes as my mind plays thoughts about Ida Wheaton. Beaten, brutalized, burned, dumped. It was such overkill. At first, I thought the carpet was an instrument of convenience, concealment. But why bother with it if you're just going to burn her in the truck and drive it into a ravine? Too much effort. Now I consider it was purposeful. Whoever hated her enough to kill her so violently must have loved her too. That's why my money's on Merritt. At some point he must have cared for his wife. Most husbands do. Then for whatever hideous reason, he strikes her with a hammer and rolls her up in a carpet to hide what he's done. Not from others. Strictly from himself.

I pass the inventive two-story mobile home and barely give it a thought.

When I near Dan Anderson's place, I consider stopping. Maybe apologizing for not getting back to him. Or say that I had my eye on the carved bear. I play all of those scenarios in my mind and am glad that I keep going. I like him. I can tell he likes me. I just can't go there. There are too many secrets to hold inside that keep me from being anything other than closed off.

The Torrance place looks exactly the same when I drive up. From where I park, I can see the note to Jared is right where it was. The goats look as though they are being taken care of, but there are no signs that any other car has been here besides Sheriff's. That bothers me a little. It's possible that Jared is someone out in the woods and gets there by walking. Maybe the mobile home with the sweet potato vine in the jar?

I scan the field and the tree line that rises up the mountains to the logging road where the truck and body were discovered. There's an opening at the edge of the forest.

Before I head in for the trail, I knock on the door. At my feet are two purple and one dark blue Croc, the world's most hideous shoe.

I knock harder.

A dark blue Croc, I know, was found not far from where Ida Wheaton's burned body was found in the pickup truck.

"Amy!" I call out, leaning toward the door. "Regina! Is there anyone home?"

I don't hear anything, but for a flash I thought I sensed a vibration on the porch.

I knock one last time, thinking of that Croc. Has Merritt been holed up here? I'm worried about the women. Something feels funny. I make a mental note to call into the office when I get in cell range. Deputies need to swing by here for a welfare check. I'll pull records on both women later.

As I move down the trail it feels as though I'm entering in a tunnel. So dark in places. Every once in a while a sharp blade of light lacerates the space. The path is wider than a deer trail, though not by much. It snakes through the forest and begins to rise about a hundred yards in.

I have the wrong clothes for such an endeavor and definitely the wrong shoes.

Should have borrowed the ugly Crocs, I think. At least no one would have seen me in them. Maybe a squirrel but I could live with that.

I remove my jacket and fold it neatly to carry the rest of the way. I can't show up looking like some derelict at Mrs. Wheaton's memorial. For all I know, Bernie notified the media.

I had no idea they were coming. Really, I'm just as shocked as you are.

The trail leads me to the exact spot where the truck went down. A deep cut in the earth shows where the tow truck driver dragged it up to the road, where a flatbed had been brought to take it for processing at the same crime lab—only to tell us that an accelerant had been used and the VIN hadn't been completely removed. The last three digits and one of the middle letters were still legible.

The truck was indeed Merritt Wheaton's.

When I get back to the Torrance house, I try the door one more time. Again, no answer.

CHAPTER TWENTY-SEVEN

Crime scene tape makes for an unsettling memorial decoration. It flaps in the breeze over by the barn and around the Quonset hut. I look at my phone, but of course, no word on the blood and hair evidence that Mindy collected yesterday. A half dozen cars are lined up in the field adjacent to the small apple orchard. I park behind Sheriff.

Before I shut my door, I smell wintergreen.

Ruth Turner is standing next to me. Behind her, a young woman of about twenty. She has long dark hair parted in the center. Her eyes are blue like her mother's.

"You must be Eve," I say.

She gives me a shy smile. "That's me."

Her mother surprises me and hugs me. I feel her body wilting in my arms. It's uncomfortable because I don't know her, but she needs it.

"I'm so sorry for your loss, Ruth," I say. "I know that words don't fill an empty space. I know that from experience."

"Thank you, Detective Carpenter. I prayed all last night you'd be here. I'm so grateful that it's over. Thank you for finding her. Ida is in our heavenly Father's loving arms. No more pain. Only the joy of being with Him."

I look up. "Damn, you, Bernie!"

A news crew is setting up.

"I'm sorry," I say to Ruth and Eve. "Let's go inside."

"I had no idea so many would come," Bernie says.

"I doubt that."

She glares at me. "Excuse me, Detective?"

I want to say *There's no excuse for you*, but I don't. Given the occasion and the fact that I'm in my almost, not quite mid-thirties.

Sheriff is drinking lemonade.

"Hey," I say, standing close. "I think I'm onto something."

"What?" he says, reaching for Sarah's homemade taffy.

"We need to go back to the Torrance place."

He wants to answer but his teeth are stuck.

He's going to lose a filling for sure.

"Later," I say.

On the beautiful cherry table her husband built is the shroud-wrapped body of Ida Wheaton. Joshua and Sarah are talking with their aunt and cousin. I approach and don't interrupt. Instead I look over the white muslin used to wrap her. The sad irony of it all comes to me. She was wrapped up after she was murdered. And wrapped a second time the morning of her memorial. I thought it would feel odd, burying someone among trees. Creating an environment that would break down a human body for the good of the earth. It didn't. In part because of the strange beauty of it all. Ida's children have decorated the outside of the shroud with orange and yellow nasturtium blossoms, bright green sprigs of spearmint and the dusty green of rosemary. It is needed and so is the fan on the window. It faces out, spewing the underlying odor of their mother's decaying body. It had been super-chilled at the morgue, but that can only slow decay. It can't stop it.

I look at my phone. No signal. In ten minutes the memorial is due to start.

"Sarah. Joshua. I'm very sorry about what you two are going through. I heard that the judge will let you stay together."

"Bernadine already told us," Joshua says. He looks at his sister. "She is really all I have. We both need each other."

Next, I say something that I never thought would pass from my lips.

"I love what you did with your mother's shroud."

I stand there for a second, thinking that while my words were sincere, they sounded like I was commenting on a pair of club chairs.

"She loved the garden," Joshua says.

Sarah looks at her mother. "I've never done anything like this, Detective."

"You two can handle it," I tell them. I want to say that there are lots of people here to support you. But there aren't—a couple of cops, an attention seeker, an aunt and cousin.

"Okay," he says. "We're going to carry our beloved mother to the orchard where Sarah and I prepared a symbolic resting place."

"Symbolic?"

Joshua shakes his head. "We can't actually bury Mom here. We're ahead of the laws, I guess. She'll go back to the funeral home and then be buried in a green cemetery."

"Sheriff Gray?" Sarah asks, indicating the table. "It's time."

Sheriff makes his way from the taffy bowl to the table.

He's going to help. Good. This will be interesting.

Ida's body lies on a cotton tablecloth, and Sheriff and Joshua each take an end. Joshua has his mother's head, all festooned with nasturtiums, and Sheriff hoists the tail end, which at once seems like a struggle for him.

I hope he can manage.

As we walk from the house to the orchard, I hear Eve talking about how hurt she is that Sarah has forgotten how close they were when they were little. If their relationship is anything like her mother and aunt's, I can't imagine they were that close at all. She'd probably seen her two or three times in their entire lives.

I hear Sheriff asking Joshua if he wants to set his mom down and rest a little.

He says no.

I know that Sheriff is the one who wants to take a break.

Next, he asks Joshua if he wants someone to ask the media to leave.

"We'll be done before you can do that."

We encircle the space where grass leads up to a rectangular space neatly cut into the black soil.

Joshua and Sheriff gently lower her onto a trestle, while Sarah brings two shovels; one's a square edge, the other rounded.

"Like I said," Joshua starts, looking around, "never done this before. I know it's what my mom would have wanted. I mean, she would have liked to actually be buried here, but she'll still be able to be part of the earth. Just not here."

My eyes meet Ruth's. Tears streak from her mascara-free eyes.

Joshua soldiers on. "We loved our mom. We will never forgive our father. When he is caught, I hope he gets the death penalty. He was garbage."

Sarah touches her brother's shoulder and he stops. He looks at her and she grips his hand.

"No one is perfect," she says. "Mom was close to it. She was always there when we needed something or when we were sick. Dad pretty much kept us away from her as much as he could. I won't say more. Everyone's said enough."

"Can I speak?"

It's Ruth.

Brother and sister step back to give her room.

"I'm very sorry that I don't know my nephew and niece better. I can make excuses, but I want you two to know the truth." She holds her breath. "Your father kept us apart too. He didn't...didn't want her to be close to anyone. I'll miss her every day. Just like I have the past six years."

Ruth Turner looks at her sister's body, bends down, and pulls a frilly blue bachelor's button from the shroud.

Her lips are tight and she's trembling.

"May I?" she finally asks.

Joshua nods and watches as his aunt drops the blossom into the open grave.

We stand there silently, then Eve does the same, so does Sarah. We all do.

Joshua sends a shovelful of loose, loamy soil over the flowers in the symbolic grave. Then another. He goes faster and faster. A strange jolt of mania has taken over his body. Two . . . five . . . six. Again, his sister intervenes.

"That's enough," she tells him. "Put down the shovel." He does as he's told, and I think it's a somewhat strange dynamic. She's younger, but she is the dominant of the two.

She takes the shovel and scrapes soil onto the now-disappearing collage of flowers.

"Bye, Mom," she says, now kneeling and pulling a flower from her hair. "Our hearts are broken. Don't worry. We're strong like you. We're fighters too." She drops the daisy into the empty grave they've made.

I look at Sheriff. He's rolling his tongue over what I'm sure is his missing filling.

"I'm going to tell them to leave," I say, indicating the TV crew.

"Yeah, tell them to get lost."

A news reporter with flawless skin, shiny dark hair, and a distinctly cocky prance in his walk comes at me. A camerawoman follows.

"Jake Jackson, KING-TV," he announces. "You're the detective on the case."

He's wearing makeup already. This is going to be one of those "live from the scene" type of stories. This was big. In the past when there was some interest in something happening here, they'd have one of the kids from the high school shoot the video and then—at their own expense—drive it to Seattle. Now just about everyone with a smartphone is doing the same thing.

Before I answer, the camerawoman chimes in.

"She's Millie Carpenter, Jake. God, you are embarrassing."

He turns red under his makeup. I don't correct her because I like the results of her mistake.

"I'm afraid we have no comment about this case. It's an ongoing investigation. We'll update what we can when we can."

"Was the killing related to a particular belief system?" He points to the orchard. "Wheaton buried in a shroud."

"In the ground," adds the dimwit with the handheld.

"Look, you're going to need to leave now. This is private property."

"Ms. Chesterfield said we could be here."

Of course, she did.

I show my badge. "I outrank her." I look over my shoulder at Sheriff. "And he outranks all of us. Please go."

I hear him say something about just doing his job, and she chirps as they turn to pack up: "Does that mean we're not going to that restaurant?"

Everyone is inside the house now, except for Ruth's daughter.

"Hi," I say.

Eve gives me a weak smile.

"Can I sit?"

She indicates the place next to her.

"I guess you heard me complaining about Sarah."

"I didn't take it as complaining, just disappointment."

"Right?" she remarks. "When you're raised like an inmate, you want a real connection with anyone outside of your home. When we were little Sarah was mine. My lifeline."

"I'm sure she feels the same way."

"Maybe. Maybe she does."

"It's a very hard day for all of you," I tell her, patting her knee.

"Yeah. That's the truth."

Ruth says she'll see me before she leaves the next day. I give Bernie a look, a glare really. The others I hug and tell them that our duty to find out who killed their mother is an extension of their love for her.

"Find her killer," Ruth whispers, as she pulls her niece and nephew close to her. "Find Merritt." Joshua's eyes widen. Sarah inches slightly to the fan that had been used to pull the scent of her mother's remains.

Just how much wintergreen can a person breathe and still survive?

CHAPTER TWENTY-EIGHT

"They keep coming, Amy," Regina says, cuddling in bed with her wife.

"You keep us safe."

"You really think so?"

"Yes, babe, I do."

Even after the fight. The really bad one.

Even then.

Even now.

Regina looks at the ceiling, and Amy's hand rests on her shoulder.

"I never should have tried to stop you, Amy."

"I know you did it because you love me. I forgave you long ago."

Regina's tears flow. She tells Amy that she hoped this day would never come. She never imagined trying to protect their own privacy, getting rid of the man's body.

"Seen his kids up that road a few times over the years," Regina remarks.

As Regina mixes rat poison into a bowl of water, she thinks back to the big fight and how it all started. It was the fall before the last. Back then, Amy barely spoke to Reggie. And when she did it was only one subject.

"I don't want to live here for the rest of my life, Reggie. We agreed it was for a few years. Great. Fine, but, babe, that was a dozen years ago. I want to move on."

Reggie ignored the remark for the longest time.

Amy finally spoke up.

"You are making me do something that I don't want to do."

That got Reggie's attention.

Amy was full of resolve, but she's crying anyway.

"I don't love you like I did, babe. I want out. I want a divorce."

Regina's eyes bulged and she dove for Amy.

"You can't leave!"

Amy pushed back hard. Regina was stronger, tougher and equally full of resolve. She wasn't going to stop until she got what she wanted. "You aren't going anywhere. You love me. You said so."

"I did. Really, Regina, but it was a long time ago."

"You little liar," Regina growled as she went for Amy's neck.

In a flash, Amy grabbed a knife from the counter, and swung it wildly, before ramming its tip into Regina's eye. Blood squirted and Regina screamed at the top of her lungs.

"What did you do to me?"

"Sorry. Sorry."

"Never leave me. Not ever."

Somehow, they'd managed to fight their way across from one room to the next. What started in the bedroom had moved them to the kitchen. Blood gushed from the spaces between Regina's fingers as she pressed over the agony that was her right eye.

However, Regina's reflexes were sharp. She knocked the knife out of her wife's hand and threw herself on top of her.

"You said you were mine forever."

By then, Amy could no longer speak. Her eyes, wide open, began to bloom blood as the capillaries burst. Regina's hands tightened around her neck. She wanted to stop. It's impossible. It's the kind of thing for which there was no turning back.

Regina stared at the ebbing life force. It's like a beautiful, nearly invisible vapor that curls above before vanishing out the window.

"You'll never leave me."

"I would never leave you," Amy insisted. "I love you, Regina. I'm sorry."

Regina sat awhile, thinking. Her eye. She couldn't go to the hospital. She made her way, nearly stumbling as she walked, to the bathroom. She took off her clothes, took a bottle of hydrogen peroxide and washed herself in the outdoor shower.

She tried not to cry. It hurt so much. Without a nanosecond of delay, Regina stepped away from the water, leaned back and poured the contents of the bottle into her eye socket. She screamed louder than she ever had in her life. Foam collected in her where her eye had been and she poured more, again and again.

Always with a scream.

That's when the idea came to her.

Amy doesn't say a single word while she watches Regina mix the powdery and crystalline poison she'd used to kill the barn rats. She's sitting up in bed, and when Regina sits next to her, Amy reaches out and touches her tenderly. She holds the juice glass with the poison; they stare straight ahead.

Regina cries from her single eye.

Amy trembles.

"I am sorry," she whimpers.

"I know."

"I love you, Regina. Always have."

"Always will."

CHAPTER TWENTY-NINE

I can't face the tapes right now. I can't face going home. I think of returning Dan Anderson's call, but that would make me feel like a jerk for not phoning sooner. So, I don't. Instead I drive to the waterfront, to the bar, The Tides, a place Mindy and I frequented back in the day. I miss seeing her. Hayden too. My list is short.

I'm feeling sorry for myself and I know it.

My focus and my brain and, yes, my emotions should be aimed solely on the case.

I don't know any of the staff at The Tides. I've hit the point in life where I'm nearing that middle part where no one sees you anymore. Service at a bar or restaurant is slower. Talking with the waiter or anyone is nonexistent. Unless I'm willing to dress a little more provocatively, I'll always be a Soup-for-One girl.

The Tides is authentic, not one of those chains that brings in some buoys and floats with netting that had never seen seawater. It's a converted warehouse at the end of the dock. It's painted blue and features a broad white and navy stripe on its awning over the door. The Tides is spelled out in thin pieces of driftwood.

I go inside and find a seat. It's next to a massive saltwater tank with a school of clown fish and others I can't name. It soothes me as I watch the fish twirl and turn in the bubbling water. One of the fish, shaped like a disk, is iridescent blue in color. Instead of thinking bachelor's buttons, my mind goes straight to Luminol.

I wonder how the lab tests are going. Maybe they'll surprise us with a sudden heroic burst of energy, but I have my doubts.

A waitress asks if I want a drink.

I order a G & T.

"Still serving dinner?" I ask.

"Yes, ma'am."

Ma'am again.

She drops off the dinner menu and, a few minutes later, my drink. First things first, I take a big sip of the cocktail that I have long thought synonymous with summer. It's lime. It's crisp. It's the drink I suspect one day will be my downfall. I know tonight I'll have two and still want another.

When the waitress returns, I tell her the New York, medium rare.

"Corn or grass fed?" she asks.

"Grass."

"Baked or fried?"

I can't do this all night, so I tell her everything she needs to know. "Baked, the works. Salad, bleu cheese, another drink."

I end by looking at my phone. Rude, I know. I'm not sorry. A text message from Sheriff is brief, but it's the first thing that has made me smile today.

Called Bernie's boss.

I give him the thumbs-up emoji. I almost send the heart emoji, though I don't want things to get weird with him. Not that he's ever been inappropriate. Not by a long shot.

I have a few texts from people in town telling me I did a good job on TV.

I wonder what they think would constitute a poor job. All I did was look hostile as I told the reporter to get off the property. And yes, I showed my badge, but honestly why does that have to go viral? It wasn't like it was my gun.

Thank God for that.

I sit there in my kitchen, while revisiting the saddest memorial I've ever attended. It wasn't only the flowers from the shroud floating downward into the darkness of an earthen hole, or even the small number of people who came to remember Ida Wheaton. It stirred more memories. Like the tapes. I thought of how Hayden and I never got to pay our respects or grieve for our stepdad at his memorial. In fact, it only crossed my mind just now that he'd probably been buried in Potter's Field. No service. No friends. No family. Just a kind of nothingness, an extension of the life we'd lived since I was little.

CHAPTER THIRTY

Ruth Turner is waiting at my office when I arrive the next morning. She's dressed in a long-sleeved blouse with a high collar; her skirt is cut below the knee. I take her to my office, where she marvels at all the "papers" I have.

"Your work looks so busy," she remarks before amending, "That came out wrong. You look busy."

I offer coffee. As expected, she declines.

No caffeine is allowed by order of her husband, no doubt.

"Where's Eve?"

"In the car. Too shy to come in."

She wasn't that shy yesterday, I think. She was upset, but she was articulate and direct when she talked about her feelings of being hurt by her cousin's indifference.

"That's too bad," I finally say. "Tell her I enjoyed our talk yesterday. She's a very smart young woman."

Ruth's wintergreen scent is so muted I can barely detect it. She sits staring at me, silent, and shifts her eyes to the window behind me. Then back.

"Ruth, what's going on?" I ask.

"I wish I knew."

She hesitates, and I prod her gently.

"Can I have some water?"

I pour her some from the Brita pitcher on my desk.

"I don't know how to say this, but something is wrong. I think those kids are a mess. They need someone to look after them. They won't come to Idaho with me. My husband said it would be okay."

"The county will provide services," I remind her. "They'll have someone to look after them. I promise."

She nods. "I think they might need more help than a weekly visit by a case worker."

I push a little. "What are you getting at, Ruth?"

She finishes her water like she's just run a marathon. She crosses her arms and pulls in.

"Tell me what you observed, Ruth. We can help."

She finally speaks. "I don't want those two separated; I just want you to pay extra attention to them."

I don't know what she means so I let silence fill my office. I've pushed her enough. I'll let Ruth tell me what she wants to tell me when she's ready.

Finally, she does.

Her hands are folded now on the table in front of her.

"At first I thought that Sarah was a little off, when she didn't seem to recall anything that she and Eve had done as children. They were close. She'd just found a way to block out memories, good or bad."

"Eve and I talked about that," I say.

"She told me. I felt it too, Detective Carpenter."

I drink my coffee and remind myself not to interject again or we'll never get to where we need to go.

"After everyone left," she goes on, "we talked awhile outside and made s'mores at the big firepit. We all went to bed. Eve and I stayed in the master bedroom. Eve fell asleep almost immediately and I just lay there, staring at the ceiling and wondering how any of this could have happened."

She sat there across from me, collecting her thoughts.

"I heard crying coming from the hallway. It was soft and plaintive. It was a kind of whimper and I couldn't put out of my mind that she'd cried so quietly, so privately, during the service. She was letting it out, trying hard not to wake anyone."

"It is a lot to hold inside," I say.

"Right," Ruth goes on. "Well I might as well be straight about it and stop beating round the bush. When I opened the door and looked out in the hall to see if I could help Sarah..."

She pauses, looks at me.

"It was Joshua. He was pretty much naked and lying on the floor crying. It was one of those things where you don't know if you should get soaked or wait for the storm to pass by. Well, then I heard another door open and a voice whisper. It was Sarah."

I lean closer and set down my cup. "What did you hear her say?"

"I'm not sure. At least one hundred percent, but I think I heard Sarah whisper through the crack of her door... 'I'll smash your hand with a hammer.'"

"Why would she say that?" I ask.

"I don't know. I shut the door and I heard Joshua's door open and close. After that, nothing. Like I said, she's a little off, but he's not doing much better. He was in the fetal position on the hallway floor, buck naked. He was crying like a baby and she was haranguing him with some nasty threat."

"They've gone through more in the past week than most of us do in a lifetime, wouldn't you agree?"

Ruth tilts her head. "Yes, but I don't know if they can really help each other. He was crying, and she was telling him she wanted to smash him with a hammer. You need to check on them, please. That case worker of yours was completely useless. Kids told me she spent all day reading magazines she brought from home. She said she was too busy when Sarah asked her to help her with the egg gathering."

I tell her that I will be extra vigilant insofar as her sister's family are concerned.

"I promise to find the best case worker we can get, and I'll personally check up on them as often as I can."

She gets up and awkwardly reaches over so we can embrace over my desk. When we can't quite do it, we both laugh, and I go to the other side of the desk. I smell her wintergreen and we hug like we know each other, like we are bonded forever.

Murders can do that.

"We'll find him, Ruth," I say as I let her go.

"Detective, one more favor," she says, looking embarrassed. "Remember, only call if it is an absolute necessity. If you capture or kill my brother-in-law, just mail me a note. I like getting mail."

She starts to cry, and I inch her out the door and wave at Eve, who cheerfully returns the gesture.

"Bye-bye now," I say, turning away from the door. I need to get on the phone with the crime lab. We deserve some help.

"Definitely not today," the clerk says in a clipped, cold manner. "Maybe tomorrow. Call this afternoon. We are very, very busy."

I don't say it, but I think it: *Yes, I know. Every time we ask for something you tell us that.*

I return back to my desk to get my purse and jacket. Since the sheriff is out doing something, I don't even need to make up an excuse. I slip out the back door and start my trip back to the Torrance place.

CHAPTER THIRTY-ONE

Record searches—criminal and civil—turned up nothing of value on the Torrances. At least, nothing that would provide any insight. Regina had a DUI fifteen years ago and Amy was cited a couple of times for minor traffic violations. All cases were King County, where they lived prior to Snow Creek. I look at the DMV photos of the women, taken in Seattle more than a decade ago. Both licenses had lapsed. Regina's eyes were blue. Amy's brown. Regina was nearly a foot taller, fifty pounds heavier than Amy.

I stand on their front porch looking at a now very familiar note. I highly doubt there's a Jared. I haven't found one after a multitude of tries.

I study the handwriting once more: it's bold and strong.

It passes through my mind that Merritt wrote it as a ruse.

I knock; as before, nothing.

"Regina? Amy?"

I try the knob and this time it's unlocked. Something is wrong. I can feel it. I draw my gun from my side holster and swing the door open. I'm assaulted by the odor coming at me. The smell is worse than the cat lady's house down the road. The air is a sweet and heavy mask, an overdose of Febreze and balsam fir scented candles. I wince. Underneath the scent is the unmistakable acrid odor of death.

Damn, I'm too late, I think, as I try to breathe from my mouth. Merritt has been here.

I move methodically through the front room. Its tidy collection of furnishings and photos of whom based on the old DMV photos I presume to be Amy and Regina are undisturbed: Regina is sturdy and quite pretty; Amy, the smaller, has a sweet smile and beautiful hair. Next, I sweep the kitchen. Everything is put away. The sink sparkles. A toy goat activated by the sun bobs its head up and down. I look toward the hall.

My gun is a divining rod in search of evil.

"Anyone home?" I ask. "This is the Jefferson County sheriff. We need to talk to you."

No response.

I make my way down the narrow, dark hall and nudge the only door open. The stench comes at me in full force. I continue to breathe through my mouth.

It doesn't help.

I can taste something dead.

The scene comes at me in pieces, my mind trying to pull what I'm seeing together in some kind of semblance of reality.

Curtains drawn.

A sliver of sunlight leads to the bed.

A battery-operated candle flickers on the nightstand.

Two figures are on the bed, side by side; the beam of light from the window illuminates a hand. It's small. A woman's? A child's?

"Regina? Amy?" I say, reaching behind me to flick on the lights, but my fingers can't find a switch anywhere. Gun still out, I reach for the curtain and yank it open.

I gasp and suck in the foul air and nearly fall to my knees.

I see a series of pulleys and wires coming from the ceiling.

What is this? What did he do to them?

My hip scrapes a wire and the woman farthest from me moves. I lose my breath immediately, and at the same time I feel a tinge of relief.

"Are you okay?" I ask. My voice is a whisper.

Her face is hidden.

The other woman, the larger of the two, stares at me with a single eye.

A dead, lifeless one. My gun feels heavy. I nearly drop it on the floor as I steady myself.

I lean down, prod her gently. She's gone. I do the same with the other, moving the white sheet that covers most of her.

I've found Amy. Or what used to be her. She's desiccated and shiny, like a preserved mummy in a curiosity shop. Her hair is a wig. In fact, I notice several now on the dresser. Her limbs, neck and arms are strapped with fabric that holds industrial-sized cup hooks. The lines that run from her body to the ceiling are a means to move her.

Amy's body is a puppet.

A doll.

The grotesqueness of the scene overtakes me. No matter what I've seen or done has never been this horrific.

A bizarre game played by one.

I can't breathe. I can't look. My brain is trying to make sense of it all.

As I spin around to leave, I see a folded slip of paper in Regina's hand. It's against procedure, I know. I take it.

I'm a ping-pong ball in the hallway, disoriented, revulsed, nearly staggering as I hurry out the door. I'm stronger than this. I say it over and over to myself. And yet, I slump on the porch. Now I'm a marionette.

The air in my lungs is purged of the vile scent of the bedroom, but my mouth still tastes the scene.

The paper remains in my hand. Actually, there are two of them. In pristine condition; treasured souvenirs of their life together, I think, as I unfold the first one.

It's not a cherished memento at all.

It's the kind of letter no one wants to receive from someone she loves. It's written in a neat cursive hand, like a veteran schoolteacher who wants her students to appreciate the beauty of penmanship in a world of texting: a completely losing proposition.

Dear Regina,

    You aren't making this easy. You don't seem to want to listen. I need you to hear me now. I love you. I really do. You will always be one of the best parts of my life.

It's easy to see where this is going. I could stop reading now. "One of the best parts" is an inimitable beginning of a goodbye.

We did something amazing here on our farm, our piece of paradise. The two of us created a world. We really did. Remember how our friends thought we were crazy? We showed them all, didn't we? I know that. I honor that. And, yes, I loved it here for a long, long time. But for a while now, I've been feeling the need for more. I can't ask you for anything because you have given me all of you. All you have. I have so much appreciation and gratitude for you.

    Here's the hard part. You need to know this. I'm no longer in love with you. I want us to separate in the spirit in which we came together. Do you love me enough to let me go? Know that I will always cherish you, but I need to leave. I'm sorry. I really am.

    Love,

    Amy

Amy's words are heartfelt. I feel sorry for her. I know about those kinds of feelings too. I left someone long ago and it was only because I couldn't save both of us. I couldn't be what he wanted me to be.

I know the next letter will be from Regina; a suicide note, I suspect. I start to read and it's immediately clear that I'm wrong.

This missive was written in a rage. Pen strokes made with such fury some tore through the paper.

Amy,

Goddamn you. I'm sorry that you made me lose my temper. You hurt me to the core. Just tossing me aside like I never mattered. You are my wife and you will always be for eternity. Our vows are sacred. What was this to you? Our life? Just test driving something that you didn't want in the first place? Seriously. You confound me. You do. It's as if we didn't really know each other if you could keep silent for so long. I wish you would have killed me. Really. Look at me. Look at you. I don't have an eye anymore. You did this to me. You shoved that kitchen knife into my face. I was only trying to stop you. I wanted to talk to you. Tell you that I would never love another like I've loved you. Look what you made me do. I didn't mean for it to happen. I know you didn't mean it either. I just wanted you to turn around and tell me that you would come back someday. And now ... Now when I hold you it will be like it was supposed to be.

Forever.

Yes, I'm angry. But I forgive you. I'll take care of you. I'll make you happy and glad you stayed.

Love,

Regina

I press my palm on the porch step and lift myself up. My stomach is queasy. Somehow, I've managed to shake off what I saw inside the Torrance house. I've pulled myself together. Tabled the horror just enough to do my job. Still processing, but clinically so. I pull a roll of crime scene tape from the trunk of the Taurus and wrap it around the posts of the front porch. Amy wanted to get away. Maybe she felt trapped. They had no phone. There was no way she could break away. So they fought. Fought hard.

Regina lost an eye. Amy lost her life. Regina preserved her body, so they'd never be apart.

I'll make you happy and glad that you stayed.

I can't even imagine what went into preserving the body. The last time anyone really saw Amy was two years ago.

I drive until I get a couple of bars of reception and call Sheriff.

"Holy crap," he says, taking in every word. "Pulleys? Wires?"

"Yes. Like a marionette or something."

"What happened there?"

"Murder–suicide. Of the ilk we never could have imagined."

Thoughts of what I'd seen start to tighten my throat.

"You okay?" he asks.

"I don't know. I really don't. I go there to find Ida's killer, so hopeful about that. So wanted to for her children and sister. Then...then this."

"We'll get Merritt Wheaton."

I glance at the rearview mirror.

I am crying.

"You need to come back here," he orders.

"I can do this."

"It's not that, Megan. There's someone here to see you. A woman wants to talk to you about her missing daughter. Thinks you can help. And only you. She specifically said she wanted the detective on TV."

"I'll stay here and wait. Sounds like another fame seeker."

"A fan, maybe," he teases me, trying to bring me out of the darkness of my discovery. "But a serious one. Deputies will be there..." He pauses and calls out to Nan. "When will those two be there?"

"Ten minutes," she says.

He repeats it, forgetting that Nan could work part-time as a foghorn.

"Come on back, Detective," he says one more time.

I promise I'll return as soon as the scene is secure. I look out as I put the car in gear. It's beautiful here. I can hear the water of Snow Creek as it careens down from the mountains to Port Townsend Bay. I think of how I'd dreamed of a big case as I waded through the property crimes that marked my routine. I'd wanted more than anything to make something so very wrong, right. And now this. In the mostly undisturbed magnificence of the Pacific Northwest is a spate of murders, dark and ugly as any could imagine.

Be careful what you ask for.

I drive back to the house and wait for the deputies to arrive.

My car window is open halfway, and it lets in the summer air, scented with spruce, fir, and blackberries. I lower it all the way. Next, I push the buttons that roll down the passenger's side, and the two windows in the back. I want air to pass over me. I want it to clean me. To take away the residue of the work that I do. It isn't about the way the house or Amy and Regina smelled. It is the idea of how murder in its various forms clings to people. For the rest of their lives. I've known this since I was a teenager.

I know it from the job I do.

My hands shake a little. This is not good, I think. Not good at all. Listening to the tapes, dealing with the Wheaton family, and now the Torrances' murder–suicide. So much in such a little time. Maybe too much? Maybe I do have a limit.

I turn onto the main road and head to the office, hoping against hope that the woman will be brief, and the lab results will be ready.

CHAPTER THIRTY-TWO

Laurna Volkmann is waiting by the front desk. She's in her forties, slender, with coral nails and matching lipstick. Her hair is blond and shoulder length. She's wearing a pale pink sweater and white pants.

It doesn't take but a beat before she's on me.

"Detective Carpenter," she says. "I saw you on the news."

I nod.

"I also saw my niece."

Right away, almost without warning, she starts to break down. I lead her to the same room where I interviewed Ruth Turner. She's already smeared her makeup by the time we get there. I push a tissue box in her direction. She takes one, then another, and dabs at her eyes, trying her best to keep the morning's work intact.

Laurna opens her mouth and her words come at me. Each is delivered on its own, a loose chain of what happened to her sister's family.

"Lake Crescent."

"Boat."

"Accident."

"All three drowned."

"Hudson, Carrie, and Ellie."

"The Burbanks."

"Ellie."

"Never found."

Laurna stops long enough to open her purse and take out a photograph. She slides it across the table. I look down, then we lock eyes.

"She's a ringer for Sarah Wheaton," I say.

"I think so. I think it is Ellie, Detective. My sister and my brother-in-law's bodies were recovered a few days after the accident. The lake is deep. We were lucky we found them. I don't think she's down there. I think she's here."

She taps a pink nail against the border of the photograph.

"That's her."

"Like I said, it *looks* like her."

"The detective told me after the autopsy, they had overdosed on drugs and were too stoned to save themselves. I disagree. They weren't druggies."

I feel for her. Family members are often clueless about what transpires between the times they see each other at family gatherings like Christmas, birthday parties, Fourth of July. What appears to be simply overindulging on alcohol on a holiday might be a daily occurrence. I can see why Clallam County ruled it an accident. It was more than plausible. Couple with a hidden addiction drags their daughter down to the bottom of Lake Crescent, one of the deepest lakes in Washington. Over the past century, more than forty-five people have disappeared, presumably drowned, and are somewhere on the bottom of the lake.

"What do you think happened to them?"

Her gaze is now steely.

"My sister and her husband were murdered," she says, her eyes firing at me.

"What makes you say that?"

"I found something. I told the detectives, they didn't want to hear it. The case was closed. No one wants a story about a family dying in one of the area's most beautiful tourist attractions. They just wanted to leave it be."

I ask for details.

"Who do you think did it and what did you find, Ms. Volkmann?"

She takes a breath. "I think Ellie killed her parents."

I can tell that saying those words are difficult for her. The betrayal of a daughter like that is rarely noted in the annals of crime. Matricide and patricide are almost always the work of a son.

"That's a pretty big leap for a teenager," I say.

"Right. I know. Listen to me. She'd been messing up at school, chatting with boys on her phone. What's typical today," she remarks, "is a nightmare for any parent. So they forbid her to go out. She was mad about that. When that didn't work, they took away her phone."

"That's like cutting off a teenager's arm," I say.

She nods. "Or their brain."

My eyes glance back to the photograph and I ask her to continue. She tells me how the police ruled it accidental and she kind of went along with it, said she didn't want to make a big thing of it at the time because she didn't want anyone to think badly of Carrie.

She stops, takes another tissue.

It was the week after the memorial service at Sunset Memorial Park in Bellevue, she tells me. Laurna Volkmann directed a Guatemalan moving crew to take some things to storage. Her sister's house was a large one, stuffed with things that became a love/hate test for Laurna. She'd watched the Japanese expert on a TV show explain how to edit down the things that do nothing for you. That even make one anxious.

As the young men helped her ready the house for painting and staging, Laurna said, so many of the things she had elected to keep were items that had a strong connection to her sister. A pair of childhood sleds she and Carrie had used every winter even when there was only a dusting over the hillsides by their house.

Pictures from a family trip to Six Flags four years ago. She also found some belongings of Hudson's that were precious and related to his family. As he hadn't any family that she could remember at that time, she put all of those in a box and then found her way to Ellie's bedroom.

Her niece's room was beginning to show the stirrings of the transition from teen to adult. The last time she'd been there, it had been painted French Poodle Pink. And while Laurna adored the color, it was almost too much, even for her. Now, the pink was gone for a pale gray hue. So was the shelving that had once held up a collection of plush animals. In its place were books and boys. One wall was plastered with images of celebrities and Abercrombie boys, their pouty lips and eyes aimed at her.

Laurna sat on the bed and shifted her gaze to the shabby chic desk. An open book sat just as Ellie had left it. Laurna sat still for the longest time, she told me, her home movies playing in her mind. It was like she was sleepwalking or something. Foggy. Sad. In need of another stiff drink.

She ran her hands over the comforter. It was silk and cool to the touch. Smooth. When she put her hands down to lift herself up, she felt something under the hand closest to the headboard.

It was a small notebook, spiral bound, with a unicorn sticker on its purple cover.

Ellie was still at that spot in life that teeters, sometimes unsteadily, toward adulthood.

She smiled, thinking of the girl that had been a joy until the past year. Ellie, Laurna knew, would have been her favorite niece forever, even if she had a thousand nieces. Carrie had complained a little and said that she wondered if she'd make it through dealing with a teenage daughter.

"Mom did," Laurna had reminded her.

Carrie gave her a knowing smile. "Touché."

That was the week before the accident.

It was the last time they spoke…Sisterhood is one of the world's most impenetrable bonds. It can only break if a husband's mother has something to say about it.

I get up and give Ms. Volkmann some water from a small table behind us. She takes it and starts drinking. I know she's weighing what she's about to tell me.

"Honestly," she goes on, lingering on the word that liars have the hardest time saying with any volition, "I didn't think much of what she wrote. It was the same kind of teenage angst Carrie and I reveled in when we were her age."

"What did she write?"

"The usual. I wish my mom or dad would die in a car crash. That kind of thing."

Her eyes widen some. She wants to say more. I want her to, too.

"All right, it seemed more like a list of ways to get rid of her folks. Not just I hate the world. I made a photocopy. Gave the entire book to the detectives in Port Angeles."

She pulls a piece of paper from her purse and hands it to me. She's right. It is a list.

There are a dozen methods listed, detailing the different ways that Ellie could get rid of her parents. Some have stars against them. Some have been crossed out. It's like she was trying to decide the best way. Her thought process, fantasy or not, seemed to err on the side of less violent murders. Poison was a possibility. It had a star. Overdosing on drugs also was underlined.

Drowning in a boating accident was the clear favorite. Two stars and two underlines.

She drew an arrow to combine the overdosing and the boating accident.

"It's what happened," Laurna says.

I scan her eyes. I think she might be right. I replay things I heard and saw. I think about how Sarah touched her brother, so tenderly. Too tenderly, I remember thinking. I remember the yelling that Ruth reported hearing the night after the memorial and how she told him to go back to bed. And how he leaned in to whisper in her ear. Something else struck me as odd: The first time I saw Joshua he was wearing the Miller beer T-shirt, and the next time she was wearing it.

But if that is Ellie, where is Sarah Wheaton?

I ask Laurna if I can duplicate her niece's note, and she follows me to the copy room. While the old machine flashes to copy, I make plans to drive out to the Wheaton place.

"Are you staying in town?"

"At the Seaport Inn," she says. "My husband and I. Hans thinks I'm being silly about all of this. *Out of my mind*, he repeated all the way here from Wenatchee. You don't think I am, do you, Detective?"

I don't know.

"Grief is powerful," I tell her. "I also know sincerity when I see it. I'll check it out. I'll call you at the Seaport."

She grasps my hand and squeezes. "Thank you. I wouldn't bother you if I wasn't so sure. My sister and her husband weren't perfect, though they did the best they could."

"No one's perfect, but how do you mean?"

"Hudson was super strict. Wouldn't let Ellie date. Talk to boys. Grounded her when he caught her. Carrie just let that happen. I guess she didn't want for her daughter what she'd had for herself. She was pregnant when they married. She was seventeen when she had Ellie. Hudson was the other half of the equation, of course, but he really put the blame on her."

CHAPTER THIRTY-THREE

After Laurna departs, I do what everyone does when they want to find out more about a potential date, a neighbor, or a teenage girl with a serious hatred for her parents. I track Ellie's digital footprints on Facebook, Instagram, and even TikTok.

I couldn't get into her TikTok, but the other social media usual suspects are an easy enough pathway to find more information.

Ellie Burbank's Instagram feed is not private and is filled with mostly those hook-armed full-body shots or the duck-lips pose that girls are certain makes them look sexy. I study the photos. There is no denying that the face on my laptop looks an awful lot like Sarah. The head shape, facial features are right. Hair color is off, but I've had a fair amount of experience dyeing my hair. The other thing that strikes me is the amount of makeup. Where Sarah favored the no-makeup look, Ellie is a true believer in heavy application. No light touch for her. Her eyelids are pink and gold hues with glitter, and her lashes are blue and long enough to leave mascara trailings on the face of her phone when taking a selfie.

It could be *her*.

Her aunt would know better than I do, I think. Or maybe the tragic loss of her sister hurt Laurna to such a grave degree that she's looking for a reason, or someone, to blame.

My pulse quickens a little as I read a post Ellie Burbank made last year.

*My parents are so phony. Everyone thinks that they are good
people. They go to church and act all perfect. If one of their
friends knew the truth, they'd never talk to them again. I feel
like a dumbass forever looking up to them.*

I scroll through others, more benign in content. Posts about
her dreams or her crushes, mostly Bieber and Drake and a couple
about Halsey. I scroll more and see rants about being homeschooled
and how she's so lonely being stuck studying in the kitchen with
only one hour a day internet time.

I look at the timestamp on the posts. They were all uploaded
between seven and eight p.m.

*At least they let me do this without their eyes all over me. I know
they have a net nanny or something like that on my laptop. I
know how to empty my history, leaving just a few things that
won't tip off my feelings for them. They won't let me have a
smartphone. Ha ha.*

Two things cross my mind. I wonder how it was so easy for me
to get into Ellie's Facebook page if she was so smart about keeping
her parents out? Had she changed her privacy settings? And when?

I also wonder about someone who posts as "Tyra Whitcomb."
She's the most active of Ellie's friends, always commenting some
sycophantic message of support. There are photos of the two of
them, in RL, as they tend to say. She's a pleasant-looking girl, a
little heavier than her best friend, but with the same affinity for a
theatrical flair with her cosmetics.

I click on her profile, though it's set to private.

Whitcomb is not that common a surname. I search on our
DMV database and find the one closest to the Burbank home; in
fact it's only three doors down.

Next, I dig up their phone number. That's easy. Just a click away. I feel like I'm the best clicker in the world. That if there was a prize for that expertise, I'd be up for it.

I dial the number.

Troy Whitcomb answers, and I tell him I'm looking for his daughter. His voice is clipped, suggesting that he's had similar call encounters with law enforcement.

"What has she done now? Do we need a lawyer?"

"Oh no," I tell him. "Nothing at all. I'm looking into the Burbank case up here and I want to talk to her about Ellie."

I hope he doesn't know the geography of the state that well because Jefferson County has no jurisdiction in the Burbank drownings. That's Clallam County's domain. Most Seattle area residents don't think beyond their immediate vicinity. Everything outside of Seattle is either the Olympic peninsula or the other two-thirds of the state, eastern Washington.

"Oh that," he sighs. "That was a tough one. Tyra and Ellie were very close."

"That's what I understand," I say.

From Facebook, I don't admit.

"I'm a couple hours away," I say. "I have errands to run in Seattle. I thought I'd call ahead to see if she was available to meet. Tonight?"

I was lying about the errands. I just wanted Mr. Whitcomb to say yes, as though the need to see Tyra was merely a formality.

"To tie up loose ends," I say, to fill the dead space on the line.

He's thinking it over.

"Yeah," he says. "I think it would be a good idea. Tyra needs some closure. This has been eating at her for a long time. Not the same girl since it all happened."

"How so?" I ask, before quickly adding, "Besides losing her best friend, of course."

He sighs. "The usual. Kids today have so many more chances to screw up than in my day."

"That's for sure," I say, looking at the time. I have a semi decent chance that I could make the ferry from Kingston to Edmonds, just north of Seattle. That's no easy feat, to be sure. Puget Sound traffic is a nightmare that just gets worse and worse.

"I'll be there around eight, Mr. Whitcomb. Will Tyra be available then?"

"She'd better be," he tells me in that clipped voice of his. "Or she's broken curfew for the very last time."

I grab my keys and fly out of the office, telling Sheriff that I'm heading out to talk to a friend of the missing Burbank girl.

"Not our case," he says.

"Could be," I tell him.

The cars are moving when I reach the ferry. Thank God. We roll on one by one, thump, thump, thump. I stay in my car, roll the window down and feel the breeze on my face as we rumble across the water. The time Hayden and I spent the night on a ferry passes through my mind. I know it's the tapes that are pulling me backward into the time that I tried to forget.

CHAPTER THIRTY-FOUR

The Whitcombs' neighborhood is an eclectic mix of vintage Craftsman and brick Tudor homes, all impeccably maintained with crisp-cut hedges and perennials that have been deadheaded all summer. Except for one house. Even if I didn't have the address, I'd know that was the Burbank place. It's dark and the lawn has missed a mowing or two. I park on the street midway between the Burbank and the Whitcomb houses. The time on my phone: 7:46. Not bad. Instead of heading to the Whitcombs', I backtrack to the Burbanks' old place. And by the way it is: old. Probably more than a hundred years. However, outside of the neglected landscaping, it would be anyone's dream house. White and gray siding with black shutters and a poppy-red door. As I approach, I notice what I think is a sprinkling of potpourri in the flower bed next to the red door.

Dried flower blossoms, stems, and some curlicue ribbons of various colors.

Flowers left to memorialize the family.

I touch a card with my toe, shifting away the floral debris.

With Sympathy
We didn't know you well, but we grieve for the loss of each of you, Carrie, Hudson, and Ellie.
The Neighborhood Block Watch

It's not much of a makeshift memorial, but that might have more to do with how insular the Burbanks were and not a reflection of bad character. I shine my mini Maglite into the front window, swiping through the dim space up and down. It's mostly empty. A few pieces of furniture, but they've been moved aside.

The oak floor has been buffed.

Ellie's aunt is getting ready to sell the place.

As I make my way around the house, a woman calls over from the backyard abutting the Burbank property.

"I'll call the police," she's practically spitting her words at me. "You have no right to be here."

"I am the police," I say. "Just following up on the Burbank case."

She opens the gate and comes over to me. She's in her fifties, with a slim build with brown hair cut in the ubiquitous Seattle bob. She's wearing pale green garden gloves and carrying a small trowel.

"Let me see your ID," she demands, her lips tight and her brown eyes looking me over as if I were a danger to the community.

I tell her who I am and show my detective's shield.

"Okay, fine," she sniffs. "We've had nothing but trouble around here when they went missing. People coming and going."

Her name is Chantelle Potter. She's lived in the neighborhood for ten years.

"Carrie and I were pretty good friends for the first few years. Hudson was kind of a loner, but he managed to make it to the annual block party. Nice people. A little different."

We sit on a bench.

"Define different," I ask.

She glances back at the house, her eyes landing for a split second on the upstairs window.

"Ellie," she finally says. "I felt sorry for that girl. She went from being part of the playgroup around here to being nearly invisible. We hardly ever saw her until the last couple of years."

I'm not sure what she's getting at and I say so.

"Detective"—she looks right at me—"I can't explain it."

"Try."

Chantelle takes a deep breath. "I saw Ellie in the yard one night and she was talking to someone on her phone. I couldn't help but overhear." She stops a moment and looks at me. "I'm not the eavesdropper type. Ask anyone."

That meant, of course, she was the eavesdropper type. My favorite type, actually, when it comes to investigating a crime. People who mind their own business, bad. People who take in every drama around them, good.

"Of course not," I say as convincingly as possible. "What did you hear?"

"She was crying. Saying that she couldn't wait to get out of the house and go to college. Her parents were riding her all the time. That kind of thing. She said her situation was worse than that of whoever was on the other end of the phone."

It sounded like the kind of conversation a million or more teenagers are having at this very moment.

She goes on. "And then Hudson came out and started barking at her, telling her to get her butt into the house and to give up her goddamn phone. She threw it over into the bushes in my yard. He came over and grabbed her by the arm. It was hard, but I didn't think it was hard enough to be abuse or I would have called you people."

She looks over at me.

"Do you think I should have called?"

What's done is done, I think.

"No," I say. "You were using your best judgment. I can see that you are second-guessing yourself now. There's no need for that, Ms. Potter."

She gives me a look of appreciation.

An eavesdropper with a conscience, better than mere good.

"What was Carrie like?" I ask.

"Sweet. Passive. Actually, she became even submissive as the years went by. We used to have a glass of wine every now and then.

One time she came over and said she'd prefer mineral water. The second time she did that I asked if she was pregnant or maybe had been drinking too much and wanted to cut back."

"What did she say?"

"Get this. She said she stopped drinking because Hudson said so."

I bristle inside, but don't show it. "Like forbid it?"

"Exactly. Her words were, 'Hudson said that I shouldn't debase my body with wine anymore. He's the leader of our family.'"

Leader? She sees disdain in my eyes.

Damn. She stops talking, like she's said too much.

I encourage her to continue. "What did you make of that?"

"First," Chantelle says, "I thought that I didn't even know this girl anymore. I knew that they homeschooled Ellie and that they went to a fundamentalist church somewhere on the eastside. Second, I felt sorry for her. I wanted to say something, ask her how she really felt. I just couldn't go there. I knew that my asking her anything would only make things worse."

"Do you know anything about the Whitcombs?"

"Do I know Troy and Tyra are liars? Yes."

"What do you mean, liars?"

"They've told everyone that she died in an accident."

I'm confused. And I look it.

"They made it up after she'd been discovered having an affair. I saw Susan two weeks ago. She's alive."

"Why make up the story?"

"Sympathy for the two of them, I guess. Joy in getting rid of her. She went along with it. Susan's like that. Weak. I'd have taken him for everything he had."

I take it all in, processing what it would take a person to lie about a loved one's death.

"Those two are messed up."

Understatement, I think.

We talk some more. I look at my phone. I ask her if we can speak again and she gives me her number.

"Detective," she says as I turn to leave, "I wish I could tell you more, but really..." She looks over at the fence that separates her house from the Burbank place. "After Hudson became the leader, or whatever, of the family, we no longer needed a fence. He'd fashioned an invisible force field between all of us."

CHAPTER THIRTY-FIVE

Troy Whitcomb answers the gleaming mahogany front door before I knock. That quick. He's older than he sounded on the phone, around sixty, I think. His hair is nearly gone, just a gray halo of duck-down-like hairs on his crown. He's crumpled, worn out. The bags under his eyes could hold the contents of a family's trip to the beach.

"Did you have a hard time finding your way here?" he asks, letting me inside. "I thought you'd be here at eight."

It's only a quarter past eight, but I offer an apology anyway.

"You know the ferries," I say.

He looks at me warily.

"Right," he says. "Extremely unreliable."

His tone is suddenly accusatory. I wonder if he's just another of the control freaks that live on that Seattle block.

He yells up the stairs.

"Tyra! The detective is here!"

For such a beaten-down figure, his voice is surprisingly robust.

"I told her why you're here."

"Thank you. Is Mrs. Whitcomb home?"

"Susan is dead," he says. "An accident."

"Oh I'm sorry to hear that. Car accident?" I scan his face, and he casts his eyes away in the direction of footsteps coming toward the stairs.

"No. Boating accident," he replies. "Please don't bring it up. Tyra was on the boat with her mom when it happened."

I nod, but inside all I can think about is the similarity between these two best friends.

One is a liar.

The other could be a killer.

Tyra Whitcomb is gorgeous. Her dark hair has obviously been the work of a stylist. I remember cutting my own hair. I had to. She has bright blue eyes and clear, pale pink skin. She'd be a lovely girl.

If she ever smiled.

I introduce myself.

"My dad says you want to ask me about Ellie."

"That's right. I understand you were close, and I know that my coming here might seem like an unwanted intrusion."

Tyra shrugs her perfect shoulders. "It's fine. I was a wreck when it first happened, but now I'm feeling okay about it. She's in a better place."

She shoots a look of palpable annoyance at her father.

"Dad, do you need to be here? She wants to talk to *me*."

Troy begins to shuffle into what I presume is the kitchen.

"All right, but watch your tone, missy," he says over his shoulder. "You're getting too big for your britches."

"Ah," Tyra snaps behind her father's back. "No one says that anymore, just so you know."

We find seats in the living room. It's decorated in the matchy-matchy style of a bad interior designer or a woman who feasted on every home design and improvement magazine.

"This room is lovely," I say.

"Mom's work," Tyra replies, rolling her eyes dismissively. "She never saw an animal print or polka dot she couldn't live without. I hate it."

"Your dad told me about your mom. I'm so sorry."

Tyra's blue eyes go from crystalline to chipped ice. She shifts her body on a zebra-striped armchair. Her fingers quietly gouge at the row of silver studs embedded the length of the armrest.

"Yes, what happened to her mom happened to mine."

She's cold and defensive.

"I've already told you people that. It's a coincidence. That's all."

I give her some space. "I'm sure it was," I say. "And really that's not why I'm here, Tyra. I'm here to learn more about Ellie. It's possible that she could be alive."

She shakes her head. "She would have called me. We were best friends. In fact, I was her *only* friend. Her parents kept her practically locked up. She used to be able to go out, and then, bam, her dad gets all weird and he makes her a prisoner."

"All weird?" I ask.

"Yeah. Like all of a sudden, he was in charge of the world. Told her what to wear. That makeup was only for sluts. That kind of thing."

"I heard he was strict," I say, leaving plenty of room for her to continue.

Tyra's fingers pick at the studs. I notice now that several are missing.

"Strict are *my* parents. Mom was the worst. Dad, I don't know. He tries to be a friend, but he's just another know-it-all. Ellie's mom, Carrie, went along with everything that Hudson wanted. She was weak, like she wasn't even a person."

I've decided I really don't like this girl. I don't show it.

"But she was a person, Tyra."

She makes a dismissive face. "You know what I mean, Detective. She couldn't stand on her own. Never stood up for Ellie."

I give her a nod. "Tell me more about Ellie."

"She was awesome. We used to talk every night. She wasn't allowed to have a phone, but I got her one and stuck her on our family plan. Told my dad that I needed two phones, one for social and one for school assignments. He never questioned me."

"What did she talk about? Did she say anything that gave you cause to worry?"

Tyra shakes her head. "No. She was fine. I talked to her the night before they went to Lake Crescent."

"Did you text or talk?"

"She'd lost her phone a week or so before, and my dad was being a real prick about getting a replacement. Said I had to learn a lesson or something dumb."

I think of the night Ellie argued with Hudson and tossed her phone into the Potters' backyard.

That was a week before the lake.

"Did she say anything about the upcoming trip to the lake?"

"Like did she say, 'I'm going to kill my parents and swim away'? No."

She's dug out a stud and is rolling it around her fingertips.

"Look, Tyra," I say, losing my patience a little. "This isn't a joke here. Your friend might be in harm's way."

"I actually don't care. If she did swim away, she never came back here. Some best friend. It wasn't exactly as though I didn't need some support. After what happened to my mom."

This girl is unbelievable. I don't want to start an altercation, but I would like to call her bluff. Instead, I press on.

"Did she have a boyfriend?" I ask, taking it down a notch. "Someone else she'd confide in?"

"None of us have boyfriends. Yeah, we see boys when we can. We just don't cling to anyone."

"Right," I say.

Wrong, I think.

Tyra tells me that she has to get back to what she was doing.

"I don't really have anything else to tell you about Ellie."

Her father appears and leads me to the door.

Just like that.

Over.

It's too dark to look for Ellie's phone. Ms. Potter would defi-nitely call the Seattle police if she caught me poking around her yard with a flashlight. I look at the time. If I hurry, I can make the ferry. Or I could take the scenic route and cross the Tacoma Narrows Bridge and get home that way.

Or I could do what I know I'm going to do.

Texting is an easier way to lie than leaving a voice message.

Sheriff Gray is in bed now anyway. I don't want to wake him. I sit in my car and type.

Missed the last boat and don't feel like driving around.
  Be in tomorrow late. Will give update then.

CHAPTER THIRTY-SIX

My room at the SeaTac Red Roof Inn has a view of a cemetery and traffic on the busy Pacific Highway, most notorious as the hunting ground of one of our many local serial killers. Gary Ridgway cruised the stretch of highway looking for dates. Dates that he would strangle and pitch in clusters, most notably along the nearby Green River.

I barely slept, and my face shows it. I'm too young to look this beat-up, tired. I don't *feel* tired. In fact, I'm energized by the case. I shower, brush my teeth with a courtesy toothbrush that leaves bristles in my mouth and I dress in the same clothes I wore yesterday.

It's the walk-of-shame look, though I'm fifteen years too old for that. And unprepared. I decide to put a change of clothes in the back of the Taurus in the future.

Just in case.

I don't imagine that Chantelle Potter is a shift worker and needs to be in the office by seven. I don't have a warrant and I need her permission to search for the missing phone. It's 7:30 when I arrive.

The drapes are open. That means, at least to me, that she's up.

As I park, the garage door opens and a Mercedes—of course, what else?—backs out of the driveway. It's Mr. Potter. He's older than his wife with a neatly trimmed gray beard and eyes that are golden brown.

I think of a goat.

When he sees me, he lowers the driver's window.

"Can I help you?"

"I'm Megan Carpenter. The detective who talked with Chantelle last night."

He gives me a nod. "Yeah, very sad about the Burbanks. Nice people. Terrible tragedy."

I don't tell him that I doubt it was a tragedy.

"Is she home?"

"She's always home," he says, with a touch of irritation. "She's on her third cup of coffee."

I thank him and go to the front door, as the sound of the garage as it rolls downward plays in the background.

Chantelle answers right away. She's dressed to the nines in a sleeveless emerald green dress and shoes on that I know cost more than a week's pay in Jefferson County. She smiles with recognition.

"Just like TV," she says. "You came back for one more thing."

"Kind of like that," I answer.

She invites me inside and I'm almost certain that none of the midcentury modern furnishings are replicas. Leather, wood, chrome. Mixed with the old are new pieces of steel and glass, electronics too. It's like a showroom of what people with money covet today.

We sit in one of those leather and chrome sofas that never look inviting but are very comfortable, and talk over French press coffee.

I tell her that I came back to look for Ellie's phone.

"If that's okay with you?"

Chantelle nods while sipping her coffee.

"No problem," she says, setting down her cup. "I'd help you look, but I have to meet my friends this morning. It's something we do once a week."

She continues to prattle on about her obligations.

I continue to covet her shoes.

"I'll get out of your way," I say. "You have things to do."

She lets out a sigh. "I do. I don't know how it is that I'm able to go on, with the loss of my friend and all. I took an extra pill last night. Just so awful to think of Carrie and Ellie that way. Even Hudson. So damn sad."

She doesn't seem sad. She wants to show me she's grief-stricken as a way of letting me know she's a very real person. None of her furnishings are fake. But her feelings might be.

"Very sad," I say. "Again, I'm sorry for the loss of your friends."

I add the "s," so she won't correct me and remind me how much she misses Ellie and Hudson.

"Thank you, Detective."

She leads me out to the backyard and points to the bushes.

"Somewhere over there. I'm sure of it."

"Thank you. I'll let you know if I find it."

And off she goes.

The yard is just like Chantelle. *Perfect.* The low hedge framing the expansive slate patio is so green and so square-trimmed that, at first, I mistake it for a painted wall. Shrubs are perfectly shaped and there isn't a weed to be had. Not anywhere. She even has a table displaying a collection of bonsai. As I make my way closer to the fence between the Burbanks and the Potters, I hear Chantelle call out to me.

I turn around. "Yes?"

"I dug this out of the garage," she says. "My son's. Like just about everything we give Matt, barely used."

It's a metal detector.

"Sprinklers come on in fifteen. Sorry. I don't know how to disable them. Good luck, Detective."

Wonderful, I think.

"Thanks," I call back as she waves goodbye.

I start scanning the landscaping along the fence, first with my eyes, then with the ungrateful Potter boy's metal detector. I'm sweeping left to right and hoping that the sprinkler system waits until after I find what I'm here for.

The metal detector is a high-tech magic wand. I *will* it to help me.

And it does as I work under an Alaskan cedar along the fence. It buzzes with such ferocity that I nearly let go of it.

With latex gloves now on, I crouch down, my knees pressing into the moist soil and wicking water to my skin. *I'm going to look like a candidate for a detergent commercial,* I think. I start crawling under the branches to the spot where the detector alerted. It's dark under the tree next to the fence. A fortress. I really can't see. My fingertips find a couple of pinecones before they touch the rectangular edge of what I know before seeing is Ellie's phone.

I crawl out with my prize and put it in an evidence bag.

My heart is pounding.

And I absolutely look like a candidate for a detergent commercial.

Just as the sprinklers start hissing, I'm back in my car for the ride home. While the phone from under the bushes is undoubtedly locked, I open the evidence bag and plug it into my charger to see if I can power it up. Just in case.

I catch my image in the rearview mirror.

I have a smile on my face.

I'm alive.

I'm doing what I was meant to do.

My phone pings with a text. I reach for it, knocking Ellie's between the seat and the console. It's a message from Dan. I don't care that he'll know I've read it. I want to see what he has to say.

I'd be a worse liar than I am if I denied he'd been on my mind.

*

Superstar detective. Saw you on the tube.

   Would like to see you. If you don't answer, that'll be your answer. Dan.

Would like to see you too.

   Meeting some friends at Hops @7. Come.

Nervously, I push SEND. I don't want to screw up my life by potentially ignoring anything that might be actually good for me. Next I text Mindy and tell her to meet me.

Safety in numbers.

She answers back right away and tells me to call her. So I do.

"I like him," I say before Mindy says a word.

"I know you do, but it's not about that, Megan. It's about the Torrance case. Not something we'd want to bring up tonight. But wow."

She is in full Mindy mode. I miss that. She is a consummate pro but couldn't mask her sometimes gleeful interest in the macabre. She loves flowers and blood spatter with equal abandon. She wanted to name her shop Pushing Up Daisies, but then thought better of it.

"What have you got?" I ask.

She takes a deep breath and then unloads.

"The Torrance case is like nothing we've ever seen before. It's reminiscent of the Carl Tanzler case out of Florida in the 1930s."

Of course, Florida.

She goes on to tell me about the obsessive radiology assistant and how he preserved the body object of his affection, Elena Milagro de Hoyos.

"He kept her in his bed for seven years, like a dead sex slave."

"Okay, that's disgusting."

"I know," she says, a little too emphatically, before continuing.

"Regina Torrance did something very similar to Amy. Her corpse was stuffed with activated charcoal and excelsior and stitched up by, get this, cat gut from an old tennis racket. She removed Amy's knee and elbow joints and managed to replace them with springs and wire."

I think of the wires and how Regina manipulated her wife's body, but I don't say anything. I let Mindy wind down, punctuating her stream of information with some *wows* and *terribles* of my own.

"You're right," I say. "We can't talk about that in front of Dan."

"Nope," she replies. "See you tonight."

CHAPTER THIRTY-SEVEN

The office is quiet. Sheriff has been away on school visits out in the county. He loves talking to young people about responsibility and the law. Lately, he told me the other day, it's been getting tougher to reach kids. In the past couple of years, he's felt a shift from the police are your friends to distrust and skepticism. Even in places like uber liberal Port Townsend, where very little violent crime takes place and where there is no racial profiling—at least none that I've heard about—there is a change in the air. Fewer acknowledgments, our blues say, when walking into a store for something after a shift.

I think of incorrigible and smug Tyra and how she cut me off. I wonder now if she saw me as the "other side" or if she had something to hide herself.

I sift through the court docket and telephone messages before I write up my interview reports—one for Tyra and one for Chantelle. Sheriff will read them later tonight, and I'll hit him up with additional details tomorrow morning.

It's almost six.

I look like I've slept in my clothes.

Which I sort of did.

Out the back door and home in sixteen minutes, I turn on the noisy old shower, so it will heat up. I tear off my clothes and let the barely hot water spray over me. Old Victorians are charming only on the outside. Unless one has an endless bank account to remodel. That includes plumbing that doesn't clang. My mind touches on the last few days and how my old life has melded with the new. The tapes. The case. I can't stop drawing out the similarities between the Wheaton kids and my own situation at that age.

I twist the knob and towel off as quickly as I can.

That my wardrobe isn't extensive is the understatement of the century—this or the last one. My closet and drawers look like a waiter's supply outlet. Black and blue cotton slacks, white shirts. Blazers that complete my daily work attire hang like a rogue's gallery of what not to wear.

I consider a dress but decide against it. Mindy will be there, and she'll give me grief later.

I can hear her now.

Gee, I forgot you had legs, Megan.

I put on my most flattering jeans, a white top that at least gives me a tiny bit of sex appeal. Lipstick and eye makeup, and I'm out the door.

Originally called Hops Ahoy, the bar was supposed to be for the tourist trade. It was all done up with nets, ship's wheels, and enormous black and white blowups of our Victorian seaport. It turned out that the tourists who came here were looking for an authentic experience, one that didn't try too hard to be a destination but was a worthy one on its own.

My heart sinks a little when I spy only Mindy sitting at a table in the bar. She brightens the minute she sees me, and I do the same. I know I'm mimicking her reaction right now. But it isn't as though I'm not thrilled to see her.

It's that Dan isn't there.

"Am I your chaperone or your excuse to leave?" Mindy asks as she indicates for the waiter to come.

"Neither."

I want a Scotch on the rocks, but I order a chardonnay.

"I don't know," I tell her. "I haven't been interested in a guy for a long time. Dan intrigues me."

She sips her wine. "Is it the beard?"

The question catches me off guard.

"How'd you know he has a beard?"

"Small town. I know things," she explains.

I look toward the door, sinking a little inside.

"And no, it's not the beard. He just seems like a nice guy. Interesting. There could be something there. Or maybe not."

"Do you want to sleep with him?" Mindy asks, egging me on like she used to when we saw each other more regularly. Her teasing feels comfortable. I've missed her. I look at my phone. It's only half past the hour. He's late. He hasn't texted that he couldn't come.

I fill her in on what I found out from Tyra and Chantelle.

"Look, before you tell me that it's not our case—like Sheriff—I know there is a connection. The girls were extremely close. They had to sneak around to maintain their friendship because Ellie was practically under house arrest."

"Wasn't she in school?"

I make a quick scan of the door.

He's not here.

"No," I say. "Her mom homeschooled her at the behest of her husband, a real control freak."

Mindy is doing what she does best. She's processing the information like it's a crime scene.

I love that about her.

"So, your theory is that, what? The girls plotted the murder of their parents? If that's the case, why is Tyra's dad still alive?"

"The plot was one sided. A game for Tyra. She was never going to get rid of her mother. She just told Ellie how she was going to do it—and then said she did."

"How could she get away with such a ruse?"

"Easier than you think. Tyra knew her friend had no internet. No way of knowing there was nothing on the news. Her phone, her lifeline, was gone."

Mindy looks up from her drink.

"That's twisted, Megan."

"As Sheriff says, 'like a soft-serve cone.'"

I look down at my phone, and I hear his voice.

"Hey, Detective," Dan says as he joins us.

"Hey," I say. "This is my coworker, Mindy Newsom."

He smiles. "We've met."

"Yes," she replies. "At the shop."

"Didn't know you worked there too, Megan."

"She's also a crime scene tech. And a damned good one."

"If I were that good," Mindy says as Dan folds his lean frame into the space next to me, "I'd be somewhere else digging up bodies instead of planting flowers."

Dan's wearing a lightweight quilted jacket over a T-shirt that stretches tightly across his chest. He smells a little like a campfire, but not in a bad way. He orders a local distillery's Scotch.

I should have ordered one too. I drink wine at home only because it goes good with fish sticks or whatever I move from the freezer to the oven when I sit at my table.

Listening to my life unspool on the tapes.

We stay clear of the Wheaton and Burbank investigations and focus our conversation on other things.

Pleasant things. His farm. His woodcarving. Dan looks at me, expecting me to dive into my life. Mindy catches the look and throws me a lifeline and talks up her family and her so far less than successful quest to develop a hydrangea hybrid that will thrive in sunny spaces.

She doesn't know my story. Not like Sheriff.

And certainly not what I disclosed to Dr. Albright.

"What about you, Detective?" Dan asks.

I shift in my chair. "Megan, please."

"Okay. What's your story?"

That question invites me to lie and I don't want to lie anymore. And yet I do.

"Parents died in a car crash when I was a kid. No other family to take us in."

He looks at me with eyes full of kindness.

"I'm sorry."

I acknowledge his concern with a slight nod. I hate that I've lived a life of covering my tracks.

"Us?" he asks. "Do you have siblings?"

"A brother. He's stationed overseas."

And he hates me. Wants nothing to do with me. It's my fault. All of it!

Awkwardness hangs over me, tightening my throat. Almost choking me. I don't want to say any more. I glance over at Mindy.

She knows me. At least enough to be a lifeline.

"Yeah," she says, touching my hand. "Megan has been through a lot, but she's the best person I know."

I feel like she's selling me, but it puts a period on the conversation.

"Didn't mean to pry," Dan says.

"It's fine."

We move the subject to the next day and what each of us is doing. Mindy's doing flowers for a funeral. Dan's installing a front gate.

And me? I've got a killer to catch.

We pay our tabs and walk out to our respective cars. Gulls perched behind the bar disperse overhead as the moon sends a path of light over the black water of the bay. It's a golden trail from Port Townsend to somewhere far away. Mindy heads to her van on the other side of the lot.

"I always park next to the road," she told me one time, "because my van is a billboard."

"Hey," Dan says, lingering by my car, "I'm going to an art show on Saturday. You know, check out the competition. If you're free, want to come, Megan?"

My Saturday is already planned as a day to catch up on bills and other things that have been set on the back burner since the start of the Wheaton investigation.

This time my lie isn't about protecting me, but about putting me at risk. In a good way, I think.

"Totally free. Would love to go."

Dan gives me his handsome smile.

"All right then. I'll text you the details."

"Good night, Dan," I say.

"Night, Megan."

When I turn the key in the ignition, the sound a phone makes when charging gets my attention. It's a soft buzz. I instinctively reach for it; it's tucked in between the seat and the console. It's not my phone. In my haste to meet with Dan I'd completely forgotten about the phone recovered in Chantelle's backyard. It's a terrible lapse and I know it immediately. I should have logged it when I got into the office. I fish it out by pulling on the cord. It's powered up. I stare at the illuminated screen. The wallpaper is of a face, though covered by a multitude of apps.

And yet I know who it is.

It's a familiar face.

CHAPTER THIRTY-EIGHT

Sheriff is in his duct-tape-upholstered chair, reading the *Leader*. Country music plays softly from his radio. An oily fast food bag pokes up through the trash receptacle by his office door. Normally, I'd remark on it, though this time I don't.

I don't even say good morning.

"I need you to come with me out to the Wheaton place. I'll fill you in on the way."

The urgency in my voice jolts him to his feet.

Just as we head out the door, Nan calls out that the crime lab is on the phone.

"Should I tell them to call back?"

I snap the receiver right from her hand. I might have hurt her, but I really don't care. She makes every moment annoying. And I'm pretty sure that's why she does it.

"Hi, Detective, it's Marley again," says a familiar voice. "Got some info for you. It's good stuff too."

I can tell right now he's of the *CSI* TV generation; you find them stuck in the mundane environment of a crime lab, thinking it would be all nonstop fun—kicked off by an anthemic, bombastic cut by The Who.

"I'm all ears," I say.

"Okay. Good. Well here's where we are: The hammer had on it the blood of three different people: we're thinking three victims; two female and one male. The hair and also one blood sample is a match for our victim, Mrs. Wheaton. The other two aren't in the system, but the female victim's DNA ladders back to both the male and Mrs. Wheaton. The only other tool found on the property that had any blood was a shovel. Again Mrs. Wheaton."

I take it in.

"Crazy, right?"

"I guess you could call it that. Same with the spatter?"

"Right. All three victims' blood is present."

"Thanks, Marley. Send the report."

I don't even wait until we are all the way out the door.

"Three victims, crime lab says," I say as we jump in his car.

Sheriff gives me a puzzled look.

"What do you make of that?"

I pull the door shut and buckle up. "Sarah," I tell him. "She might actually be a Seattle girl named Ellie Burbank."

He's all ears on the drive out to Snow Creek. I tell him that Ellie, in fact, might not be at the bottom of Lake Crescent, and that Susan Whitcomb is more than likely alive—her supposed death was merely an inspiration for the Burbank homicides—and he updates me about the Torrance case and how national media has already started calling.

"And her aunt is sure that's Ellie? Not Sarah?"

"That's what she thinks."

"All of a sudden, we're Ground Zero for murder," he says.

I don't disagree.

"We need to find Merritt Wheaton," I remind him. "He's out there somewhere."

"Right. This is only the beginning."

I look out the window thinking that this case has been the most bizarre I've ever been involved with.

At least in an official capacity.

CHAPTER THIRTY-NINE

Bernadine Chesterfield, grandstander and attention seeker extraordinaire, a woman who would snap her gold-framed ethics code in a million pieces just to be in the middle of something noteworthy, sits by the road in a sagging heap.

We pitch to a stop and get out.

I loathe this woman, and I'm not alone. She's crying and hunched into a big ball. She looks like she's had the wits scared out of her.

It's not quite that. It's something else.

Sheriff approaches first, and I follow a step or two behind. Bernie and I have a history. A decidedly mixed one. She doesn't know that he's the one who made the complaint about her conduct with the media during the Wheaton memorial service. Short as it was.

As fake as it might have been.

"I'm so stupid," she says over and over. "So damn stupid."

No argument comes from me—or Sheriff.

She doesn't need any prodding. She unfolds herself and starts talking. Her blue slacks are torn and there's blood on her sleeve.

She sees us looking at her clothing and the blood oozing from her arm.

"I'm fine. That's just a scrape. I ran like hell."

"What happened?" Sheriff asks.

She steadies herself against the car.

"I came out here, you know, to see how the kids were doing. They seemed so lost. Really. I just wanted to help."

I don't ask if she was making a court-mandated visit because I know she wasn't. I know her MO.

"The house was quiet, and I went looking for them. I thought maybe they'd be in the orchard, but they weren't. I got kind of worried. With everything going on around here, I wasn't sure what to do. I mean, I thought something had happened to them."

I want to tell her to cut to the chase, but I don't and Sheriff nudges her along.

"I went back into the house to leave a note. My cell doesn't work out here so I couldn't call."

"None work out here, Bernie," Sheriff says.

She nods. "Right, so I wrote a note and as I went back to my car, I thought I heard something coming from the barn. It sounded like a hurt animal or something. Real muffled. I went inside, oh God. I saw something that I shouldn't see."

"What, Bernie? What did you see?" I ask, knowing that I'm not a patient person, the way Sheriff is.

"I called out their names again. And then I found them. They were in the back of the barn. Joshua was crying, and Sarah was telling him everything was all right. He stopped when he saw me. And when he turned to look at me, I don't know . . . I saw that his pants were unbuttoned. He saw my eyes and turned away, while Sarah just snapped at me."

"How so?"

"She just got mean-eyed and told me that I didn't see anything. I lied, and asked her what did she mean I didn't see anything. Then Joshua looked at her and said something like, there's nothing to see here. I took a few steps backward and told them that I was just checking on them and was going to be leaving. And did they need anything? I could make a run to the store. I got out of there and hurried to the road. I didn't even go get my car because I'd have to pass by the door of the barn."

Sheriff looks at me, then back at Bernie.

"What is it that you think they were doing?"

"Sex," she whispers. "That's what I think was going on. They were having sex."

I don't tell her what I know. I just keep my poker face.

"I don't know what I was thinking, approving those two. I just...I just thought they should be together, brother and sister."

I pretend to care about her. "It's not your fault. You didn't suspect anything wrong. You did a thorough evaluation, right?"

Bernie knows what I'm doing. I'm not always as clever as I think. Or maybe I am? I want her to know that like the rest of Jefferson County law enforcement, I'm onto her. She's been milking this job for years. Everyone knows it.

She wraps her arms around her body and mimics a shudder.

"I know you have a good heart," Sheriff says.

She sniffs as though she's been crying. "I do. I really do."

"Do you have your phone on you?" I ask her.

She shakes her head.

"Take mine. I want you to take my car and drive where you can get service, a couple miles. Patrol is in the area. Tell them we need some backup here."

Sheriff nods.

He knows what I know.

CHAPTER FORTY

I reach for my gun, but Sheriff motions for me to put it away.

"We don't want to incite something we can't handle here." His voice is quiet, almost a whisper. "We want to bring this to a calm conclusion."

I say I agree. At the same time, I know what we're dealing with. I know that Ellie is the master here. I've seen her kind more than a time or two. She's got Joshua wrapped around her little finger. His family is dead because she wanted them gone.

Just like she wanted her mother and father gone.

Gravel on the road crunches. Backup is here.

Sheriff motions to the deputies to stand back, out of direct view.

We make our way to the barn.

The lawn is green, and I can make out footprints where the blades have been crushed. The scene is a Hallmark card at its surface. The house. The workshop. The barn. The orchard where Mrs. Wheaton's memorial was held. Apples are ready for picking. Goldfinches have started to lose their bright yellow plumage in favor of fall brown and winter gray.

Joshua appears in the doorway of the barn. His shoulder is bleeding, turning his white T-shirt into a Rorschach of blood.

He staggers toward us. His eyes are wild, full of fear. Confusion too.

"She stabbed me," he says. "She tried to kill me."

He falls to his knees onto the dust- and straw-strewn ground.

"Where is she?" I ask, bending down and giving him my jacket.

"Gone. She's gone."

I press the jacket against his wound.

"Hold this. You'll be okay," I say, though I know that is far from the truth. He'll be in prison for the rest of his life.

Sheriff speaks up. "What happened?"

Joshua looks lost, bereft. I see tears in his eyes. It's a trick, I think. She's in charge of everything. When they talk, what they say, Ellie rules it all. She has more power over her lover than Delilah had over Samson. When we find her, she'll point the finger directly at him.

He's in love enough that he'll let her.

Sheriff lets me take the ball. He doesn't owe me that, but he respects me enough to give me my moment.

My words are simple and brimming with what I think he needs to hear. They are aimed at getting the truth.

"Joshua, we know what happened to your family. We know that Sarah isn't Sarah."

"That's a lie. She is."

"What about your parents, Josh? You know what happened to them. We do too. Your father didn't kill your mom, did he?"

Sheriff indicates for the backup officers to come forward. He tells the younger of the two to radio for an ambulance.

He looks at me.

"Cuff him. We'll clear the barn and then work as a team over the property."

I nod.

"Son, you need to tell us what you know about Ellie's whereabouts," Sheriff says. "You won't have much to help you when you go through the process, but this is one chance to make things go a little smoother."

As if a triple homicide could be smooth.

"Let's clear the barn," Sheriff orders. "We're looking for the girl."

Joshua's eyes flutter as I secure the handcuffs. His pupils are filling his iris. He's going into shock. He needs medical attention.

The officer in the car heads toward me. I wave for him to hurry and he yells at me.

"Look out, Detective!"

I see Sheriff lunging in my direction, but it's too late.

"She's got a knife!"

Ellie has thrown herself on me like a missile. I'm facedown in the dirt and she's wielding a blade against my neck.

"Make a move and this will go through your throat," she says, coolly, a tone that suggests she means it. Maybe even had done it before. She's fishing for the keys to the handcuffs, but they are in my front pocket and I'm flat to the ground. Her hot breath rakes against me, her fingers like a hundred spiders searching my body.

"You don't want to do this, Ellie," Sheriff pleads.

Her eyes dart away from me to him.

"You have no idea what I want to do."

She presses the knife against my throat and speaks to Joshua.

"You did good," she says.

I'm gasping for air in the dirt and feeling as stupid as I've ever felt in my life.

Despite the seriousness of Joshua's injury, it's a setup. She used Joshua as bait. And we fell for it.

We should have known.

I should have known.

Blood from Joshua's wound puddles.

"We know you are Ellie Burbank," I say. "By this time tomorrow, everyone will know your face and your name. So stop. Stop now. Stop before you lose everything."

Ellie seethes. "You stupid bitch. I'd rather have the nothing I have now than anything I'd ever had before. I don't care about anything that people like you think is precious. Even freedom."

She finally locates the key.

"Get up, Josh. Get over here."

He slithers in the dirt, making guttural sounds.

She twists to give him the key, and I know it's my chance and I make a rookie move.

I grab at the knife. Stupid. My hand is cut, and I yell out in pain. I turn myself over with such ferocity that it pushes her up and over to Joshua, who lets out a gurgled scream.

And then, a staccato, guttural "I didn't kill her."

Ellie slides off of Joshua. Her eyes appear frozen and empty.

"He raped me," she cries. "He kept me prisoner. I thought he was a good guy. He's a monster."

I know who the monster is.

She's young. Pretty. Evil.

"Nice try," I say as Sheriff and the other officers converge around us, the blood oozing from my hand and Joshua's body turning the dust into a red mud.

Sheriff, panic in his eyes, pulls me away and immediately stems the bleeding with a Miller High Life graphic tee found in the barn.

And as he does, I look down at Joshua.

He's alive.

"Someone stop his bleeding," I say.

The first ambulance roars away, its sirens and flashing red and white lights amplifying the horror of the scene as it careens toward the hospital.

I sit on the back of the second ambulance. I'm at once embarrassed and proud. I know I did good investigative work. My failure was in letting my guard down. I watch Mindy lead the others collecting evidence, securing the scene. They walk with precision, avoiding any area that might reveal additional evidence.

Sheriff pours some hot coffee from a thermos into a paper cup. I hold the cup in my now bandaged hand. I don't need a cardboard sleeve to protect me from the heat. That's about the only thing good about my injury.

"He's going to make it," he says.

"Good," I answer. "Dying would be the easy way out."

He knows my comment is about justice, not a bitter statement—a comment born of my own background.

"How are you, Megan?"

"Okay. Just thinking."

"What about?"

I down the coffee. It tastes good and I know I need a boost of caffeine. I refused pain meds because I want to be here in this moment. Right now. The girl in the portrait posed with her brother is on my mind.

"Sarah Wheaton," I say. "We need to find her."

"Or her body?" he asks.

I study the car holding Ellie from my ambulance perch.

"Right. There was a third party's blood, a female, on the evidence we processed. Joshua said he didn't kill her. Was that 'her' Sarah?"

"All good questions," he says.

I get up. "Excuse me, Sheriff."

I walk over to the cruiser transporting Ellie for processing at the Jefferson County Jail. I tap on the window and ask the officer if I can have a minute or two with her.

"Alone."

He tries to dissuade me from what he considers a dangerous situation.

"She tried to kill you."

I want to tell him others have too, but I don't. It would only add speculation from some of my peers that I come from a fucked-up situation. No parents. No family. Car wreck? Murder–suicide? I've heard the gossip.

And I know they couldn't even imagine.

"But she failed," I say instead. "Just a few minutes, okay?"

He gets out and I slide into the driver's seat. I look at her only through the rearview mirror. Her face is a grid through the steel mesh that separates us. She doesn't acknowledge my presence.

I pull the phone from my pocket and turn it on. Without turning around, I hold it so the screen faces her. The wallpaper is a picture of Joshua. Most of his face is hidden by the small tiles of her collection of apps. Near the center left of the screen is the unmistakable "M" from the beer logo shirt he wore the first day we were out here.

And she wore it the next time. It stuck in my mind and I might have figured out their relationship without the phone.

And without Bernie's discovery.

Her eyes flicker a little, but she betrays no discernible emotion.

"Techs will unlock it and we'll follow your text trail, Ellie. It will lead us to Josh, and you know where else it will go, don't you?"

She's stone.

"You killed your parents."

"You don't know anything, Detective. You'll see."

She's defiant. She's playing tough, but I see behind the mask. I see a sociopath who knows she's undone. She knows that there will be no way to wriggle out of it.

"Where's Sarah?"

Her eyes meet mine directly for the first time.

"I wouldn't know. They were all gone when Joshua took me."

"Took you?"

She releases an impatient sigh to let me know she's frustrated.

"That's what I said, Detective. He held me captive. He raped me. I was a prisoner."

She's sticking to her story. A flimsy one at best.

"The phone, Ellie. What you're saying won't hold up. You know that, right? We'll follow the trail you left on this phone."

She watches as Mindy's van pulls away. Next, the ambulance pulls out.

The officer taps on the window.

"I really don't care what you think or what you find," she says as I turn around to face her. "I'm glad it's over."

"It's far from over, Ellie. For you, this is only the beginning."

CHAPTER FORTY-ONE

My hand needed five stitches. I'm grateful that I wasn't injured elsewhere. I don't want the doctors at the hospital to see the other marks on my body, scars that were waypoints on my fight for survival. It's the same reason I don't go to the beach. I wonder if anyone has noticed that and assumes that I have some kind of body dysmorphia or am a cutter.

I would actually love for either of those to have been my problem.

At least those would have been options of my own doing.

Very little evidence was recovered from the Wheaton residence and outbuildings. Bernie's belief that Joshua and Ellie were having sex, however, was backed up by DNA collected from Josh's bed. It appeared that Ellie brought nothing from her old life when she arrived in Snow Creek. A burn barrel in the yard, however, was filled with some of the remains of Ida and Merritt's clothing. The wedding photo that had been reframed was there too.

"Ellie's got a lawyer from Bellevue," Sheriff says as he scoots into my office with the daily paper and a couple of blueberry muffins his wife made.

"She says it's the lemon that makes them."

I smile. He's probably eating his third muffin of the day.

"A lawyer from Bellevue," I repeat. "Sounds pricey."

"Rolex-type guy."

"Aunt Laurna?"

He takes a big bite. "Yeah."

I shake my head and put down the muffin. "Her niece killed her sister and brother-in-law."

"The aunt refuses to believe it."

"She'll be in for a rude awakening when we unlock the phone."

"Could be. Remember, it's not our case. It's Clallam's."

Of course, I know that.

"Right. We're opening the phone for our case, and if we stumble onto something that'll help Clallam, we're good with that, right?"

He eats the rest of his muffin.

I dial Laurna right away. She answers after several rings. I don't even bother with a hello.

"Laurna, what's going on? You know what Ellie did."

"Look, Detective, I saw it was you and I wasn't going to pick up. I am told by Ellie's lawyer that I shouldn't talk to any police. It could hurt her case."

I'm exasperated, and my tone shows it. "What case? You know what she did, Laurna."

She breathes into the phone.

She's thinking. Deciding. Maybe preparing a lie.

"Yes, I do. I know. She said she was abused. I believe her. I have a way of connecting with her that allows me to see through the veil of any lies she might be telling."

My heart sinks lower and lower. I don't even know what to say. I hold my tongue and let her finish.

"She's my sister's child. I don't have any of my own. Surely you can understand that every young person's life is worth fighting for."

I want to tell her she's right, the kind of PC remark that fills Twitter when people are outraged.

I don't.

"Take care, Laurna," I say, hanging up.

Good luck with that, I think.

CHAPTER FORTY-TWO

At 11 p.m. my phone pings on my nightstand.

I think I was asleep, but I'm not sure. I'm in that state somewhere between thinking about the events of that day and revisiting old wounds by facing things that I thought better forgotten.

It's Marley Yang from the crime lab.

Detective Carpenter, my techs got the Burbank girl's phone opened. Tons there. Sending what I have now. Want to go over it in person. More work to do. Need direction. I'll be at your office at 7:30.

I resist calling him back right then. He's got small kids and a wife that can only be so understanding. Work at the crime lab is never a nine-to-five.

At least it shouldn't be when there is so much at stake.

I open the first of several folders and plow through the content as quickly as I can. I read the texts between Ellie and Joshua as fast as possible. I'm no longer tired. I'm energized. Morning can't come quick enough.

Finding out the truth is the shot of adrenaline that keeps detectives going where others never tread.

Truth, it turns out, is our drug of choice.

Marley Yang is sitting in a state vehicle in our parking lot when I arrive at seven. He swings open his door, lugs a big black briefcase, and hurries to greet me. He's short and compact, a wisp of facial hair on his chin and a head of hair that anyone—man or woman—would envy. Longish, black, luxurious, thick with bunched up locks in the back that indicates he wears it in a ponytail or, God forbid, a man bun.

He's also carrying a tray of coffees.

I smile at the balancing act.

"Your files kept me up half the night. Coffee is not only appreciated, but desperately needed, Marley."

He indicates a clear envelope nestled in the coffee tray. Inside, a flash drive.

"Champagne might be in order."

"I like champagne. Sheriff does too."

Sheriff meets us inside and we head to a darkened conference room while Marley sets up the flash drive and turns on the projector. He opens his briefcase and sets out a stack of printouts. It's thick. More than three hundred pages. Details of what he'll be showing. He told me one time that if he could do anything other than working for the state crime lab, he'd be a professional poker player.

He loves holding his cards to his vest before the big laydown.

I don't mind.

"There are literally thousands of pages of content on the phone. Texts and photos. Also, the history of Ellie's web search and downloads, too."

"That sounds daunting," Sheriff replies.

"It is, though I've organized the content to what would be most helpful right now. After we go through it, we'll take your direction on how to proceed as you build your cases."

"Cases?" Sheriff asks.

I know Marley dropped that on purpose, so I give him a nod as the screen lights up.

"Let's start with the text messages first," I say. "I was up all night reading them."

Marley nods. "Yeah, Ellie was a practiced texter. Maybe world-class. Hardly a day went by until three weeks ago that she didn't text several hundred times."

"My thumbs hurt just thinking about that," I say. "Did you organize by date or recipient?"

He opens a folder on the screen.

"Both."

Sheriff gives me a look of approval.

He likes where this is going too.

"I focused on the primaries that Detective Carpenter noted in her report. Tyra Whitcomb's number was aligned with contact name Ty. She was a primary focus of Ellie's attention on social media and texting for quite some time."

He indicates the screen. "Most of the texts were of this nature."

The screen is filled with a grouping of texts.

Hey girl what's up? Want to hang out?

Want pizza?

Got new shoes.

"I call these mundane," Marley says.

"I call them inane," I reply.

"Right. So there are literally thousands of these. The girls chatting back and forth about clothes, podcasts, celebrities. They come at all hours of the day and night."

"I thought you couldn't text in class," Sheriff says.

"You couldn't smoke on school grounds back in the day either," I say, a gentle nudge to his old habit. "Besides, Ellie was homeschooled. And Tyra didn't strike me as a girl who cared much about her education anyway."

"Right," Marley says. "All of that's true. And all of that changed early in the summer."

Like a novel reader cheater, I'm skipping through the pages he'd handed out.

"How so?" Sheriff asks.

Marley opens the second folder on the screen.

"Again, all of these are between Tyra and Ellie. In the spring the subject of their parents comes up more frequently. Mostly from Tyra who complains about how her dad is always belittling her mother."

He points to a group of messages on the screen from Tyra to Ellie.

It's my job to be a bitch to her. Not his. Jesus! My dad won't let up.

My dad's the same way. My mom's no better.

This isn't about you. God, can't you just shut up and let me vent. Seriously.

Sorry. I was just saying.

"It goes on and on like that for some time. Tyra going off on her mom being weak. Fat. A loser. Just every ugly thing she can come up with. And by the way, she's skilled at trashing her mom."

"That fifth one." I walk to the screen and point. "This message from Tyra took my breath away last night."

Dad hates her as much as I do. He wishes she'd just die. Last night she was so drunk and messed up on her pills when she passed out, we just left her on the floor. She puked and everything.

I return to my seat. "Two weeks before the boating accident."

Sheriff speaks up. "That's not our case."

"Right," I say. "I know they are related."

"She's right," Marley confirms.

"This text." I run a yellow highlighter through the words on the printout in front of me.

Dad got Mom more meds. Maybe that will fix things.

"That's a week before the accident. Troy Whitcomb got new meds. How? Clallam told me that she was only on Paxil and Ambien. They couldn't account for the Oxy. Troy had a bad shoulder from golf. He had Oxy, but he barely used any."

I'm flipping through the date sequences. Marley makes a face yet gives me what I need—room right then.

"And here," I say, tapping my marker against the paper. "This one is two days before the accident."

My dad wishes she'd just die. I told him that wishing for something is stupid. I told him to divorce her. He said that he'd lose half of what we have, and I'd have to live with her. Fuck that.

"She wanted her mother dead?" Sheriff says.

I nod and look at Marley.

"Right," I say, "both she and her father did."

"I can see that, I guess. But..."

"Right, not our case."

Marley isn't annoyed. He actually seems to be enjoying the exchange between me and Sheriff as we untangle what Tyra wanted to happen to her mother and what actually happened to Ellie's parents. It wasn't as I'd thought. Tyra hadn't hooked her friend into a let's-get-rid-of-our-parents murder scheme, after all.

"It inspired Ellie," I say.

Marley runs his fingers through that amazing hair of his and nods.

"Let's break down Ellie's communication first with Tyra, then Josh," he says, closing the Tyra folder and opening one named Ellie.

"Tyra wrote thousands of texts to all sorts of people, mostly during the period before her mother died, including to Ellie; Ellie, on the other hand, had only two main points of contact—Tyra and Josh. Ninety percent of Ellie's communication with Tyra was in answer to a text from Tyra. In fact, many of her texts directly to Tyra were unanswered or only responded to with an emoji."

"The lazy way to respond to someone," I say, looking over at Sheriff, who sends a thumbs-up or a smiley face to most of what I text to him.

"Right," Marley says, "but also passive. You see, Ellie was actually the alpha here. It was Ellie who encouraged Tyra, supported her. I expect a psychologist looking into their relationship would see what was really going on."

Sheriff looks up from his papers, lowers his eyeglasses. "I don't get it. Tyra was hating her mother all on her own."

"Okay," Marley says. "Look here, at this exchange, where Ellie's replies are all emojis."

I wish my mom would die.
:)
She treats me like crap.
>:(
I wish she would just die.
Happy Dance.

"Throughout all this time, Ellie was encouraging her," I say. "Feeding Tyra what she needed to hear. I suspect she was living in her own fantasy world of wanting to see how far someone could go. How far with a gentle and persistent nudge?"

"Okay, but what does it have to do with our case?" Sheriff asks.

"Turn to page 245," Marley says.

"Already there," I answer.

"First," he goes on, "the highlight reel." He opens the folder marked Joshua. "This one has photos too. Let's start with the timeline. Joshua and Ellie meet online two months before the murder of her parents, overlapping what happened to Tyra's mom."

"How did they meet?" Sheriff asks.

I take this one. "On a social media site for kids whose parents don't understand them."

He rolls his eyes. "What? Does it have 100 million members?"

"Make that 2.5 million," Marley says.

"I thought he was forbidden to be online. Her too."

"You don't have teenagers, Sheriff," Marley replies. "Kids find a way."

"So they connect on the site and start talking," I go on. "His parents are too controlling. His dad is a religious freak. Her dad is the same. Her mom is clueless. And so forth. Innocuous at first as they try to one-up each other on how bad their dads and moms are. Then the relationship started to move to a romantic vibe."

Ellie: I feel so lonely. So trapped.
Josh: Hate that you feel that way.
Ellie: Wish I could be with you.
Josh: Rents won't let me date until I'm 21.
Ellie: Oh God. Mine are the same way!

"She makes a mention of Tyra's mother's purported accident a couple days after the incident," I note, pointing out the text.

Ellie: Sorry so quiet. BF's mom drowned.
Josh: Wow. That's terrible.
Ellie: I don't know.
Josh: What?
Ellie: You'll think bad of me.
Josh: Never.
Ellie: She was a very cruel woman. I'm not sorry. My friend is better off.
Josh: I don't know what to say.
Ellie: I shouldn't have said that, babe.
Josh: I wish my parents were dead.
Ellie: If mine were gone, we'd be together, wouldn't we?
Josh: Forever.

I indicate the timeline. "Two weeks later her parents were dead, and Ellie was presumed drowned."

Sheriff narrows his brow as he thumbs through the pages.

"They don't plot to kill their folks?"

"Not online," I answer. "The phone was used only for another few days. The last call, however, was between Joshua and Ellie. We don't know what they said. At some point after they talked, it was tossed into the neighbor's yard where I recovered it."

I look at my phone.

"Joshua has been released from the hospital, arraigned on first-degree murder charges for his mother's homicide. He's not talking."

"I wonder why," Sheriff says.

Marley nods.

"The interesting ones never talk until they've been in custody for a few years."

I smile.

"Yeah, it's kind of lonely there."

CHAPTER FORTY-THREE

Aunt Laurna, Ellie, and her lawyer—resplendent in an Italian suit that I'm immediately convinced the likes of which have never crossed our county line—sit in a row behind a table in the jail's visiting room. Ellie's youthful beauty has been eclipsed by her jail-issue jumpsuit. She wears no makeup. Laurna, the foolish do-gooder, is dressed in a smart suit of her own, a thick gold chain around her neck, equally costly, and garish gold earrings dangle like wind chimes.

As I sit down, I can't help but label each of the three.

Denier.

Killer.

Mercedes.

Mercedes introduces himself. His name is Clifton Scott; he's a partner with blah, blah, blah.

"I'm representing Ellie here," he says.

I change his name to Obvious.

Laurna nods at me but doesn't say a word. I wonder if she's hired the high-priced attorney out of guilt for coming forward after seeing Ellie's picture. Her loyalties are a mystery. The girl sitting to her left killed her sister and brother-in-law. I'm thinking now that their family album is a book of horrors.

Ellie just sits there, smugly and silently. It passes through my mind that this might be a new role for her. No longer the one pushing buttons herself but enlisting a lawyer to do so. I set that aside straight away. She had Joshua do her bidding.

"Why are we here?" I ask.

"I've negotiated a deal with the prosecutor's office."

"I've heard you were trying."

"Well, that's why we're here, Detective."

I know that the deal is contingent on Ellie's disclosure on a matter related to the case. I also know that she's going to do time in our system for the assault on her accomplice, Joshua Wheaton, and threatening an officer. And yes, the murders of the Wheatons. She's tangled up in that too.

"We have evidence that proves she wasn't there when the Wheatons were killed, but that's not what we need to tell you."

"You don't need to tell me anything, Mr. Scott."

"No. I don't. But in exchange for the information I'm going to tell you, the prosecutor has agreed to lesser charges and an immediate extradition to Clallam County, where they will charge my client with the second-degree murder of her parents."

None of this surprises me. Girls like Ellie always manage to land on their feet.

"Okay, fine," I say through slightly clenched teeth. "Testifying against Joshua Wheaton isn't exactly a surprise to me. I figured she'd flip the second she had her fingers and palms scanned and had a mug shot taken."

Clifton Scott gives me a condescending half smile manifested out of reasonably natural veneers. Laurna pats Ellie on the shoulder, wind chimes tinkling. Ellie shrugs and her belly chains rattle the table.

The lawyer speaks up. "Ellie has agreed to give you the name of Mrs. Wheaton's killer."

I crinkle my brow. "We know who that is already. What we don't know is the location of Sarah's body."

"I'm prepared to tell you both, Detective."

The drive to Leavenworth, Washington, is among the most beautiful in a state known for its scenery. The highway cuts up and through the Cascades, with drifts of snow and conifers stunted by altitude and ice.

Before leaving, Sheriff told me to contact local law enforcement and asked if I needed backup from here. I told him I'd already made the call and that I was fine.

"Bring me back a murderer," he said.

"Will do."

"And one of those German pretzels too."

"That goes without saying."

Leavenworth is distinctly an American oddity. Nestled in the Cascades along tumbling Icicle Creek, it bills itself as a Bavarian village, a gamble to save the town from dying by mandating a makeover. It worked. It's a town dripping in gingerbread, beer steins, women in dirndls, and men in lederhosen. Every business from the grocer to one of the countless cuckoo clock purveyors is required to adopt the Bavarian theme in signage and architecture. Whether it makes sense or not.

Hence, Der Kentucky Fried Chicken.

I find a spot in the parking lot at Chelan County Sheriff's Office. Before going inside, I make a call to the school that Ellie had offered as part of her arrangement with the prosecutor's office. I speak briefly with the head administrator, Paul Singer, asking if the subject is there. I tell him only very little, but I can easily sense his distress. I text him a photo.

"Yeah," he says, "that's her. Can you come after the kids are out? Staff stay an extra hour or so to plan the next day."

"That would be perfect. I'm at the sheriff's now and will be there no earlier than four."

"Okay," he replies.

CHAPTER FORTY-FOUR

Paul Singer sits silently in his bleak, impersonal office, a white-board, some drawings his dad had made when he was in college, a poster of the private school's mascot, a falcon. The call from Jefferson County Sheriff's Detective Carpenter has rattled him big time. She'd indicated that his most recent hire was in major trouble. *Criminal trouble.* Sweat begins to bloom under his arms. He's made a mistake, something he was loath to do.

A big one too.

He thinks back to the new teacher's interview at tiny Orchard School. Becky Webster was everything the kids between Leavenworth and Cashmere had hoped for in a small school. Young, kind, and beautiful. She wore her hair shoulder length and dressed in stylish clothes. The kids at the school were a lively mix of disadvantaged locals and seasonal agricultural workers who toiled up and down the West Coast. Teachers worked there for the love of what they did, certainly not for money.

While the detective didn't specifically say what trouble Becky was in, he knew the fallout would not be pretty. He was worried for himself, of course, but also for the school. The work they were doing was important.

He reaches for the tissue box to capture the excess moisture under his arms.

Becky told him that her paperwork was in her luggage that had been lost on the train, but her credentials were solid.

She was so damn beautiful.

No problem, he'd told her, smiling. It was a lingering smile.
His jaws tighten, then relax.
He looks down at her application, remembering.
Sorry about your folks.
Car accident. Went off into a ravine in the mountains out west.
That's awful. No emergency contact? Sibling, maybe?
None.

CHAPTER FORTY-FIVE

I check my rearview mirror: two deputies follow my Taurus as we speed past row upon row of apple, cherry, peach, and plum trees. Ripening fruit dangles from propped-up branches, and I crack my window. I'm not sure but I think I can smell the Honeycrisps that are my go-to apple. I peek at my phone, noting new texts from Mindy and Dan. I don't read either. My focus right now is to bring home a killer.

Orchard School is at the end of a long, narrow gravel lane, bordered by farmland and homes that appear, sad and slumped into the landscape. It's a world just barely getting by. It reminds me of Snow Creek and how the lottery of where you're born directs much of one's life. The main building has a cinderblock façade that's been painted with what I expect are school colors: bus yellow and midnight blue. A school flag of a bird of prey flutters under the American flag on a pole adjacent to the entrance. A dozen cars are parked to the west of the building; beyond those are a playfield and two large trailers, which I presume are used as classrooms when enrollment is up.

I tell the deputies to keep back.

"Guys," I remind them, "let's keep it low-key. I'll park and go in. I want you to stay back and come in five minutes later. Set a timer or something. Alarming her in a place like this could make all three of us famous for all the wrong reasons."

I check in at the front desk and am quickly escorted to the administrator's office.

Paul Singer looks up from the job application.

"You wouldn't come this far if this wasn't bad."

I slide into a seat across from his blank, hospital-clean desk. I want to ask how long he's been there, if his clean office is an indication that he's ready to bolt if he gets a better offer. But I don't. He's sweating, and I find it hard to keep my eyes off the leakage oozing out from his armpits.

"It's serious. But this will go down easy."

I show him the photo I'd sent over.

"You sure this is her?"

He takes my phone and studies the photograph.

"Yeah. I'm positive. She seems so nice. So normal."

He reminds me of the neighbor of a just-discovered serial killer.

"Want me to buzz her now?"

"Tell her you need to go over some paperwork or something."

He looks wary as he presses an intercom button.

A woman answers.

"Ms. Cathy, is Ms. Webster there?"

"Yep. I'll get her."

"Tell her to come down to my office. One of her students is moving away and her mom is here to thank her for the extra help she gave her in reading."

"Nice," she says. "On her way now."

CHAPTER FORTY-SIX

The clacking of heels announces Becky Webster's arrival even before she knocks on the door to the administrator's blank little office.

"Come on in, Becky."

The door opens to reveal a lithe blonde with blue eyes and only a touch of eye shadow.

She looks at me, then at her boss. A confused expression comes across her pretty face.

"Cathy said there was a parent here. I don't recognize you. I'm sorry."

I tell her to sit.

"I recognize you, Sarah."

Her neck grows taut, like rubber bands nearly stretched to snapping.

"My name is Becky, not Sarah."

I hold out my phone and show her the same family portrait that had hung on the wall in the Wheaton living room.

Her hands grip the arms of the chair.

"That's not me. I mean, it looks like me. It's definitely not me."

She's pulling herself under. Inside she's clawing at the surface and trying with all she can to find a way out.

There is no way out.

"I know what you did," I tell her. "That's why I'm here."

"I honestly don't know what you're talking about. I didn't do anything."

In a flash she bolts for the door. She's unsteady. She's a blinded deer on an icy road. My new best friends from Chelan County are right there to stop her. She sinks to the shiny linoleum floor, splayed out like a broken doll.

Her face is flushed and she's sobbing.

"Sarah Wheaton, you're under arrest for the murder of your parents, Merritt and Ida Wheaton."

I finish reading her rights while cuffing her on the way to the car, thanking the Chelan deputies for their help and promise to follow up when I get back to the office.

Sarah is a sad, broken record.

"I'm sorry. I'm sorry," she cries, taking her place in the back seat. "I didn't want my brother to do it. I told him that it was wrong. That he could go to jail."

She's been following the news.

"Remember," I caution, "anything you say can and will be used against you in court."

I tell her she can have a lawyer appointed free of charge.

"I know," she says. "But I really didn't do anything wrong."

I merge on Highway 2 and head west. I didn't get the pretzel, but I did bring home a killer. Sheriff will be both elated and disappointed. I want to call in with an update. But I don't.

Sarah wants to talk.

"My mom and I came into the workshop. Joshua had just killed our father." She stops to remember or to fabricate her story.

I'll know in a moment which.

"My dad was molesting me, Detective Carpenter. He had been for years. When Joshua found out he told me he was going to put a stop to it. I thought he was going to call the sheriff. He didn't. When my mom and I went into his workshop that night it was because we heard them fighting. Fighting more than normal."

As she speaks my eyes leave the road longer than they should as I watch her in the mirror.

"Your father was molesting you."

She senses my sympathy and pounces on it as some kind of common ground that will work some magic and somehow save her where her brother had failed.

"Yes. It was terrible."

"And no one knew."

"Not until I told my brother."

While I'm an accomplished liar, I sometimes hate the game. This is one of those times. She's young and out of her league. What she'll tell me next, I think, will be a lie.

"Your mom didn't know."

She shakes her head.

"Really," I say.

"Yes. She had no idea."

"What happened to her in the hut that night, when the two of you went inside to find Joshua killing your father?"

She stays quiet for a long time. I'm hopeful that what she'll say next will correct the record.

No such luck.

"My mother ran to help my dad, and Joshua went crazy. He hit her with the hammer. She went down to the floor. Blood everywhere."

"Ellie told me another story."

"Ellie wasn't there."

"You're right. But she knows things, doesn't she?"

"She couldn't know anything, Detective. I was gone before she got there."

"I said I believe you were molested. Don't screw things up by lying to me, Sarah."

She looks out the window. Tears flow from both eyes. She's being pulled under again.

This time, for real.

"Okay. I'll tell you."

Sarah Wheaton promised herself that she'd been violated by her father for the last time. She lay still in her bed as he passed by her room. She prayed that he wouldn't return for a second visit that night. Sometimes he did. Other times, weeks would pass, and she'd tried to convince herself that what he'd been doing to her since she was four was over. She told herself that, at sixteen, whatever had attracted him to her as a little girl had finally outgrown him.

Wishful thinking, she found out, takes the mind on a journey to false hope.

What Sarah told Joshua the year before, though, had made it sound as if it had been only one time, and it hadn't been full-on intercourse, but merely fondling her while she slept. Her story was sketchy on purpose. She wanted Joshua to draw more out of her, help her. False hope. He said that he'd stick around until she was eighteen and then both of them would get out of there.

Nothing happened.

She finally summoned the courage to tell her mother.

The two were outside planting bare-root roses up against the house. Her brother and father had gone to town to the feed store.

"Mom," she said. "I have something to tell you."

Ida looked up from the bundle of ruby rugosas they were planting.

"It's bad, Mom. Really bad."

"What is it?"

Sarah started crying. It was as if the words were caught in her throat.

"Mom," she spat out, "Dad has been abusing me."

Ida returned her attention to the roses and started, vigorously so, to dig a hole.

Sarah stood there. Frozen. Confused. It was neither of the responses she'd imagined. The first was a hug and a promise to help. The second scenario was denial and a call for proof. But this response? It was as if the wind had carried off her words into nothingness.

"Did you hear me? Don't you believe me?"

Ida continued digging.

"I heard you, honey. Yes, I believe you. I know it is true."

Her mother's last words jolted her.

I know it is true.

"How do you know?"

"Your father told me. Years ago. He told me he had a sickness and had been praying on it. And after a while, he said that God was allowing him to continue."

"God let him continue to rape me?"

"I'm sorry that you don't understand. In time, I know you will."

"I could never, Mom. How could you let it happen?"

"I am my husband's wife first," she said.

We're not there yet on her story. It will come. I look at the time and consider asking if she needs a bathroom break. I don't. I'd rather have her pee on my backseat than hand her a single minute in a stall to rethink telling me her story.

"I'm sorry for all you've been through," I say.

"Thank you," she says.

I watch her in the mirror. She's looking out the window again, watching the world go by. She's thinking about what happened and the lie she'll tell me.

What really happened.

I play the game.

"What happened, Sarah? What happened to your parents?"

"I don't want to get Joshua into any more trouble."

"Tell me," I say. "I am a victim of abuse too. I know what it's like. I want to help you."

I think just then how Mindy and Sheriff will laugh at that one. I'm a lot of things, but victim will never be one of them.

"I don't know if I should say anything."

To me that means she can't wait to lay blame.

"I know it is difficult," I tell her. "The right thing to do isn't always easy."

Her eyes catch mine in the mirror and she gives a little nod.

"That night when Joshua came home, I told him what happened. How I'd told Mom and how she just stood there saying that she already knew. Had known for years. He just lost it. He was so mad. Scary mad. It was like some kind of switch had been turned on."

I urge her to take a breath.

"What happened, Sarah?"

Slowly, deliberately, she paints a picture.

Joshua found her later that night. She was crumpled into a ball, crying in a corner next to the workbench.

He dropped to his knees to comfort her.

"Are you okay? Are you hurt?"

She shook her head,

"Josh, I told Mom what Dad's been doing to me."

"Seriously? What did she say?"

"That bitch didn't care. She said she's known for years that this has been going on."

Joshua didn't understand.

"For years? You said it was one time."

"I said that because the truth was too much for me to put on you. I thought you might do something crazy. And I didn't want that. I just wanted someone to help me."

Josh's face went white. His eyes stayed on her.

"I let you down, didn't I?"

"It's okay."

Joshua stood up and turned to the door. Their father stood there.

"What are you ungrateful kids doing in here?"

"Just talking," Joshua said.

"I heard what you were talking about and it's complete bullshit. Your sister is the biggest liar in the county. She's full of shit. Never touched her once."

Joshua put a hand down to help Sarah get up.

"We're going to go to the sheriff, Dad. You're going to stop."

Merritt started for Josh. His eyes bulged from his face. He looked as angry as Joshua and Sarah had ever seen their father. He wasn't holding a belt to beat them, but his bare hands.

Just before he reached Josh, the teen grabbed a claw hammer and swung it at his father's head. After one strike, the big man fell to the floor.

He struck him a third and fourth time, sending a spray of blood upward.

"What just happened here?" Sarah screamed.

"I saved you."

A few minutes later, Ida came looking for her husband. When she entered, she processed the chaotic scene. She looked at her kids and rushed to Merritt.

"What did you do?" she asked.

Then the hammer went down.

We drive in silence for a while as I think about the blood evidence.

"That's not what happened, Sarah."

"It is too."

"The evidence says otherwise."

She doesn't say another word for at least a mile. I stay quiet, letting my challenge to her story sink in. I wonder if Sarah is thinking of a way out of what she said or giving in to the reality of her situation.

"Joshua did it all. He did it to protect me."

"That's a story, Sarah, and you know it."

"I don't understand what you're getting at, Detective Carpenter."

My eyes burn into hers through the rearview mirror. I'm thinking of the evidence that's never been mentioned, or thought of as inconsequential.

"The shovel," I say. "Let's start there."

She looks away. "What shovel?"

"The one you used to kill your mother."

She doesn't say another word.

It doesn't matter. I know what happened. The evidence and what Ellie told me in the jail interview room is all a jury will need to convict.

CHAPTER FORTY-SEVEN

The Jefferson County Sheriff's Office is a madhouse. It seldom sees press action of any kind. The place is one story, so nondescript that people often pass by thinking it's a former nail salon or dollar store that's been stripped of its signage for the next big thing. Whatever that is. Especially here. When I go inside the moron TV reporter is already setting up. I wonder if he and his camerawoman made it to that restaurant—and a motel room.

I tell Sheriff I need to leave. I don't want to be on camera again. A lot of good it did me last time. I shudder at the very idea of it.

"You need a scorecard to talk to the press?" I ask. "Don't forget to add Ellie killing her mom to the list."

He gives me a side eye and a shrug.

"I've got this," he says.

I nod, and he actually reaches over and hugs me.

I can't think of the last time anyone did that.

"You are the best person I know," he says.

I don't deflect. I'm *not*, but he means well. He cares about me.

"See you later," I say.

He gives me a quick nod and makes his way to the TV people. I hear him bark at them and tell them no one is making any statements.

I read through my text messages before I start the car.

Mindy notes that dogs alerted on the firepit at the Torrance property.

Found a femur and a human jaw. Tool marks on both.

I don't need a forensic dentist to tell me who the jaw belongs to. I know. I followed the trail. Just like Regina Torrance did.

As I drive, I consider that the murders were a chain of broken links. Not completely connected but interlocking in peculiar ways. The first to die is unrelated to the sequence, but I count it anyway because the last death—Regina's—bookends everything. Her reason for dying was the hidden crime that was sure to be discovered. It starts with Regina's wife. Amy was murdered, or killed by accident, at least two or so years ago. A dark, hidden crime. Then, this summer on the other side of Puget Sound, Tyra Whitcomb tells Ellie she killed her mother, Susan. That in turn inspires Ellie to kill her parents, Hudson and Carrie; all three murders are set up to look like boating or hiking accidents.

Except one was a lie. Tyra never killed her mother. She and her father just made her disappear the old-fashioned way.

With a threat and a check.

At the same time, or shortly thereafter, Ellie urges Joshua to do the same thing: to kill his folks and sister so they could be lovers in a world of their own.

When Regina finds Merritt's body on the edge of her property, she becomes frightened that her secret will be discovered, so she disposes of his body in the firepit.

Who could do something like that?

Considering how she managed her wife's corpse, my bet that dismembering and burning Merritt's body wasn't the hardest thing she'd ever done.

Why didn't she do the same with Mrs. Wheaton?

My thinking is that she just didn't see her. It was dark in the woods and her vision was poor. In addition, the body was wrapped in a carpet.

All of that is conjecture informed by the evidence.

My phone pings and another piece of the puzzle falls into place as Mindy provides an update from processing the women's bodies.

Regina poisoned herself. Tox will tell us more. The other one. Wow. Still can't get over Amy's corpse being filled with charcoal. Like a bean bag. Let's do lunch next week.

He's drinking a Scotch and soda while I down a shot of tequila and a PBR. The burn of the alcohol feels good in its own way as it travels down my throat. I don't even bother with the lime.

"You drink like a guy," Sheriff says with a smile.

"You do too. Sometimes."

We laugh and then stare ahead at the back bar while the bartender, a portly man in his late forties, chats up a young pretty brunette nursing a gin and tonic. She's acting interested, but I've seen that look before. Used it myself even. She's talking to him because no one better has sidled up next to her.

Not yet.

"I knew you'd be the best detective I'd ever hired," he says, unsuccessfully motioning for a second Scotch.

"I don't know. You sure took a chance on me."

He knows some of the baggage I carry with me, but not the worst of it. I doubt he'd have hired me if he knew.

I know I wouldn't.

It feels uncomfortable just then. It's me, of course. Compliments are hard to accept. I think that it's because, deep down, I feel like a fraud. Dr. Albright warned me that it would be a lifelong battle and I might never fully believe that I am a good person, that the sins of my past don't define me.

I immediately segue to the case. I resist the urge to write on the cocktail napkin. It's complicated, but Sheriff knows all the pieces. Just not how they all fit.

"It was through Sarah that Ellie met Josh," I say.

"Through the hate-my-parents social site."

"Correct."

The bartender looks our way, finally, and Sheriff indicates one more. I shake my head. I'm fine with my beer.

"Sarah had logged on to the site first, then introduced her brother to Ellie. Ellie, in turn, played Joshua in the same way his sister did. She wasn't in love with him. She only needed a place to stay until everyone moved on."

"Yeah, she lived in the mobile home with the sweet potato vines."

"That's what she said. She didn't move onto the property with Joshua until after it was all done."

"Let's run down your theory," he says.

"Okay, Ellie claims she was only a sounding board to Josh. She didn't make anything happen. I'm not so sure about that."

I sip my beer.

Sheriff speaks up. "It doesn't matter anyway. She cut a deal and is off to face charges for murdering her parents."

"Right. So, here's what I think happened—backed up by the evidence: Sarah was looking for the right moment and she found it when she and Ida were planting the roses. She swung the shovel, striking the back of her mother's head. The autopsy indicated multiple blows. The back of Ida's heels indicated that she'd been dragged."

"Back into the workshop," he says.

"So, she was the first to die."

I nod. "Merritt was lured into the workshop by Sarah. Josh, who believed her rape story, was lying in wait. He used the hammer and beat his father to death, while Sarah egged him on. During or right after the bludgeoning, Ida stirred."

"She wasn't dead. That's what you think?"

"Her blood was on the hammer. No real castoff. Just a couple of blows to finish her off." We stay quiet and watch the brunette wrangle a free drink.

"Cold. Calculating," he says.

Though I know he's talking about the Wheaton kids and Ellie, I resist adding that a free drink's a free drink.

"There were three sources of DNA on the hammer. Mr. and Mrs. Wheaton and a third. Sarah's?"

"Lab will let us know. But I suspect so."

"How would it get there?"

"Not sure. Maybe she put it there."

"To throw us off?"

I look at the foam in the bottom of my beer glass. "Maybe so. Maybe she's smarter than we think."

It's what I would have done.

Sheriff shifts the conversation to Sarah's purported defense.

"Do you think Wheaton was molesting his daughter?" he asks.

I shrug. "I honestly don't know. My guess is that will be her defense. Her brother's too. It might work. However, there isn't a shred of evidence. No school counselor. No doctor's visits. No friends to say she confided in them."

My own story passes through my thoughts.

I'd never told another person about what happened to me until I met Karen Albright.

CHAPTER FORTY-EIGHT

I idle in the drive-thru at our local burger place and order the works. Even a chocolate milkshake. When I get home, I go for the tapes right away. It's like there's a poltergeist in my house putting those little cassettes in my face and telling me to PLAY them.

So that's just what I do.

I can't resist.

I'm a moth to the flame.

I eat slowly and listen to every word. I also see every single thing that my younger self is describing. I am reliving it all. I want to stop the player, but I can't; I'm an addict. I'm someone without the good sense to throw the damn thing into the trash.

The garbage disposal. That is if I had one.

Run over it in my car.

"Go on, dear," Dr. Albright says in her sweet, yet urgent voice. *"You're doing fine. You're revisiting a time and place that made you... but doesn't have an iron grip on you. You can be free. Acceptance is what we're going for here."*

It's almost laughable how those words spoken a decade ago still ring false.

I finish my milkshake, making that sucking noise that kids do when they want to get every last drop.

I close my eyes and allow a memory to fill my head.

*

Hayden was asleep in the bedroom across the hall from mine. The house was quiet; I could actually hear the clock in the foyer ticking away the time. My thoughts had been racing, looping, spinning, since we'd arrived in Idaho. I padded downstairs and found Aunt Ginger in the darkened living room, the curtains still drawn. The TV was still on mute. The light flickering over her face altered her appearance a little. She didn't look like my mother at all. Her eyes were darker; her hair was long and lifeless, without even the faintest trace of a shimmer. By the time I took a seat next to her, I had already learned everything I could about her by studying the photographs in the hallway, and yes, digging through every drawer that I could when she was getting our rooms ready. I knew that she was single. She loved the scent of lavender. I knew that she was estranged from her son and daughter. I didn't know exactly why, and when it got right down to it, I really didn't care. What I did care about was the truth. What I cared about was finding my mother.

> *Dr. A: Rylee, what did your aunt tell you? About your mother?*
> *Me: Sorry. Just thinking about it. How incredible and awful it all seemed to me.*
> *Dr. A: But you're here now. You're safe.*
> *Me: (pause) I think so. But I don't know for sure. No one really does.*
> *Dr. A: I suppose that's so. You're no longer in imminent danger.*

I don't say it, but I remember thinking it at the time. *That's what you think, Doctor.*

I see our conversation in pictures. My aunt sitting on the sofa, looking away from me to tell her story. I play the whole scene in my mind.

*

"When I was twenty, your mom was sixteen," she told me. "She was coming home from feeding the neighbor's cat. It was summer, and the dahlias were in bloom. We had planned to go out shopping after dinner. She needed a new outfit for a party at the end of the month." Aunt Ginger hesitated, lost in a memory that might have been bittersweet and horrific at the same time. I gave her a minute. I have memories like that too; the kind that take me far away from the present.

"No one saw it happen," my aunt said, back from wherever her thoughts had taken her. "I mean, she just vanished. It was as if Courtney was just lifted up away from home by a helicopter or something. There was no trace of her. Nothing."

She stopped short.

I wanted an answer. "What happened?"

Again, Aunt Ginger weighed how much she'll say. I wanted it all, but she looked at me and sees a kid. She had no idea how much strength I had or what I would do for my family.

"How much do you know?" she finally asked me.

"I know who my real father is, if that's what you're asking."

Me: Aunt Ginger tells me she's so sorry, or something lame like that. I just let it float away from me. I didn't want apologies, Doctor. I wanted to know. I mean, here I was fifteen and my bio dad was a serial killer and that meant we shared a ladder of DNA code steeped in violence and murder.

Then she tells me. "Your mom was abducted by a monster. That's what happened." It was so empty. So, nothing. It was what I'd already known from the letter and clippings. I asked her for more. I needed to know details. If he took her again, then I wanted to find her.

Dr. A: How did she react?

Me: Weird. She said a couple of things. That I wouldn't be able to find her and, here's what I thought was so wrong, she said my mom wouldn't want me to find her. She was insistent that we'd be better off just moving on or something.

    Dr. A: How did that make you feel?

    Me: Pissed. I told my aunt that no way was I going to just let my mom die. And that she'd left all the things in the safe deposit box, so I could find her. Even a gun.

I turn off the tiny machine. I know every word of what's to come. I go to the refrigerator and retrieve a bottle of water. I don't want wine. I don't want beer. The window facing the Port Townsend Bay calls to me and I go to it, looking at a car go by on the street in front of my house. A dog running around loose. A woman with a crackly voice calling for that dog to come home.

I think of Aunt Ginger crumbling under the weight of her story. I had come unannounced and reopened a wound that had not yet healed. Not in sixteen years. I never thought about that until now. I never considered her situation. Only mine. Only Hayden's and mine.

I watch the scene outside my window, but I only see my aunt and me, sitting in her darkened living room.

"Start," I say to her. "Tell me everything."

She inhales half the oxygen in the room. It's a long pause. Not of the kind to create drama, but the kind to stoke some courage.

"Your mom said she stopped to help someone who was trying to load some things into the back of a truck. The things weren't heavy, she told me later. Just awkward. Your mom is like that. Always helping people. When she wasn't looking, he came from behind her and put something over her mouth. Chloroform, she thinks. It could have been something else..."

She let her words trail off. I give her a moment. Reliving whatever happened to Mom is painful.

For her.

For me.

Her words pummel me: "captive, abused, tortured." She says that my mother was subjected to the vilest of humiliations. She says that only the sickest, most depraved mind could conceive of the things done to her. Now that she started, it all comes tumbling out, and my aunt seems to be in another, horrifying, world until her eyes focus back on mine, realizing who I am. How old I am.

I remember her staring at me with her pale, penetrating eyes. She wanted me to understand the next part, to embrace it.

"A weaker person would have folded and given up," she says. "Courtney is the bravest girl who ever lived."

How she could say that? Mom, brave? We'd been running all of our lives. Exactly how is hiding brave?

"How did she get away?" I ask.

"She said she was able to drug his coffee. She doesn't even know what the pills she used were. She should have cut his throat while she had the chance. It was the biggest mistake of her life. She regretted it more than anyone could ever know. She said she was too weak to kill him, no matter what he'd done to her."

"Why didn't she just go to the police and have him arrested?"

"Look, I can see you don't really understand. Not every criminal is caught. Not every victim is believed."

"I know that, but I still don't understand. It's worth a try, right?"

"Your mother did file a report. And she had her body probed and scraped for evidence. She said it was nearly as humiliating as what he'd done to her. She even told me once that she felt the police and the doctors were almost an extension of her captor's crimes. Their questions were like acid poured over her wounds. They didn't think that she had been abused, raped, whatever. Our mother—your grandmother—didn't believe her. Even I wondered about it."

"But why didn't anyone believe her?"

"Because she'd been captured once before."

A pause.

"Or she said she was."

Now I am confused. Completely.

"The year before she was raped," she goes on, "your mom disappeared. She claimed she'd been kidnapped, well..." I can tell by the way she's wringing her hands that this part is hard for her to disclose. The torture of my mother was, oddly, easier. "She'd run off to be with a boy. She had gone to the coast. She was afraid she would get in trouble, so she made up a story."

My aunt catches the look on my face. She pounces. "She *was* kidnapped. She was brutalized by that monster who raped her. She wasn't lying about any of that."

Her explanation placates me only a little. "So, if she made a complaint to the police, why did he carry on stalking her? If it was all out in the open, he had to know that even if he wasn't arrested that the police would be watching his every move."

I go back to the kitchen table and fast-forward through the last bit of the tape, the words that changed my life.

And made me do what I did.

Me: Aunt Ginger said the police didn't believe her... past incident... might have been more to it...

Dr. A:... must have been painful... how could it be?

Me:... friends in the sheriff's office... made evidence disappear...

Dr. A: Why didn't the rapist just leave her alone?

Me:... got away... he is.

I speed to the end of the tape. Much of it seems blank, just hissing. I'm almost to the point of flipping it over when I hear my voice say my mom had something my biological dad, her attacker, wanted.

I hold my fingertips to my lips. Tears tumble down as they did that evening in Aunt Ginger's darkened living room, and later, in Dr. Albright's room.

Me: My aunt started to cry. And then I did. Even before she said another word. It was like she was warning me. Or breaking a trust with my mother. I don't know. Her words came out one at a time.

You.

He.

Said.

He.

Wanted.

You.

My stomach roils. My eyes mist over. I suddenly feel like I'm being sucked inside of my past. I need to talk to the only person who knows the story—at least most of it.

CHAPTER FORTY-NINE

It's against department policy and I know it, but I find Karen Albright's address through the DMV database. She's in her sixties by now, retired from her practice, and living in Woodland, a small community not far from the Oregon/Washington state line. As I drive southward on the interstate, I think about what I want to say to the doctor who saved me from where I was going. She led me to what I needed to do. She didn't preach. She didn't convince. She simply let me know that what I am can be good.

No matter where I came from.

Mindy and Sheriff only know bits and pieces. Not all of it. Not the really terrible things I did and why.

Hayden does. Most of it. He'd never betray me.

I loosen my grip on the steering wheel. The cut on my hand has reopened. Red blooms through the layer of medical gauze. Red. The color I know best.

Dr. Albright's house is a lively seafoam green and trimmed in cream. I've never been there, but I know at once it has to be her place. Out front is a massive forsythia bush. It's fully leafed, yet its spider-like limbs betray it. When I first went to see her, she had a vase of bare branches in her office.

"Not pretty now," she had told me. "Just wait. Beauty comes from the most unlikely places, Rylee. You'll see."

It was February and the world outside was cold and gray. It was the way I had felt inside too. Also empty. Hurt. It was as if I was floating on a sheet of ice in the middle of a lake with the shore completely out of reach. Hopeless.

The next time I had gone to see the doctor the twigs had sprouted a hundred bright yellow trumpet-shaped blooms.

"See?" she'd told me. "You're like those budding branches. We'll get you to bloom again."

I get out of my Taurus, smiling faintly at the memory of those flowers and how she forced blooms from naked twigs.

I knock and the door swings open right away.

Even though it has been more than a decade, Dr. Albright looks the same, just a kind of bleached-out image of exactly how she was. Her hair is even whiter than I remembered, and her skin now is a page of wrinkled paper.

Recognition immediately comes to her face.

"Rylee!"

"Dr. Albright, I wasn't sure you would remember me."

It was kind of a lie.

Actually, a big lie.

I didn't think she could ever forget me or what I had told her.

She immediately gives me a warm look and wraps her arms around my shoulders.

"You are all grown up," she remarks. "I'm so happy to see you."

I pull back a little and look deep into her pale blue eyes.

I don't blink. I just hold her sympathetic gaze.

"I've been playing some of the tapes."

She lets out a sigh. "I knew you would someday," she says, leading me inside the house.

Her living room is a mix of antiques and contemporary furnishings. I recognize the large crystal vase from her office; it's on a table next to the sofa. The room is like she was when I was her patient: comfortable, smart, and warm.

"I've been following you," she says.

"You have? How?"

"Photo search matched an image from your police academy graduation."

"I see."

"I'm not a stalker. At least not a real one. I'm happy for you, Rylee. I always had such faith in you."

She did. I didn't doubt.

"When did you listen to them?" she calls from the kitchen.

"Like I said, I haven't listened to all of them."

"That will take some time. There are hours and hours to go through. It will also take the right frame of mind."

I swallow. "That's right."

"Tell me how I can help you, Rylee."

I haven't been called that name in such a long time that it almost makes me feel as though she's addressing someone else.

"I'm not sure. Just some perspective, I guess. You're the only one who really knows me. What happened. Why I did what I did."

She gets us water and sets a glass on a coaster on the coffee table. Embarrassed, I move mine to one right away. I wipe the ring from the table's gleaming glass surface. Looking down, I see my face. I am who I am. I will never be like anyone else.

I'm no longer really listening to Dr. Albright.

"I can only reiterate what I know to be true and what I told you all those years ago during therapy. You could make a choice to live a life that would keep you safe and still allow you to be the kind of person you were meant to be."

"Sometimes I am. Sometimes I wonder what it would be like to be with someone, to really share myself. Be loved."

"No one knows you? Is that it?"

"Sheriff knows. He fixed things for me so I could be in law enforcement. Nothing illegal, but certainly not completely ethical either. I owe him a lot."

"Does he know everything?"

I shake my head. "No. No one does but you and me. Not even Hayden."

She brightens a little at the mention of my brother.

"Are you in touch?"

I look down at my water glass, appropriately half empty.

"Hayden is in Afghanistan. We email sometimes, and I'll see him when he returns to the states. Our relationship has always been a little strained, but we're working on it."

I wonder if she still can tell when I'm lying. I'm working on the relationship with my brother. However, it's a solo effort. Hayden doesn't want a thing to do with me.

"I'm glad to hear that," she replies.

She can't tell anymore. That's good, I think.

"Are there any other tapes?" I ask.

She looks at me quizzically. "No. Just the ones I gave you. Why?"

I'm not accusing her, but I need to know.

"No copies?"

She pulls back. "Of course not. I told you when I gave them to you that they were the original recordings and that no copies or transcriptions were ever made. For obvious reasons, Rylee."

Obvious reasons, indeed.

I let out a sigh of relief.

"I'm going to destroy them when I finish listening to them. I just needed to make sure that, you know, nothing ever got out."

She suddenly looks defensive.

"I would never do that," she says. "You know that. Don't you?"

My face feels warm.

"Sometimes I don't know anything. Sometimes I'm going along, and I feel like a regular person. And then bam, I see something that reminds me of what I did. My parents. All of that. I want to shed my past and live without it bombarding me every now and then. You know what I mean, Dr. Albright?"

"I do," she replies, getting up and moving closer to me. Her white hair is framed like a halo in the light. Her blue eyes seem even more watery.

I hurt her.

"You need to know that even if it weren't the law," she adds with an air of indignation, "I would never disclose anything about you. Not to anyone. That isn't how I operate. No good psychologist does. However, that's almost beside the point, Rylee. I have always wanted one thing for you...to live life free from all that bullshit from the past."

I think that's the first time Dr. Albright ever used a swear word in front of me.

She puts her hand on my shoulder and invites me to stay for dinner.

"Nothing fancy," she goes on. "For someone with eastern European ancestry, I make a pretty decent lasagna. It's in the oven."

I smile. "I thought I smelled something wonderful."

A half hour later, I sit across the table and look at this kind and generous woman and wonder how it was that she was able to rescue me.

And how it was that I could doubt her.

She tells me about her life, her pet iguana, her recent trip to Hungary and the Czech Republic. There is very little shop talk between bites of pasta and sips of cabernet. I tell her that I have the occasional bad dream and some generalities about the Wheaton case.

"You're doing what you're supposed to do, Rylee."

"I think so," I say.

"I know so," she says.

I give her a warm smile.

If I had a pet iguana or a pet anything, I would have told her about that too.

CHAPTER FIFTY

He wanted me.

As I drive home, those words from my taped session with Dr. Albright play in my mind. Actually, it plays *at* me. Like a cat, claws out, toying with a small bird. It wants blood. It wants to win. I know it's the reason I felt the need to see Dr. Albright after all these years. I would like to tell the world that there is great help in psychotherapy. It's what we tell everyone we see as they struggle through things, visible and invisible.

I remember everything about that moment when my aunt told me. She changed from rose dusting powder to a lilac scented one. It was strong, but pretty when she left the room. At least it wasn't wintergreen. The clock over the mantel chimed. I could smell the cinnamon rolls she'd baked that morning.

Everything.

The drive is long. Each flashing headlight is the beat of a drum. It's foiling my efforts to move my mind to another topic.

When I get home, I feel defeated somewhat. I try to shut the past away by getting something to drink. I stream Maren Morris's first album. From the refrigerator, I pour some orange juice. And then I do what zillions of other people do when searching for a distraction, I stare down at my phone.

I'm unable to resist.

I check my email. Of the fourteen new ones, one has to be from my brother.

Shooting in Denver. Fire in downtown Portland. A protest for the homeless in LA.

I immediately start to delete.

I hesitate on one. It sends a chill down my spine.

Its subject line:

It's You, Rylee.

It seems non-algorithm-created, not spam. The spelling of my name is a challenge for just about everyone, as they always assume RILEY. I don't recognize the sender. It's a guy named "Wallace."

I open it anyway.

And I forget to breathe.

Saw you on the news. Good work. How's the weather there in Port Townsend? Maybe I'll come by and we can talk about what you did.

I snap my phone to the table so hard that it tumbles to the floor. The glass face shatters.

I'm shattered.

Someone knows.

God, help me. Someone knows.

A LETTER FROM GREGG

I want to say a huge thank you for choosing to read *Snow Creek*. If you enjoyed it and want to keep up to date with all my latest releases, just sign up at the following link. Your email address will never be shared and you can unsubscribe at any time.

greggolsen.com

I come from the rainy and murderous Pacific Northwest near Seattle. We know a thing or two about serial killers here because we've had some of the most notorious call our neck of the woods home. I can look across the water from my home and see the city where Ted Bundy first killed a girl. Gary Ridgway, the Green River Killer, dumped several bodies in a cluster within a mile or two of where I worked at the time. Robert Lee Yates, a serial killer from Spokane, dumped a body one road over from where I live today.

Here's the thing…my characters, like brilliant but damaged Megan Carpenter in *Snow Creek*, are rooted in experiences I've had as a true-crime writer. Hanging out with cops, talking to victims of crimes, and living in the atmospheric and rugged Pacific Northwest are genuine creative forces behind my novels. Megan's only getting started. And so am I.

I hope you loved *Snow Creek*, and if you did, I would be very grateful if you could write a review. Reviews are your way of introducing others to books that have intrigued or maybe even scared you. I'd love to hear what you think, and it makes such a difference helping new readers to discover one of my books for the first time.

I love hearing from my readers—you can get in touch on my Facebook page, through Twitter, Goodreads, or my website.

Thanks,
Gregg Olsen

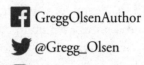

GreggOlsenAuthor

@Gregg_Olsen

@GreggOlsen

ACKNOWLEDGMENTS

It is often said that it takes a village to really get something done. Publishing is that way too. I am grateful to the awesome Book-outure team: Publisher Claire Bord, who brought one of my most beloved characters to adulthood in a series I just couldn't shake from my dreams. Much appreciation also goes to each and every member of this amazing team: Leodora Darlington, Alexandra Holmes, Chris Lucraft, Alex Crow, Jules Macadam, Kim Nash, Noelle Holten, and Natalie Butlin.

To my copyeditor Janette Currie, proofreader Liz Hatherell, and, last but not least, cover designer Lisa Horton. Each of you are innovators and masters of disciplines and programs that are unrivaled anywhere in the world. Thank you all!

I'd also like to pay tribute to my agent Susan Raihofer of David Black Literary Agency, New York, and my personal assistant, Chris Renfro, for all that you do to keep things moving at a rapid-fire clip.

Finally, to Liz Pearsons, you have my undying gratitude on so many things. I know you know that. But at the top of the list at the moment was your recognition that I had a need to write this book and you paved the way to make it happen. I adore you.

Special appreciation for the care Kirsiah McNamara gave this print edition.

**Detective Megan Carpenter returns in her
next crime thriller from the #1 *New York
Times* bestselling author Gregg Olsen!**

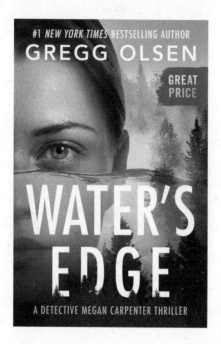

When a body is found in a secluded cove in Mystery Bay,
Washington, Detective Megan Carpenter is one of
the first on the scene. The victim has telltale marks on her
wrists, ankles, and neck where she has been bound.
But that's not all. Next to the body lies a puzzling clue—an
unusual symbol scratched into a rock. Megan must crack
the clue fast if she is to catch the twisted soul
before they strike again.

Please turn the page for a preview.

CHAPTER ONE

The streetlights on the corners were dim. Young men—teenagers, mostly—stood in the yards or between houses in small groups, smoking, laughing, staring at her small car as she passed as if challenging her to encroach on their territory. She had heard all the talk about this part of the city. She'd read the newspaper accounts and seen the raw footage on television. And still she came. His invitation had been so shy, embarrassed, charming.

She had rushed home from her shift at the tavern, showered, and tried on several different outfits before she decided on the one that would highlight her figure and accentuate the red of her hair.

Green.

That was her go-to color. She studied herself in the mirror.

She'd been called pretty, even beautiful a time or two.

Yet never by the sober.

Or the especially handsome.

That evening he'd called her beautiful.

She had been working in a coffee shop downtown and just started taking shifts at the tavern. Tips were better at the Sandpiper, but the clientele had bottomed out on the disgusting scale. The coffee shop had been full of New Age creeps and wannabe writers. The Old Whiskey Mill had drunks and more drunks, and it was a cop hangout. Drunks were more generous than coffee sippers.

She ran her fingers through her hair and thought about him.

He looked familiar. Not overly so. Just enough to make her lean in when he spoke. He ordered a Jack Daniel's, straight up, and smiled at her. She'd said something like: "Do I know you from somewhere? Are you famous?"

The moment it passed from her lips she felt schoolgirl silly.

"Afraid not. I'm sure I would remember a beautiful woman like you."

It was a very old, very worn-out pickup line, but he'd blushed.

And yet, there it was: a real, honest-to-God blush.

She remembered asking if he worked in town, and he answered with a straight face.

"I work for the CIA."

She blinked and was about to say something, but he laughed and said CIA stood for the Culinary Institute of America. CIA. He was a chef in search of employment. A recent graduate of the Culinary Institute of America in Napa Valley, California. He said he was going to prepare something special for her.

He sheepishly explained he still lived at home with his father and would she mind if his dad ate with them?

That made her mind up. She had felt silly that she had almost turned him down. She hadn't gone out with anyone for a long time. Especially someone she'd just met. She'd said yes much too quickly. She regretted that now. She didn't want him to get the wrong idea.

Or maybe she did?

She knew what her mother would have said if she were still in her life. "Leann Truitt, just what were you thinking?" It was one of her mother's favorite lines, a dart meant to hurt. It was true that sometimes she hadn't been thinking, but she was a grown woman now.

"Shut up, Mom," she said to herself. "We'll find out soon enough what I was thinking."

The house was on the corner and faced north. It was badly in need of a makeover and was exactly as he'd described it. But her stomach dropped as she drove around the corner. The house was dark except for a flickering light behind thick yellowish curtains. It looked empty. She looked at the clock on the dash, thinking she was early, but she was actually a few minutes late.

She parked and walked across the cracked cement of the sidewalk to the side gate. She lifted a black latch and pushed the gate open. A walk of original brickwork led to the door. The bricks were covered in green moss, and she had to step carefully to keep her high heels from slipping. If she twisted an ankle, she wouldn't be able to work—and, even worse, would miss this wonderful evening.

And yet something niggled at her; a little doubt crept in.

She looked for a doorbell but there wasn't one; there wasn't even a knocker. She raised her hand to knock and hesitated. What if his father disapproved of her coming for dinner? This place was older than old. It smelled of mildew and rot. It reminded her of one of her father's rental dumps.

"I'll get it, Dad," a voice said from inside.

She heard footsteps. A shadow appeared behind the glass and the door opened.

He took her hand and led her inside the darkened foyer.

Her eyes adjusted and she could see that both walls of the wide hallway were lined with boxes and stacks of clothing and dolls and appliances and lampshades. There was a narrow path and he was leading her through the clutter. Then she stepped in something sticky. Adrenaline coursed through her. Something was wrong.

"Maybe I should..." she managed to say, before he turned and slammed a fist into her face.

CHAPTER TWO

I sit at my desk at the Jefferson County Sheriff's Office with posters of the craggy Olympic Range on the wall behind me. I can see into Sheriff Gray's office to my left. His door is open and he's leaning back, too far back, in his roll-around chair, the springs squeaking whenever he shifts his weight.

So annoying.

I swear, the chair could be used by the CIA to get confessions from the most hardened terrorist. I want to take a full can of WD-40 and douse the springs.

But I don't.

I turn to the disheveled woman sitting in a chair beside my desk. She is holding a toddler with one arm and attempting to corral her eight-year-old serial-killer-in-training with the other.

"Miss Gamble, let's move to an interview room," I say, partly because I don't want to cause her more embarrassment and partly because her kid can bounce off the walls in there. Literally. In the kids' interview room are soft toys, carpeting, soundproof walls, and posters of breaching orcas, the PAW Patrol, lighthouses.

Miss Gamble gladly gets up. Her ears are bleeding also. Whether it's from the squealing made by the chair, the squalling toddler, or the whining, nasal, nasty mouth of her son is unclear. If I thought a can of WD-40 would work on the eight-year-old, I'd use it. But it's not Miss Gamble or her kids that are getting to me. It's her situation. It sparks memories. I try to set it aside. Sparks can be bonfires.

Miss Gamble is unmarried, trying to raise three children by three different fathers, and trying to do it alone. She is on public assistance, living in public housing, using food stamps in an unwise manner—for example, trading them for illegal substances—and I deduce from her belly bump she might have another baby on the way.

She leads the ones she already has into the children's interview room. The interview room for adults is not like this space. Not even close. This one is meant to soothe and mollify. The adult side is designed to irritate and get them to confess just to get out of the room. I can testify that it works. At least, some of the time.

I take a seat, pick up the paperwork provided to me by the Port Hadlock Fire Department, and look at Miss Gamble, then at the eight-year-old.

She remains silent.

"Did you know your son was setting things on fire?"

It's a straightforward question. Yes or no. She doesn't answer. Just gives me those big brown eyes. I can't sympathize. I don't know enough about the family dynamics. Maybe the kid's been abused?

When I ask the question, her little firebug's eyes light up and a half smile plays at his lips. The sheriff is in the next room. I want to continue the questions, but I get up, go into the outer office, shut the door behind me, and return to my desk to clear my head. I wonder if he's a bedwetter. If so, I know how the textbooks would classify him, and it stings me. I know from experience that while bedwetting often indicates a child's future behavior, the trajectory is somewhat changeable.

I hear the sheriff's chair give an emphatic squeal and know he's gotten up. The floors vibrate under his plodding gait as he comes over to my desk.

"You okay?" he asks.

"Why wouldn't I be?"

"Is that kid really setting animals on fire?"

"Fire marshal says so." The fire marshal actually said more than that, but Sheriff Gray doesn't need to hear the descriptive language he used. The man was very upset. I've never seen a grown man cry, but after seeing the pictures of a family's beloved pet, I don't blame him. I felt queasy thinking about it, and it takes a lot to make me queasy.

"Well, I'm going to do you a favor," Sheriff Gray says, handing me a Post-it note.

I read and look back at the kids' interview room. I can hear banging on the wall. "What about them?"

"I'll take care of them," he says. "I'm the sheriff. I can do a referral to juvenile court the same as you, and I've done this job longer."

Outside of a multiple murder in the Snow Creek area, the cases I've had lately have been thefts and high-dollar vandalism. The note the sheriff handed me has eight words printed in his perfect, steady hand.

It reads like a telegram.

Marrowstone Island.
Mystery Bay State Park.
Cove.
Floater

A floater is a tasteless but accurate descriptive term we use for bodies found in water. I haven't been on the job very long—two years—but this is the first time I've heard of a drowning in the little cove of Mystery Bay, Marine State Park.

"Homicide?" I ask.

He gives a little shrug. "They want a detective. You tell me after you get there."

I grab my windbreaker that doubles as a raincoat, thinking the sheriff is done.

He's not.

"Detective Carpenter, meet Reserve Deputy Marsh."

A younger version of me, but with red hair instead of blond, steps in front of my desk with her hand held out. A smattering of freckles high on her cheekbones are visible through the makeup she's applied. The hand is perfectly manicured.

Those nails won't last the day, I think.

I can't help but notice my own hands just then. My skin is dry, tanned from spending time in the sun. Nails somewhat chewed but practical for this kind of work.

I already don't like her, but, to be fair, I don't know her.

I remind myself to get to know her first and then not like her.

Her grip is like water, soft. She is wearing a blue pinstriped suit with a white silk blouse billowing out in front. She probably got the idea for her getup from a television show where all the female cops are busty, with longish styled hair, and dressed in high heels. Her ridiculous outfit will last about as long as her nails before it's ripped or covered with mud or puke or blood.

"Ronnie Marsh," she says.

"Nice to meet you, Ronnie." I don't mean it. I've got a case to work, and in my mind I'm already heading to Marrowstone Island. I let her hand drip through mine, and I slip into my windbreaker. As I turn for the door, Sheriff Gray stops me with a hand on my shoulder. I don't like to be touched, but I'll make an allowance for him.

"Take her with you, Megan."

I work alone. Always have. I work alone for a reason. I don't want complications. I don't want relationships. Working together qualifies as a relationship. Relationship equals abandonment. That's what life has taught me. My brother, Hayden, hates me because I left him in Idaho with a veritable stranger. My mother betrayed and lied to me in the worst way.

Everyone does eventually.

Reserve Deputy Marsh can ride along with me for today, but that's it.

"You've got her for a week."

I shoot him a look. I don't care if the reserve sees it or not.

"I'm swamped, Sheriff. I can do today. Maybe you can give her to someone else?"

"Swamped with what?"

I stay mute. He already knows the answer. I'm tempted to say, *Sheriff, you and I both know I'm not working shit right now. So why don't we save some time here and you hand her to someone that wants to work with her.* But I don't say that because Sheriff Gray gave me a job when probably no one else would. Because he knows things about me. Because he has helped me erase some of my past mistakes. And, more than anything, because he is about the only person I can trust.

He doesn't remove his hand from my shoulder. "You might as well take vacation time, Megan. It's so dead around here."

I wish he wouldn't use that word: "dead." It has a way of multiplying trouble. Like a virus.

Just then, Nan, Sheriff Gray's assistant, shows up. She is also wearing a suit. She and Marsh could be twins. I change my assessment of where Marsh got the idea for her attire. She must have seen Nan.

That doesn't bode well for her.

"Sheriff," Nan says, "Marine Patrol wants to know if they need to respond to the drowning." She's looking at me, smiling at Marsh, and talking to the sheriff. She's perfected multitask ass-kissing. "Should I tell them you're both with a suspect and can't be disturbed?"

Reserve Deputy Marsh speaks up. "I just completed my rotation through Marine Patrol. Captain Martin gave me a good write-up. He said I was his best intern yet."

I'd met the captain one time during *my* academy rotation. He was good-looking, in a Ted Bundy sort of way. I remember he was always partial to the female cadets. The guys, no matter how adept they were on the water, barely squeaked by with a passing grade.

"I can see that," I say.

Nan and Marsh were exchanging looks and giving each other a knowing smile. It's no secret that Nan has a picture of Captain Marvel—that's what I call him—displayed on her desk. He is at the helm of his boat, bravely sailing into a perfect sunset. I remember a while back he gave Nan a ride on his personal boat. The next day she came to work in wrinkled clothes, messed-up hair, no makeup.

I just rolled my eyes when I saw her.

Sheriff Gray looks at me for a response.

"I won't know if I need the Marine Patrol guys until I get there. What's their location?"

Nan gives me a stare. "The captain didn't say. He just asked if he should respond."

"I'll call Captain Marvel when I get there." Then I change my mind. "I'll call the captain on my way," I say, and try to leave.

Sheriff clears his throat. "Aren't you forgetting someone? Take Deputy Marsh with you." He says this like I should stand to attention and salute.

I head to the parking lot, and Deputy Marsh trails behind me with her high heels clacking all the way. I get to my old Taurus and hit the unlock button on the key fob. I forgot that the key fob doesn't work anymore. The good thing is the car is old enough that it still has a regular key on the fob. The bad thing is the car is old. I've asked for a new car. I won't get one until I have to drive with one arm out the window holding the door shut.

The day just gets better and better.

I open the door with the key and hit the inside unlock button. Nothing happens. I lean across and unlock the passenger door. Ronnie Marsh waits until I pull out of the parking lot before she starts what will become stream-of-consciousness chatter. I tune out somewhere around her graduating from middle school at the top of her class.

CHAPTER THREE

The drive to the scene isn't a long one. We cross over the narrow causeway to Indian Island and a second causeway to Marrowstone Island. I turn left on State Route 116, which is also Flagler Road. Every now and then a cut through the thickets of ferns and old cedars reveals the sun reflecting off the waters of the bay. It reminds me of my little brother, Hayden. In Port Orchard we lived not far from a little creek, where he would look for salamanders. He was seven. I was fifteen or sixteen. I read *A Tale of Two Cities* for English class. Charles Dickens said what I was feeling about those times in Port Orchard. "It was the best of times. It was the worst of times." There's enough time and distance from those days that I choose to remember the good. The bad is too painful. Hayden remembers only the worst of days and my screw-ups. He has little contact with me, and that is more painful than the memories.

Mystery Bay is to our left, the state park straight ahead. I see a sign for the boat ramp and slow down. A state patrol car is parked several hundred feet down the road with the emergency lights on. In front of it is one of our Sheriff's Office vehicles.

Further down is a relic: a red or oxidized brown Ford Pinto.

A young man, teens, early twenties, stands behind the deputy's cruiser, one arm wrapped around his chest, his free hand twisting the hair of a skimpy beard and stuffing the end in his mouth. His hair is long and black and curly and looks like it hadn't been washed in . . . well possibly, *ever*. He wears camouflage army boots with the laces tied so loosely, I can't imagine how they stay on his feet. His faded jeans are cuffed and tattered.

The trooper's corfam dress shoes are dirt- and mud-free. So very shiny. If I'd been inclined, I could use the toes for a mirror. There's not a fleck of lint or dust on his sharp-enough-to-cut-you pressed trousers. I look at the statie's name badge: *MacDonald.*

"Your deputy is down with the body," he says flatly. "No need for both of us to get dirty. Besides, one of us had to stay up here to keep the road closed to civilians."

I glance at the pair of cruisers with their emergency lights flashing and then return my gaze to him. I want to say that I would have totally missed the police cars with the Christmas lights going and driven right past. But since I have a trainee with me, I shift gears.

"That's what I figured. Good thinking." I give him "the look" so he knows he didn't pull a fast one on me. To my pleasant surprise I hear my trainee giggle.

Maybe she'll be okay.

"Is that the person that found the body?" she asks.

The young man stopped twisting his beard long enough to offer his hand. He says nothing and I don't take the hand. I doubt anyone would.

Trooper MacDonald speaks up. "This is Mr. Boyd."

I nod. "I'll need a statement from you, Mr. Boyd. Why were you down there?"

I didn't see a boat trailer or any fishing gear. He isn't dressed for anything outdoorsy.

He appears surprised by the question. I half expect him to ask if he is a suspect and then invoke his rights. To which I might respond that he has no rights until he becomes a suspect. The truth is everyone is a suspect until they're not. I have learned that from experience. He doesn't disappoint.

"I'm not a suspect, am I?"

"Absolutely not," I lie.

He looks skeptical. "On TV the person to find the body is always a suspect."

That was also true in real life.

"That's TV, Mr. Boyd."

"Robbie," he says. "My name's Robbie. I go to school at Olympic College. I'm taking criminal justice."

"Great choice," I tell him. "So you know how this goes. Tell me: why were you down there?"

He stuffs some of his scraggly mustache in his mouth and chews on it.

Gag.

"I heard about this place from a friend at school," he finally says. "I don't have to give you her name, do I?"

"No," I say.

Not right this minute, anyway, I think. I'll let him tell me all he knows and then I'll get the name out of him.

"Okay," he starts. "I was looking for a new hiking trail. I'm parked right over there." He turns and points at the Pinto as if I hadn't noticed it or it might have mysteriously moved. "I'm a hiker and a rock climber. I was looking for some cliffs. I'm very strong."

"I can see that." He looks all skin and bones in his grimy T-shirt and well-worn jeans and hiking boots.

He smiles and warms to me. Everyone does. I can charm when I need to.

"So," he goes on, "I headed down to the bay—to the boat ramp, I mean—and I started looking for a trail."

He stops a beat.

"This isn't going to be on the news, is it? I'm supposed to be in class. I skipped a test and told them I was sick."

It's going to be in a full-length movie if you keep asking stupid questions, I think.

"I don't think your name will come up," I say.

He seems a little disappointed, so I pivot again. "But I can't promise the news media won't track you down."

He brightens a little. That was the correct response.

"Well, I guess if I have to talk to them..."

"Finish telling your story," I say.

"Okay, so I walk that way"—he points—"and I come to a place where I found a trail. I went into the trees and followed it a bit and that's when I found the place."

Ronnie interjects: "What place?"

"The rocks," he says. "I'm a rock climber. You ever been rock climbing?"

She shakes her head.

I want to shake her for interrupting the interview.

"Mr. Boyd," I say, "you found the body. Can you tell us about that?"

"Okay. Sorry. I just really like rock climbing."

I gave him a stern look. I am running out of patience.

"Anyway, I came up to the little cliff, bluff, whatever." Boyd has warmed to the subject. "It was only, like, thirty feet high, but it was sheer, man. I mean, it was straight down: 'Do not pass GO, do not collect $200,' if you know what I mean."

He gives other expressions of this stupidity and I let him talk until he runs out of "likes" and "you knows" and appears to be wrung dry as far as skirting the subject.

"I was going to climb down. I left my climbing gear back in the car, but it looked like I could make it. Then I saw I didn't have to. Someone left a perfectly good rope tied off to a tree. It was coiled up and I almost tripped over it. I pitched it over, checked the knot, and over I went."

"The body," Ronnie says.

I can see she is getting impatient too.

Good girl.

"So I got down to the bottom and there's a bunch of big rocks and a tiny strip of sandy beach. I pulled on the rope to make sure I could climb back up. I didn't want to fall down in those rocks. Some of them are sharp. Anyway, I was about to climb back up and I saw what looked like a foot sticking out between the rocks. I couldn't see any way to get to this beach except by climbing down. I thought maybe the person had fallen off the cliff. At the same time I wondered how they could have, 'cause the rope was coiled up at the top of the cliff."

He stops and looks at us.

"Aren't you going to take notes?"

"I have a very good memory," I say. "Go on."

He sighs. "Okay. Fine. I go over and look and it's a woman. She ain't moving and looks banged up. I thought maybe she had fallen but then I see she's not wearing anything but her panties and a bra. So I think maybe she tried to swim to the beach and got tossed up on the rocks. I climbed back up and called 911. Then I thought maybe she needed help and I got in my car, but it wouldn't start. Then the officer showed up and he called for a deputy and, well, here we are."

I question him again, walking him through his story. It doesn't change. He climbed down, saw the body, climbed up, and called 911. Boyd swore he didn't touch anything or take any pictures, although I don't believe him, because he still has his phone. He'll probably hightail it back to campus and show pictures to his buddies or sell them to the news media.

I say to him, "So when CSI gets here and takes fingerprints and collects DNA samples, yours won't show up anywhere?"

He swallows and I hear his Adam's apple click in a dry throat. He shakes his head. "I don't think so. You can't get fingerprints off a rope and that's all I touched. Honest to God. And the rocks where I was climbing down."

"We have a new technology that's called Touch DNA. You probably heard about that in class."

He stays silent.

"And it's what the name says. When you touch something, part of your DNA gets on the item, body, whatever. Then, using the FBI and Homeland Security database, we can then trace it back to the person through family lineage and down to a specific individual."

Boyd stops chewing on his beard and begins rubbing the side of his face.

"Well, to tell the truth, I might have walked out in the water to see better. But it was too deep, and I didn't want to get that wet. I didn't never touch her, I swear."

The bottom half of his jeans are still damp.

My rule of thumb is that when someone says, "I swear," what follows is going to be a big fat lie. I believe he didn't touch the body but maybe he took pictures. Maybe even a selfie. People are sick. I should know.

"Can you let him sit in back of your car?" I ask MacDonald.

MacDonald does so reluctantly.

As he is getting in the back seat Boyd says, "I'll give a full statement to your partner, Detective Marsh." He smiles at Ronnie. She smiles back, turns to face me, and scowls.

"I'll take his statement if you like, Detective. They taught us how at the academy. I've got a voice recorder on my cell phone."

I've used my phone recorder to take confessions too. But the person giving the confession didn't know I was recording them. Tricking them didn't bother me.

MacDonald is cold. I need to turn on the charm.

"I'm Megan," I say. "Can I call you Mac?"

"No. It's State Patrolman MacDonald."

CHAPTER FOUR

Seriously.

He wants me to call him *State Patrolman MacDonald.*

Not a chance.

This is going to be a long morning.

"Okay," I tell him. "Is the rope still there, or did Deputy Davis have something of his own to climb down with?"

"He used the witness's rope," MacDonald says.

I was afraid of that. It's too late to collect the rope. I follow the beaten-down grass path through a stand of huge big-leaf maples to a smaller fir where a climbing rope is tied off. The rope extends down the side of the cliff. I step out as far as I can but don't see a body or my deputy. I return to the cars and MacDonald.

"Deputy Marsh will stay up here to wait for Crime Scene. Do you have crime scene tape?"

He nods.

"Can you help me out and string some along both sides of this road? We'll need to search both sides for any evidence or tire marks." I look directly at him.

He doesn't say anything. He goes behind the car and opens the trunk.

"Unless you have hiking boots and work clothes in your handbag," I tell my erstwhile deputy, Ronnie, "I want you to stay up here and take a statement from the witness."

She looks down at her shoes. "Sorry. I thought we'd be staying in the office today. Tomorrow I'll be better prepared, ma'am."

Ma'am? Seriously?

"Don't call me 'ma'am,'" I tell her. "I'm Megan for today. Okay?"

"I'm really taking Mr. Boyd's statement?" she asks.

"Might as well get your feet wet. I want you to write his name and personal information down. And get the license information."

She takes a notebook and pen from inside her jacket. It was so tight fitting I didn't see anywhere she could have hidden them. "And while you're at it, search his car."

"We don't have a warrant. Is he a suspect?"

"No," I lie again. "Just see if he'll let you. If it makes you feel better, you can ask him to let you search his car while you're taking the statement. If he says yes, it will be on the recording."

She doesn't look convinced.

"I've been at this awhile, Ronnie. Trust me."

"I do. Trust you, I mean."

Now, that's a start.

"I'm going down to see what we have." I go to Mac's car, open the door, and ask Boyd, "Are you sure there's no other way down there besides climbing?"

"I guess you could swim around."

Smart-ass.

I return to Ronnie.

"Are you going to call Marine Patrol?" she asks.

"I'll call from down there." Mac approaches with a roll of yellow-and-black tape. "Thank you for helping. This is Reserve Deputy Ronnie Marsh."

Ronnie offers her limp hand and he takes it long enough for it to drip through his fingers and says, "Nice to meet you."

"She will be taking a statement from Mr. Boyd."

I know Mac will gladly let Ronnie take the statement so he can avoid going to court or testifying. I don't warn him that once Ronnie starts talking, there is no off switch. The witness is on his own.

I follow the trail through the trees again and stand at the top of the cliff. It's about thirty or forty feet to the bottom. Rocks ranging in size from a football to a dinner table cover most of the beach. I scan for the body again, but I can't see it from here. I turn around and start descending hand over hand, shoving the toes of my boots in any crack they can find. I get about ten feet from the top and look down again. Can't help it. I don't care for heights. I can't even see the deputy. I start down again and don't dare look anywhere but straight ahead. I hang on to the rope and try to lean away from the rock face like they taught in the academy.

"Watch out for..." a voice comes from below.

My foot picks that exact moment to find probably the only loose shale on the side of this cliff and I slip. Two things save me. There is a small sandy area where Deputy Davis is standing four or five feet below me.

And I land on top of him.

We look like a Jenga puzzle game, all arms and legs askew. The breath is knocked from me, and I can hear Deputy Davis grunting. He'd better not be enjoying himself. I roll off and he helps me up. He begins brushing the sand and dirt from the back of my jacket while I use my fingers to comb the sand out of my hair. He brushes the back of my butt and I move away.

I'm armed.

"I owe you one, Deputy Davis," I say.

Actually, I owe him two—black eyes—if he touches me again.

"Not necessary, ma'am. I mean Detective Carpenter."

Deputy Davis is a year younger than me. He has thick brown hair and a mustache that screams vintage porn star. Or maybe cop. Cop is much better. He's not particularly overweight, but his stomach somehow manages to roll over his coaster-size buckle. He's a good cop and a total pleaser as evidenced by his willingness and ability to make the climb down. I've tried, unsuccessfully, to break him of the habit of calling me "ma'am" and he tries. I have learned to accept it. He is being a gentleman. It's the way he was raised. He explained to me that his mother taught him to call all ladies "ma'am" and all men "sir."

My mother taught me to lie, manipulate, betray, and worse.

"Show me what we have, Deputy Davis," I say. He likes to be called "Deputy."

He climbs over some of the bigger rocks and I try to keep up. I can see the water lick at the rocks thirty feet away. I still don't see a body. I wonder how Boyd saw a foot. I reposition myself on a large rock and look toward the water and I see it. A bare foot, ankle, and part of a lower leg. Toes pointing up.

We make our way closer until I can see the body. A woman. White. On her back in a small sandy area, a twenty-by-ten-foot stretch of beach. Her legs are pointed toward me, her head toward the cove. Her legs are spread with the rock between them. I look to the left and to the right. Boyd was correct: the rocks block any entrance to the body without going into the water. I will have to go over the rocks to get to the body. Or swim from the boat ramp.

I climb on top of another rock and look directly down on the body. Long reddish hair covers half of the face. My guess is she's in her mid-twenties. Just as Robbie Boyd said, she's wearing only a bra and panties. I look around but don't see clothes. Her face is battered; her bottom lip split so much that I can see teeth through the cut. Dark, indented marks circle her wrists and ankles. A wider one encircles her slender neck. Her skin is light blue, but I see deeper blue or black marks on her torso.

It appears she's been beaten or kicked.

I take out my cell phone and breathe in. I've got two bars. I'm tempted to call Ronnie and ask her to climb down. Instead, I call Captain Marvel of the Marine Patrol and advise him of the situation. It will take half an hour for the patrol to arrive.

I also phone Jerry Larsen, our coroner. Since he's in his sixties, he won't be able to make the climb. When he answers, I tell him to meet me at the boat ramp where Mac is parked. He can take the boat. I'd rather not get on the boat with Marvel.

"Do you have a camera, Deputy Davis?"

Davis reaches for his backpack and proffers a digital Nikon.

"Take all the pictures you can," I tell him. "Some of where we climbed down and from there to where I'm at now. How high do you think that cliff is? Thirty feet? Forty?"

"Over thirty, ma'am." He starts clicking away. He doesn't have to be told to get close-ups or to tell me if he saw something unusual. Davis has worked crime scenes before.

"Captain Martin will want to take his own," Davis reminds me, and I say nothing.

Captain Marvel can do whatever the hell he wants as long as he gets the body out without destroying evidence, and gets it someplace where I can get a better look. I always assume homicide until I know different.

Davis says what I'm thinking.

"I don't think she was swimming."

"And she didn't fall from the top of the cliff unless she was running about forty miles an hour before she jumped," I add.

"How long do you think she's been here, ma'am?" he asks.

"Long enough to be dead," I say, and immediately regret being smart with him. "We'll have to wait for the coroner."

I trace a way to move from rock to rock and maybe get down to the body, and I go for it. I slip only once and bang a knee. That's going to leave a bruise. I'm on the gravelly, sandy shoreline now. Ten feet from the body. Her legs are pointed inland. She had to be brought in by boat. Pulled up into the rocks. Dumped. Posed. The tide has erased any drag marks in the sand. The body is at least fifteen, twenty feet from the water, but she has been pulled in between some rocks large enough to hide her body from the water. If Boyd hadn't climbed down the cliff and spotted her, it might have been some time before she was found.

"Damn," Davis says, and I turn toward him.

"What?" My heart is pumping a little.

"I ran out of film," Davis says.

"That's a digital camera. Stop fooling around."

"Sorry, ma'am."

He doesn't sound sorry, but I forgive him. It's the first time he's ever shown any type of humor. He's usually so focused and eager to please that I want him to loosen up. Humor is law enforcement's way of pushing emotion away so you can function under pressure. I wonder what is stressing Davis out. He has worked horrible scenes with me before and seemed okay. I would ask him, but I don't want to see another grown man cry today. I had that earlier with the fire marshal.

As I look over the body, I wonder how she got there. Maybe she was kidnapped, beaten, taken on a boat to be dumped at sea. Then she jumped overboard and ended up here. She would have had to have been pretty desperate to do something like that. I don't even want to step out into the cold water.

The more I look at the position of the body, the more I see a dump site. She was brought here by someone.

I'm punching the sheriff's number into my phone to update him when my phone rings. I answer.

"This is Nan. I've been trying to call you for half an hour."

Nan is an administrative assistant, not my boss. Not anyone's boss, for that matter. Even so, she acts like one.

"Sorry, Nan. The reception is sketchy here. I was just getting ready to call Sheriff Gray to tell him there are body parts everywhere and...oh, crap!"

"What?"

I say with a wicked grin, "I just stepped on a finger. At least, I think it's a finger. Or maybe it's a small—"

"I don't want to hear," Nan says. "I just want to tell you that a state patrolman named MacDonald has been calling and asking for your phone number."

"Did you give it to him?"

"I didn't think I should. I told him I'd pass the message on to you. Do you want his number?"

"Yes."

She provides the number.

"Is the sheriff done with the Gamble family?" I ask.

"I can go ask him."

I know she's lying. She knows everything about everybody. Except me. "Never mind. Tell him to call me," I say. I disconnect before I yell at her. I don't know if she's really stupid or if she's just trying to get my goat.

I call Mac.

"I hear your Marine Patrol is coming here."

"In a while," I say. "Where are you?"

"I'm with my car. Do you need me to stay?"

Now I'm getting pissed. "Is there anyone else up there with you?" *Besides my brand-spanking-new reserve deputy*, I don't add.

"Roger that," he says, and the phone goes dead.

Jerk.

"I looked around the rocks, ma'am, but it might take a couple more guys to do a thorough search," Deputy Davis tells me. "I saw a couple of soft drink and beer cans and put down flags to mark them."

I don't have to ask if he has crime scene flags in his backpack. He probably has a full forensic kit in there. I didn't think of bringing anything. I didn't even want to bring Ronnie of the blue power suit with me.

CHAPTER FIVE

Captain Marvel and one of his crew show up. They anchor the *Integrity* outside the cove and make their way to the shore in a bright yellow Saturn inflatable boat with a five-horsepower motor. The captain eases the inflatable near the rocks at the east end of the beach while his crewman jumps out and ties it off.

Captain Martin comes ashore last. He checks to see that the boat is tied up securely before heading in my direction. If this were a movie, there would be golden sunlight behind him. He's wearing faded cargo pants, but his boots look as expensive as my car. He doesn't say anything to me. Just looks the scene over. He smiles, and I can see why Ronnie is hung up on him. He has a square jaw, piercing cobalt-blue eyes, perfect white teeth, and wavy blond hair cut stylishly. The cargo pants are tight on his triathlon-built frame. I expect him to pose with a hand on his hip, his cape billowing out behind him. I unconsciously smooth my hair.

He nods toward the other deputy, who is wearing an almost identical getup. He's the same size and build as Captain Marvel except he has long, curly brown hair.

The captain introduces us: "Deputy Floyd, Detective Megan Carpenter."

"Floyd."

"Detective."

At least he didn't call me "ma'am."

Floyd digs into his backpack and pulls out full-body waders. They cover his legs and chest with straps going over his shoulders.

He takes out a camera—not as nice as the one Deputy Davis has—and begins wading out to photograph the body from the water, then wades forward until he is only a few feet from it.

"Floyd brought a scuba outfit," Captain Martin says. "He'll check around out in the water while Crime Scene is working the beach."

"That will be good."

I call Mac again. "Has my crime scene guy arrived yet?"

"Yes," he snaps. "I've been trying to call you, but your secretary wouldn't give me your number."

"Hold on," I say, and ask the captain, "Can you go to the boat ramp and pick my guy up?" He nods and goes back to the inflatable.

"The coroner just got here," Mac says.

"Captain Martin is going to meet them at the bottom of the boat ramp. Can you give the phone to Deputy Marsh?"

Ronnie gets on the line. "Deputy Copsey and the coroner are here, Megan."

I hear the barely contained excitement in her words. "Captain Martin is coming to the boat ramp to pick up everyone. Are you finished taking the statement from Boyd?"

"Yes. Should I come with them?"

I ignore her question. "Did you let Boyd leave?"

"He let me search his car. I took pictures of the inside, the outside, the tires, and the plates. I got the information from his driver's license and his address at the school. He wanted to leave. Said he had to get back to school, and if he wasn't under arrest—"

"Okay, I get it. I would have you come with Crime Scene, but you'd have to do it barefoot."

"They always have an extra pair of rubber boots on the boat."

"Hang on." I turn and raise my voice so Deputy Floyd can hear. "Does the captain have an extra pair of rubber boots on the inflatable?" He gives me the thumbs-up. I turn away again and say to Ronnie, "You can come, but you're probably going to ruin your nice outfit."

"It's an old one."

She says that like it's disposable.

"What's your cell phone number?" I realize I never asked that. She tells me. I don't have to write it down. I'll program it into my phone later. "Can you put Larsen on the phone? The coroner."

Larsen gets on the phone. His voice never ceases to amaze me. He's well past sixty, with longish white hair, a six-inch white beard, and laugh lines at the corners of his eyes—all topped off with a merry tone in his voice. He's taller than me, which isn't surprising, and thinner as well.

"I'm coming down, Megan," Larsen says. "I haven't been rock climbing in years. An adventure is in the making."

"You don't want to come that way." I say this nicely. He can be grumpy if I try to tell him what to do. "I've sent a boat to pick you and Crime Scene up at the boat ramp."

"Oh. Okay." He sounds disappointed. He can be pigheaded too, but I can't let him get hurt. Sheriff Gray would disapprove, and Larsen is the only one with authority to order the autopsy.

"I fell on the way down," I say.

Not a lie.

"You would have to be lowered down in a sling," I go on. I know he won't go for that. He stays quiet.

"What is it?" I ask.

"I don't do boats," he says. "I get sick. Don't repeat that to anyone."

"We'll bring the body to you, then." It will be a while. He'll have time to go home, have lunch, watch television or take a nap, then come back. Jeez. I really don't like being in charge. I almost always work alone. This is why.

"How am I supposed to examine the scene from here?"

Good question. I want to tell him I can have him airlifted in, but I don't want to get that sarcastic. He's a good guy. I can count on him to give an honest off-the-record opinion.

I hear Ronnie start to chatter in the background.

"I can use FaceTime on my phone. I can hold the phone where the coroner can view the scene and the body."

"Is that okay with you?" I ask him.

"If I can get a cell phone that has that Face-do-hickey on it."

"Put Ronnie on." I hear him asking in the background if she is Ronnie. Then she comes on the phone again. "Ronnie, give your phone to the coroner."

It's not long before Captain Marvel is back with Deputy Copsey and blue power suit girl, who is becoming my appendage. She is smiling and chatting everyone up, especially Captain Marvel, who is favoring her with his strong profile in tight pants. I reluctantly admit he's a good-looking man.

Deputy Copsey is the first off the inflatable and helps Ronnie onto the shore. She's wearing bright orange rubber boots at least four sizes too big. Captain Marvel hands off several plastic cases of gear to Copsey, then jumps off himself.

My phone rings. It's Larsen wanting to know what's going on.

Ronnie has gotten Larsen fixed up and I have her give the phone to Davis. I don't want her to get too close to the body until they have cleared the scene. Larsen gives Davis directions where to point the phone. Davis moves the phone around to different angles and up closer, then farther away. Larsen says something about very little blood and tells Davis to gently feel around the victim's neck and head. He does.

"There's a knot on the back of her neck, Jerry. Feels like the bone is sticking through the skin. I'd have to move her to tell you more."

"Lift the face up a little and hold the phone so I can see it."

Her long red hair is partially covering the face. Davis smooths some of it away and gently lifts her head. He holds the phone close to her face.

Her lips are deep blue, her eyes open. Davis cants her head to the side. She is younger than me.

Open contusions on her cheeks and chin and several big splits on her lips mar what was once a pretty face. If she washed ashore, the rocks might account for almost every injury. However, it can't account for the dark blue ligature mark around her neck or the positioning of the body.

She was strangled and deliberately posed.